USE
ME

WM *William Morrow*

An Imprint of HarperCollins*Publishers*

USE
ME

HarperCollins books may be purchased for educational, business, or sales promotional use. For information please write: Special Markets Department, HarperCollins Publishers Inc., 10 East 53rd Street, New York, NY 10022.

FIRST EDITION

Designed by Deborah Kerner

Library of Congress Cataloging-in-Publication Data

Schappell, Elissa.

Use me / Elissa Schappell.—1st ed.

p. cm.

ISBN 0-688-16557-5

1. Fathers—Death—Psychological aspects—Fiction.

2. Fathers and daughters—United States—Fiction

3. Young women—United States—Fiction I. Title.

PS3569.C474 U84 2000

813'.54—dc21   99-052549

2   3   4   5   6   7   8   9   10

In memory of my father,
Frederick Schappell

Acknowledgments

My greatest thanks to my editor Rob Weisbach, without whom this book would not have been possible. For their guidance, enduring generosity, and inspiration I am eternally indebted to Helen Schulman, Eddie Villepique, Michael Hainey, Elizabeth Gaffney, Jennifer Gilmore, Rachel Urquhart, and Aimée Bell. I am also grateful for the advice and encouragement of Joy Harris, Leslie Daniels, Dr. Judith Brisman, Betsy Sussler, Ken Foster, and Meaghan Dowling. For their abiding faith and support, Connie Schappell and Andrea DeLuca are deserving of more gratitude than I can express.

Finally, I am in awe of the love that Rob Spillman, the last man standing at the weenie roast when it started to snow, has bestowed on me.

Contents

Eau-de-Vie *1*

Novice Bitch *37*

To Smoke Perchance to Dream *68*

Use Me *102*

The Garden of Eden *130*

Sisters of the Sound *153*

Wild Kingdom *186*

Try an Outline *224*

In Heaven, Dead Fathers
Never Stop Dancing *254*

Here Is Comfort, Take It *285*

USE
ME

EAU-DE-VIE

"Pouilly-Fumé, Chardonnay, Pouilly-Fuissé, Sancerre." I chant my mantra in the backseat of our white rental car, Josephine, as we speed through the Loire Valley countryside, past chateaus and vineyards and endless rows of grapevines.

It's not fair that all my friends get to be normal and go to the beach, and I have to go to France and be a total albino. I barely ever see the sun because my parents are constantly dragging me and Dee through every museum, church, and restaurant in France. We spent two whole days in the Louvre!

On the road I lean as much of my body out the window

as I can without attracting my mother's attention. At least today we'll be outside, not during peak tanning hours, but God, I'll take it. I love that feeling of sun soaking into my bones. My dad says the sun turns the grapes' blood into sugar. "You can taste the sun in the grapes," he says, "the way you can taste dirt in a tomato."

Dad is speeding because we're racing to make the tour of some vineyard where they produce a prized Pouilly-Fumé (whoop-de-do) and a brandy called Pear William (ditto the whoop-de-do). My mother has been *dying* to go to this château place ever since she "discovered" it in *Gourmet* magazine. You know, she showed me that picture three times before we left. Each time I saw the same thing: a bunch of pear trees with wine bottles roped to their branches, and inside each bottle a tiny pear was supposedly growing. I tried to make out the pears. I never could, but I guess a magazine wouldn't lie about a thing like that.

My little sister is eating a yellow pear out of a handkerchief. My mother says that's how the French eat them. Their skins are so soft they bruise brown when you touch them and rip open so easily they nearly dissolve in your mouth. Big deal. All I know is Dee is getting the whole backseat sticky and drawing flies. As far as I can tell, anything good draws flies.

Dee eats only fruit, bread and butter, and *pommes frites.* Oh, sure, she'll say, "Yes please, yes please," when my parents offer her poached salmon in béchamel sauce or foie gras on toast. Dee always says yes—she wouldn't want to disappoint you—but Dee, she won't eat one mouthful, and because she's so cute, so small and blonde and pretty, with her big blue doll-baby eyes, she gets away with murder.

My dad's going to put us into a ditch if he doesn't slow down. It doesn't help that he's got his arm around my mother, who is wearing her Jackie O sunglasses and a black and purple silk scarf tied around her long blonde hair like a gypsy. I'm just thankful she's not wearing her toe ring. I can't wear an anklet because "it looks tacky," but she can wear a toe ring. Explain that to me. She's just showing off because she has feet like the statue of Venus de Milo. My dad pointed this out in the Louvre. "Look," he said, dragging us over to inspect the goddess of love's feet. "See, the second toe is slightly longer than the big toe, it's perfection."

He even made Mom take her shoe off in the museum and compare. She acted like she was embarrassed, you know— "Oh, Chas, honey, stop stop"—but she did it. For Dad. I bet she's sorry now she didn't pack that toe ring. It's not like she'd need it. France is like Spanish fly to my parents. Ever since we got off the plane they've been pawing each other. More than usual. Which is saying something, believe me.

Dad looks mostly normal. His black hair is a little on the long side, but he's dressed in a regular Levi's denim work shirt, jeans, and the sneaks he wears to cut the grass. The only problem is that my father, who has shaved every day of his life, even on weekends, is now growing this horrible little black beard for my mother. With her head scarf and his beard, they look like pirates who've escaped the suburbs, taking me and Dee along as hostages. It doesn't help that my dad is also wearing these black wraparound sunglasses that my mother bought at a gas station. I've never seen my dad in sunglasses. It's creepy. I know he's wearing shades in case we get pulled over for speeding, so the cop can't see his eyes are all blood-shot from drinking wine at lunch. He also reeks of cigarettes because he and Mom smoked Gauloises after lunch. The thing is, my parents don't even smoke!

"We're getting close," Dad says, and leans over to kiss my mother on the mouth. Josephine jerks to the right, and Dad accidentally flips on the windshield wipers for only about the hundredth time. He shouts, "Jesus Christ, I'd like to strangle the guy who engineered this car!"

Dad should have both hands on the wheel, seeing as how he drank almost a whole bottle of red wine at lunch. Mom had just half a glass, it gives her a headache. Red wine and frog's legs, you can't have one without the other, according to my father, who it seems has read every book about France ever written, so he must know best.

My dad is on a quest to cram culture into us, so we don't have to pick it up late in life like he had to. See, Dad never went to Europe as a kid. It wasn't just that Grandpa was a plumber and so there wasn't lots of money for travel; the family never went anywhere, except to the lake, or hunting.

Dad says his father and mother never traveled because Grandpa was uneducated and feared the unknown. It was the same reason he forbade my grandmother to have a job or drive, and why my dad could never learn to ride a bike.

Of course, my dad, he felt he wasn't doing his fatherly duty unless his little girls saw every pane of stained glass, every splinter of the One True Cross, every crappy druid stone formation, every scenic panoramic view, and anything that could be considered "art" in all of France. I don't know which is worse. At least at a lake I could lay out.

At lunch today Dad offered to lend me his ratty old copy of *A Vagabond's Guide to Paris in the '50s.*

"I think you'll like it. It'll give you a sense of history. It's *cool*," he said as he sucked the meat off a tiny jointed frog drumstick. I thought I was going to pass out. You know, what the Fu Manchu happened to the rest of the frog? Was there a bucket of stump frogs in the kitchen, and if so, were they still alive and flopping around?

"Hmmm, chickeny," Dad said. He smacked his lips. "I think you'd like this. Give it a try."

"Frog? No, thank you."

"How can frog taste like anything but frog?" Dee asked. She leaned down to pet one of the stray cats lurking under our table, living it up on all the food Dee "accidentally" dropped.

"Oh, come on. Be brave, puss, take a chance," he said. He reached over to mess up my hair.

"Dad," I said, for like the hundredth time, and swatted at his hand. I'd just spent all morning trying to de-frizz my hair. Unlike my mother, I didn't go for the natural I-am-woman-hear-me-roar hair thing.

"Oh, sorry, sorry, the hair. I forgot, don't touch the hair." He let his hand rest on my shoulder for a second, like he didn't know what to do with it.

"This is animal cruelty, Dad."

"You know, Tommy Ford had rattlesnake once," my mother said. "He said it tasted like chicken too. Same with emu." She dove into a plate of escargots that the waiter insisted had been farmed from birth on parsley and thyme. My parents were eating so low on the food chain it was ridiculous; this stuff was like bait.

"Really? Gee, that's too bad," Dad said, sounding genuinely disappointed. "Listen, you never know, maybe to some people *everything* tastes like chicken."

"Daddy, you *just* said *frog* tasted like chicken," I reminded him. My mother had a fleck of parsley wedged between her teeth. I wanted to scream.

"Mom," I said under my breath, "Clarissa."

"What?"

"Clarissa," I said louder this time. *Clarissa* was a family code word that meant you had food in your teeth.

It came from a girl I went to arts and crafts camp with named Clarissa, who always got food stuck in her braces. My mother sucked her teeth in this embarrassing way. "Gone?"

I nodded. Thank God. Sometimes just listening to her chew can make me feel I'm going insane.

"Is it so wrong for a father to want his children to try new things, to actually have a foreign experience? If so, sue me."

"It doesn't taste *chickeny*. You lied. I can't believe you lied."

"I'm not going to argue this with you, Evelyn, it's ridiculous." He slammed his hand down on the table so the bread jumped in its basket.

Man, was he ever getting riled up.

"What about the sweetbreads?"

"Grace, more wine?" he asked, ignoring me.

"Dad?"

He bit his lip like he was trying to control his temper.

"I told you right off the bat that sweetbreads were fried thymus."

"Okay, but *duh*, who knows what a thymus is?"

"Then you, little lady, should have paid more attention in biology class. The point is, you liked them."

"I hated them. The texture was all wrong, weird and spongy, *and* I'd never have known that's what they were if I didn't just happen, by mistake, to see in the guidebook that they were glands. Sex glands!"

Dad shrugged like it was no big deal. Like all the cool people went around eating sex glands.

"You didn't tell me that," I said.

"That's right," he said. "You would never have tried them. You don't know what you could be missing, Evelyn."

I had almost spit the sweetbreads out. I knew from the minute it touched my tongue that it was dirty, that a person would be crossing some line even having it in her mouth. But my father was looking at me like he was so proud, so I just swallowed it. I almost gagged. I bet giving somebody a blow job was disgusting like that. These thymus glands were responsible for creating sexuality in animals. I wondered if it was possible to have them removed, or if I could have mine checked out, without having to take my clothes off, if possible. I was a little afraid that I was way too sexed up. It seemed every boy that went by on a Vespa looked good to me, even the ones with acne and snaggleteeth, and that wasn't right. Everybody that passed by, I thought, What about him? What about that one? Maybe something was wrong with me. Left alone for five minutes, I couldn't keep my hands out of my pants. Not like I was doing anything, I just liked resting my hand there.

"So, are we going to be able to drink liquor at this place or what?" I call up to the front seat, even though I know it's hopeless.

My parents both answer at the same time.

My mother says, "No, we'll get you a soda, or an ice-cream cone if you'd like."

Dad says, "We'll see."

This is as good as a yes, and I'm shocked. There's a wonderful, disturbing quiet in the car; my parents rarely disagree about anything, ever. They are a team. Dee gives me a curious look. She's still on edge from dinner last night, when my mother accused me of making eyes at a busboy. I didn't mean to.

"You are never borrowing that dress again," she said the minute he left the table. She was so angry, her hands were shaking as she tried to tug up the straps of the clingy black sundress. Was it my fault I filled it out better than her? Was it my fault she was as flat as two fried eggs? When she wore one of her slinky dresses she'd just slap Band-Aids over her nipples so they didn't poke out like party hats.

"You said I could wear it."

"You nearly caused a riot walking here, and I mean it, no more of that swishy walk—where did you pick that up? Have you been watching Marilyn Monroe movies, or some T-and-A Battle of the Network Stars thing, what? It's so objectifying. Gloria Steinem would—"

Dee knocked over her milk glass. "Oops," she said, but

my mother barely batted an eye. I swear, Dee did this all the time, just for attention.

"What are you talking about?" I crossed my arms over my chest. I was starting to blush. I tried not to laugh—it wasn't Suzanne Somers or Barbi Benton. It was just me.

"You know what I'm talking about, young lady. That walk will get you into trouble, so unlearn it now. It won't always be cute boys on motorbikes whistling at you," she said, grabbing my arm across the table, her nails digging into my skin. Since arriving in France three days ago she'd painted her nails red, much darker than any color I'd ever seen her wear at home, and had also started wearing a dark wine-colored lipstick that looked very chic, but forget about me telling her that now.

"Did you see the old guy offer me half his ham sandwich?"

"Yes, I did. Not to mention all those disgusting sucking noises they make, that makes me so mad. Who do they think they are treating women like that? Don't laugh, Evelyn, it's not funny. And it wouldn't happen, *Charles*, if you walked with us, all together, like a family."

"What?" my father said, looking up from the menu and wine list. He blinked his eyes like somebody was shining a flashlight in his face.

Dee said, "Daddy, I spilled my milk. See?" She pointed to her plate. A piece of fried fish and some carrots floated in a sea of milk.

"Dee, honey, watch your elbows, please," he said, and tried to mop up the milk that had splashed onto her jumper. I thought he'd be mad, but he was perfectly cool.

My mother was just heating up. "I said, dear, on the way

home she's wearing your sport coat and you'll walk on one side of her and I'll walk on the other. Let's see if we can get Miss Sexpot home in one piece."

"Uh-oh," Dee said, and slid down in her chair. "Somebody's a sexpot."

My father put down the napkin and focused on me. He hardly ever looked right at me anymore, it was like I was a stranger he didn't want to get caught staring at.

"Listen to your mother, Evelyn, she knows what she's talking about."

"But, Daddy . . ." I was afraid I was going to crack up. It was none of their business in the first place.

"You heard me. Cut the crap."

It was clear: now that I was fourteen I belonged to my mother.

I hated them both.

In the hotel room that night, while my mother was in the bath brushing her teeth and Dee was playing with her stuffed horse, Twinkle, I went over to where Dad was sitting at a desk, the map stretched out in front of him, planning our route to the winery. I wondered if he was mad at me. He hadn't looked at me once during dinner. Walking back to the hotel, he'd given me his suit coat to wear, and he walked with us most of the way back, but I kept my head down, and he didn't say much. Dee and Mom made up funny lyrics to "Frère Jacques" and sang all the way home. Every time my father got slightly ahead of us, my mother would call him back; each time it was like he forgot why he was supposed to be playing chaperon, then, remembering, his face would cloud up. He resented having to baby-sit me when he wanted to explore side streets, to go as he pleased. But my mother would have it no other way. By the time we got to the hotel I wanted to kill my mother.

We were all sleeping in one room that had two big beds. I brushed my teeth, got into my Snoopy nightshirt, and crawled into bed with *A Vagabond's Guide to Paris in the '50s.*

When my mother went into the bathroom to perform her nightly toilette, I got out of bed. I couldn't help it. I couldn't stand him being mad at me.

"Hi, Daddy," I said, nudging my way into his lap.

"Oof," he said as I sat down, like I was heavy.

"Gee, thanks, Dad," I said, then, "I'm sorry if I made you mad earlier."

"What do you mean?" He looked confused, like he wasn't sure exactly what I was talking about.

"You know," I said.

"Ouch," he said, and moved his legs so I was mostly on just his right knee. It wasn't too comfortable, so I scooted closer, and fixed the hem of my nightshirt so it would stop riding up.

He frowned but didn't say anything, and went back to studying the map. I waited for him to say something, to get mad, or put his arm around my waist, or hug me, or kiss my hair, but he didn't. He just continued to look at the dumb map, tracing the road with a mechanical pencil.

"Daddy, rub my back," I said, raising my shoulders up and down. "My back hurts."

He acted like he didn't hear me.

"Come on, please."

He sighed, and without even looking at me, he clamped

his hand onto the top of my shoulder and gave it one hard squeeze.

"Ouch, softer. That's like a Vulcan death grip." I laughed, leaning back closer to him, resting my back against his shoulder. "Come on, do more. Please."

He sighed and once again squeezed the top of my shoulder in the same place, again too hard.

"Ouch, Dad . . . pay attention, yikes, it hurts." I shook out my shoulders, then straightened up tall, like my back was now a clean slate to start over on. I was willing to forget.

"That's it," my father said, and started to stand up. So I had no choice but to get up too.

"Daddy," I said.

"That's it," he said again. "It's bedtime."

"Are you going to keep that beard?"

He sort of laughed and stroked his face, like he'd forgotten it was there.

"No, I don't think so."

"Good."

Maybe things would get back to normal once we were back home.

"Dad, don't you think it would be all right for me to have just a little taste of wine at the vineyard?" I press. "I mean, we are supposed to be having a *foreign experience*, right? I can get soda at home," I say, knowing this logic will drive my father nuts.

"I don't think so," my mother says, cutting her eyes to catch my father's attention. For all of my parents' outward coolness, they're so old-fashioned when it comes to stuff like calling boys on the phone, white bread, and underage drinking.

"We'll discuss it," my mother says, drumming her plum-colored fingernails on the side mirror.

"Mom."

"I said we will discuss it."

"So ... let's discuss it."

"Your *father* and I will discuss it."

"Oh, fine."

I launch back into my mantra.

I know all about mantras because my mother started taking yoga classes last year, when she turned forty. "I'm giving it to me as a gift from myself," she said, as if anybody could deny that woman anything. My mother's mantra is "I'm free and I'm enough."

My mother was so free and so enough that she posed half naked for her painting teacher last summer. The teacher gave Mom the painting, and Mom gave it to my father as a gift. The painting is of Mom in blue jeans, no shirt, no bra. Topless. Just hanging out. Looking right at you. Like somebody surprised her in the middle of getting dressed. Every day for weeks, I'd take that painting down from their bedroom wall and stuff it under their bed. I mean, what if one of my friends saw that?

Word was already all over school that my parents often had dinner parties—none of my friends' parents were ever invited—where they played Creedence Clearwater, the Grateful Dead, and the Rolling Stones and dinner wasn't served until nearly midnight, and then it was often Chinese or Thai, or something in a communal pot you ate with sticks. There

were no pigs in a blanket, no chicken divan, and absolutely
no pudding in a cloud. After they'd finish a bottle of wine,
my father would take it and roll it across the dining-room
floor, and it would bang into the wall with a crash, and they'd
all laugh like they were the funniest damn people on earth.
How did they think any kid could sleep through that? Sometimes guests fell asleep on the living-room couches, and somebody would throw coats over them. Once the beanbag chairs
ended up in the back flower bed, and an antique end table got
smashed one night when it was used as part of an obstacle
course in the living room to determine who was the least
plowed to drive home.

Finally, my parents just stopped hanging that damn portrait up.

"Good grief," my mother said, when she confronted me.
"It's art! The female body is beautiful."

"It's not the female body," I reminded her. "It's *you.*"

But it wasn't just the possibility that my friends might
see it and think my mother was a slut or a nudist weirdo. And
it wasn't my dad looking at it all the time; he never seemed
to care one way or the other whether it was hung up. It was
me. I couldn't bear seeing her like that. It made me sick knowing one day that would be me.

The portrait was still under my parents' bed, Mom's lib-
erated boobs gathering dust bunnies.

"Oh, Woogey," my mother coos, and leans her head on
his shoulder. He kisses her.

Even from the backseat I can see my dad going in for the breast grope. I shut my eyes.

"Would you just cut it out!" I yell. "We're children, for God's sake!"

"I should think you'd be comforted by the fact that your mother and father are so in love," my mother says. "In this day and age, when divorce is on the rise, isn't it nice to know your father and I are going to grow very very old together?" She plants her hand on his thigh.

"No," I say under my breath.

Dee laughs.

"What was that, honey?" my mother says, but in that fakey voice that means she heard exactly what you said.

I tear the rock 'n' roll magazine we got at the airport out of Dee's hands. If she got Keith Moon sticky, I have license to kill her. Dee likes Roger Daltrey because he has long wavy hair. I love Keith, because he's a wild man. He once set off a bottle rocket on *The Ed Sullivan Show* and that's why Pete Townshend is deaf in one ear. I like that he's a drummer too, not the show-offy guy out front. You have a better chance of getting the drummer than the lead singer. Of course, my mother loves Mick Jagger. She and Dad have seen the Rolling Stones three times! Have I seen them once? No, of course not! I'm too young!

My father says he isn't threatened by my mother's crush on Mick. Yeah, right.

"You're speeding, Daddy," Dee says. She leans over the seat and sticks her finger in his ear.

"Yes, sweet baby. We have to speed if we're going to

make the four o'clock vineyard tour. The light should be about perfect for photos."

My father had been driving us all crazy on the trip, stopping the car over and over again and hopping out to go shoot a church, or a town square, or a field of poppies. Even Mom was starting to get annoyed with him. But I bet she'd like a picture of those pears growing inside those bottles.

"Don't you want to see the caves, Deedle-dee?" my father says in this silly voice, and reaches around into the well behind his seat to grab Dee around the ankle and give her foot a little shake.

"They're full of bats, right? Bats with gooey ears that fly into your hair," Dee says with a screech, and leaps over onto my side of the seat. I punch her in the back, and she pinches the soft inside of my arm and twists it.

"Girls!" My mother whirls around and glares at us. "This is my vacation, and I will not tolerate fighting! Don't make me come back there and sit between you."

As soon as she turns around, I kick Dee again, hard, that time for my mother.

"Do you want me to pull over!" Dad shouts. For an instant I think he's going to cross two lanes of traffic and do it. "I will, I will pull right the hell over if you two can't behave yourselves!"

We are silent. My father is scary when he's mad, which is seldom. He seems even scarier with the beard, like he's a kidnapper. I chant my mantra, stopping at Pouilly-Fumé. I remember *fumé* means smoked. I imagine that the Pouilly-Fumé grapevines are set on fire to make the wine—snakes of flame crawling slowly along the thick curlicued vines, sparks bursting from the leaves, the grapes plumping with heat, then disappearing under heavy blankets of smoke.

"How do they smoke the Pouilly-Fumé grapes?" I call over the backseat. Dad likes it when I ask him questions.

"It's not smoked," he says, accelerating around a turn like he's driving a race car.

"*Fumer* means smoke, or fire, in French. I know I got it right on my vocabulary test," I say.

"Well, in this case," my mother interrupts, "*fumé* refers to the morning mist that lies across the landscape and the fact that when the sun burns off the mist it looks like smoke is rising from the fields."

"So it is smoke, in a sense," I say.

"It looks like smoke, but it isn't," she says. "I wish I'd brought my sketchbook, I'd love to capture that," she says.

"That's stupid," I say. "Why confuse people?"

My mother sighs. "Anything you don't understand is stupid. Anyone who doesn't think just like you and your girlfriends is stupid. It must be nice to be so perfect."

"Smoke is smoke," Dad says. He shakes his head, like I've committed some failure of imagination.

Nobody talks. It's quiet in the car.

"So, Dad," I say, "what's the deal with the Pear William?"

I know it's an eau-de-vie, but I'll play dumb if it'll make him happy.

"It's an eau-de-vie," he says.

"Oh, water of life, right?" See, Dad, I think, I speak French. I'm learning.

"Well, that's the pretty name for it," my father says. "It's really just brandy distilled from the fermented mash of fruit."

I can't win.

"I think I'd like to experience this eau-de-vie," I say. "I don't see why I can't have one little glass." I lean forward and put a hand on my father's shoulder. "There's no drinking age here, kids as little as Dee have wine with their dinner. Why can't I?"

"Because *I* said so," my mother snaps. "Please, Evelyn, let it go."

"You're not old enough to drink," Dee says in this annoying told-you-so voice. She doesn't even care that her hair is all mashed to her head, or that she's wearing crappy Tweety Bird sneakers.

"I am so old enough," I snap. "This is France, idiot."

"You can't let her, you can't, Mom," Dee says in this pleading baby voice. "What if she gets drunk? Who knows what she'll do!"

"You wish, you spaz."

"Listen, your mother knows best, Evie," my father says. I try to catch his eye in the rearview mirror, but he won't look at me.

"But Dad, you said I could!"

"Well, I thought about it some more and I made a mistake. Don't think your old dad doesn't occasionally make mistakes," he says, and shrugs. I glare at him.

"Listen, let's play a game, okay?"

My father always does this after he's gotten us lost and he's yelled, or it's going to take longer to get where we're going.

"All righty!" says Dee. "Whaddya wanna play?"

"A new game, it's called magic or true—is that agreeable with you, Evie?"

"Evelyn?" my mother repeats when I don't answer.

"Whatever," I say. I know what they think, but I won't forget that he said I could drink booze.

"Okay," Dad says, eager to play. "Magic or True is a game we used to play in school when I was a kid. You'll like this one." He laughs. "It is possible to remove the skin from an entire apple in one long continuous peel. Magic or True?"

"True," Dee shouts out, pleased with herself.

"Of course," I say. It's so dumb, so simple it has to be a trick question.

"Smart girls. Smart girls. When I was a boy I said, 'That's impossible, that's got to be magic,'" my father says, driving a little too fast up the road and into the parking lot, gravel shooting out from under our wheels like bullets.

Dee laughs. "No way, Daddy. No way you were that dumb."

The tour is just getting started when we arrive.

"Right on time," my mother says as she locks her door. My father slips his money belt under his shirt and the two of them link arms. My mother winks at my father and he gives her a long kiss, a kiss that seems staged just to get under my skin. Then he grins, like he's pleased with himself for getting here without killing us.

"Yay Daddy!" Dee sings out, and my father bends down and launches her up into the air and onto his shoulders. My mother puts her arm around my dad and sticks her hand in the back pocket of his jeans so her hand is on his butt. I don't need to see this. You can bet if I ever did that to some guy my parents would cut my arm off.

"Oh, just give me a break," I say, and hang back. Dee is clapping her hands like a deranged monkey, but for a second I'm jealous of her. When I was younger Daddy used to carry me upstairs to bed when I fell asleep on the sofa or in the car driving home from dinner out at somebody's house. I remember the feeling of being weightless in his arms. Even when I'd wake up as he carried me up the stairs I'd pretend to be asleep and keep my eyes closed tight so he'd carry me into my bedroom and tuck me in.

I hurry to catch up with them. I wrap my arm around my father's waist. I'm embarrassed by how good it feels to be so close, the four of us, but he doesn't put Dee down to put an arm around me like he should. Instead he reaches up and places both hands on the small of her back, like he's protecting her from falling backward.

"Hey, kiddo," he says, barely looking down at me.

I try to hold tight to him so we can all walk together, in sync for a moment, but my mother's arm is in the way, and it's hard to keep ahold of him when he won't put his arm around me, so I just let go. I watch as the three of them move on ahead of me, until anybody seeing us wouldn't even know we were together.

"Okay, Princess, you're killing your old man here. Down, down," my father says, and lifts Dee from his shoulders like she doesn't weigh a pound.

"Wow, this is something." He motions to the big château and the gardens. "Very nice."

"C'est magnifique," my mother says in her goofy French accent. Unless I am wrong, this whole crappy trip is about my mother's happiness. France itself exists just to amuse her. It's so unfair I can barely stand it.

Our guide is a plump, bald-headed man in a rumpled black suit; the pants are floods, so you can see his yellow socks. As we assemble with the dozen or so other tourists, he straightens up and smiles at us, the way teachers do when they want you to stop talking. My parents squeeze to the front of the pack. My father has his hands in his back pockets, his head tipped back admiring everything, like he's taking notes. He lifts up his camera and snaps a few pictures. Dee clings fast to my mother's leg like it's a fence post and she's facing a hurricane. She tugs on my mother's jeans and my mother takes off her sunglasses and hands them down to Dee, who slips them on. She looks like The Fly.

I stay at the back of the crowd. There's a cute French boy, who looks about seventeen. I bet he rides a Vespa. His black hair hangs over one of his catlike eyes. He smiles at me. I turn away for a second because I'm blushing. He's staring at me like he's wondering what I look like in a bathing suit. Why can't American boys be into me like this?

He walks right up to me and stands there, inches away. The boy has a scar cutting through his eyebrow that looks like a knife cut from a fight, or maybe he gashed his face climbing over the barbed-wire fence of his reform school. He is so close I can smell his b.o. and I don't even care, it doesn't even seem that gross. In fact, maybe I like it. How come French boys can smell but American boys just stink?

I lag behind the group as we weave through the vineyard toward the château. I look at the hard bunches of black and green grapes and wish they were burning right now, wish that the air was full of smoke. When my father scans the crowd with his camera and the lens fixes on me, I just flash him a quick smile that lets him know I see him looking at me, and I'm fine, but I don't wave or do anything that might tip the boy off that I'm with my parents. My father doesn't act like he sees me at all, but he lingers on me for a second, adjusting his lens, and I wonder if he's taking my picture. I wonder what it is he sees.

My mother turns her head to look for me. Posing in profile, I nod at her, willing her to stay where she is, and she flashes me her I-am-giving-you-space-to-be-an-irrational-teenager smile. The same annoyingly patient smile she gives me when I won't let her hold my hand when we cross through the parking lot at the mall.

The last leg of the tour is through the fruit orchards. Small hard peaches dangle from the branches, their pink-and-pale-yellow skin covered with fuzz, like a girl's mustache. The air is full of flies and bees that cling and crawl on the puffy and split skins of the overripened peaches that have dropped onto the ground.

Our guide pauses and waits for us all to assemble in the pear grove. "There are several varieties of pear grown in France." He pauses. "The tender yellow *cuisse-dame* pear, which translates into English as 'lady's thigh,' " he says, and his icky lips pucker a little like he's dreaming right now of sinking his teeth into the soft white skin of a woman's thigh. "There's also bright green *tant-bonne* pears, which some of you may know means 'so good,' and the *brute-bonne* pear," the guide says with a sneer, "is brown and stout and ugly, but oh, she tastes like heaven."

Some of the people laugh like this is such a surprise, or it isn't a surprise but it should be.

But the pear that sounds the best to me is the *Louise-bonne* pear, which the guide says "was named to immortalize a woman in Les Essarts, but no one knows why or who she was—it's still a mystery," he says with a romantic sigh.

"Sort of defeats the purpose, huh?" jokes a man whose wife is wearing an identical khaki outfit, pockets bulging with phrase books and Kleenex. This is just the sort of romantic thing that an American man can't understand.

God, what would it be like to be loved like that? I imagine holding a *Louise-bonne*, my heartbeat being absorbed the same way a pear absorbs the sun. I look at the French boy with the sexy scar and imagine the letters we'd write each other, mine scented with my mother's Chanel No. 5, his with bike grease and sweat.

We follow the guide up a grassy path that winds through the pear trees. The boy pauses on the path and looks up at the sun like he can tell the time this way, as if he's had to live by his wits and instincts like some kind of alley cat, and for a moment I'm afraid he's going to bolt. I smile at him and catch his eye, cocking my head like, Come on. I signal him, Keep up. My heart is going crazy as I turn away and unbutton another button on my shirt. Up ahead I notice a weird glimmering in the flat green leaves, light bouncing off of something crystalline, a shimmer like heat trapped in glass. When we reach the glen, I stop.

Here is the pear orchard my mother had seen in the magazine. I turn to look for her, imagining her getting right up close to the trees and checking them out, but she and Dad are standing back from the group holding hands. Dee is back up on his shoulders. Standing on tiptoe, I can spy the pears growing inside the bell-shaped bottles. Some branches have pears that are tiny and hard looking, little green baby fists of fruit, others are pulled down low with the heavy, fully grown and ripened pears. Some of the pears are pale brown and have long tapered waists and big broad bottoms, others are nearly spherical gold balls. All of the pears look like the bodies of women grown in bottles, captured women slowly being lowered to earth. I wonder if this is what was so interesting to my mother, if this was what she wanted me to see.

The French boy reaches out and touches a bottle, turning it in his hand so that the little pear inside jiggles on the branch, nearly snapping loose. He grins at me, like that bottle is my body he's handling, and my stomach scrunches up.

"*Ah non!*" the guide cries out, and screams something in French that I think means "Touch that again and I'll break your neck!"

The boy shrugs and curls his lip in boredom like it's no big deal, and socks his hands down into the pockets of his blue jeans. If the guide had yelled at me I think I'd want to cry, but the boy just laughs it off. As soon as the guide turns his back the boy has his hand back up in the branches, his fingers leaving faint greasy butterfly-shaped prints on the bottles.

"How're you supposed to eat the pear?" someone in the group calls out.

"Ah, the fruit is too hard to eat," the guide says dismissively. "But it doesn't matter, no one buys Pear William to eat the pear anyway," he snorts, and the group laughs along with him, like they all knew this.

The boy and I lag behind the crowd. His eyes travel up and down my body like he's checking me for damage. I could kiss this boy in a second. I am ready. For months I have been practicing by kissing the palm of my hand, not too hard, not too soft, very little spit. Still, practicing on your hand or a pillow isn't like kissing a boy.

As I think all this, the boy's eyes are boring into me. He jerks his head back toward the pear trees like he wants me to slip off with him, but suddenly I'm all nervous. What if my mother sees me and drags me away? She'd say, "You're too young," or "A woman needs a man like a fish needs a bicycle." Except for my father, of course.

What if my father finds me with his camera and takes my picture—how could I deny that I wanted this boy? I smile and pretend I don't understand what he's saying. *You've got to keep them guessing. Be mysterious. Be playful, like a tigress.* That's what the magazines tell you. I keep walking, but slowly, moving my hips side to side like I've practiced in my bedroom mirror. The walk that is supposed to drive men wild. Then he is behind me, speaking in French, and it's like some wonderful dream. "What is your name? You are so pretty. I want to kiss you . . ."

· · ·

Back at the château we enter the caves, which aren't caves at all, but big, low-ceilinged rooms dug out of the earth. It's a little like a bandit's hideout or a root cellar, but fancier. Coming out of sunlight into the murky dark, it takes a few moments for my eyes to adjust. I stand in the dark and feel how cool and dry it is in the cave, how the air smells spicy. The walls are lined with giant wooden casks of wine, and further back in the gloom are metal racks stacked with hundreds of bottles lying on their sides like they're sleeping. The room is lit by a chandelier of candles, and many more little white candles stuck in the hollowed-out walls of the gloomy room. I've lost sight of the boy; I hope he hasn't cut out. I want him to see me in this light. *Seventeen* says that candlelight is the most flattering light there is; the next is a red lightbulb, or a red scarf thrown over a white lampshade, to make your skin look pink.

Set out on top of some giant wooden barrels are dark green bottles of Pouilly-Fumé and a clear, almost bell-shaped bottle of Pear William that is half empty. The pale yellow pear juts out of the remaining pool of eau-de-vie like a woman reclining in a bathtub. What I want is to touch that pear for just a second.

There are also glasses full of Pouilly-Fumé and Pear William. They gleam with the light of hundreds of tiny candle flames, leaping against the glass. The glasses' stems are shorter and the bowls smaller than the wineglasses we have at home. I wonder if this French wineglass is the one *Cosmo* says the perfect breast is supposed to fit into? Or was that a champagne glass?

Everyone, including my parents, is hovering around the

guide, who is describing a wine as tasting of meadows and figs with a pineappley nose. No one is paying any attention to me, so I snag a glass of Pouilly-Fumé. As I take it into my mouth I realize that the *fumé* is the fire, the sting on my tongue, the burning in my throat. I don't smell any vanilla or taste any honey, but I pick up another glass and take it off into a dark corner of the cave to sip it alone. Not that anybody would notice me anyway, seeing as everybody, even Dad, seems hypnotized by our guide, who scolds a woman for picking up a cork and smelling it.

"Ah ah ah, one reads a cork, one does not smell a cork," he says condescendingly. "The cork, she smells like cork."

I scan the room for the French boy. I feel a little light-headed from the first glass of wine, but I think now that the wine tastes good, and it's relaxing me. I'm good at this.

I spot the dark-haired boy as he picks up two glasses of wine like he's at a bar, like he does this all the time, and starts to walk over to me. I drink my wine quickly, watching out of the corner of my eye as Dad swishes wine around in his mouth like Listerine. My mother sniffs her wine, then takes a loud sip, sucking the wine into her mouth. It's too embarrassing to watch. Dee is standing between them, pouting, and still wearing the sunglasses, which must make the room pitch black. Poor Dee really believed that there were bats in these caves. Even when my mother told us my father was joking, even when she told us, "And it's not cave, it's cahh-v." Dee still wouldn't let go of the possibility. To her, cave-cahv was no different than vase and vah-z. Same diff. Dee didn't want to get it.

"You like, yes?" the boy says in my ear, and hands me a

glass of wine. I sip it, it's the Pear William, it's thicker and much sweeter than the wine. Eau-de-vie tastes like syrup with heat.

"*Merci,*" I say, hoping I don't sound too nervous, or too American, although he must know I'm not French, since all I do when he speaks is grin like a baboon. I could speak with him, but I'm just too nervous now—my parents are here, not to mention Dee, who is always spying on me. I wish I were wearing my mother's tight black sundress instead of a camp shirt and cutoffs with sandals. I've got a Band-Aid on my knee from where I wiped out racing Dee in the hotel parking lot two nights ago. I look like a stupid kid. He stands close to me and drinks his wine down in one gulp, his eyes fixed over the top of his glass on my breasts. At least I have those.

I look back at my parents and Dad's eyes are on me. He looks a little confused, like maybe he isn't sure if it's me, or not. After all, it is dark, and this guy is standing right in front of me. Then he looks away. It isn't me, it isn't his daughter.

"*J'aime le poire,*" I say, pointing to the pear lying there in the last bit of brandy.

"You want?" he asks, with a shrug.

"*Oui, je voudrais.*" I would like, I guess, but too much more and I will be *très* drunk.

"*Le poire?*" he asks, checking with me, although I don't know what else he thinks I mean.

He picks up the bottle and gives it a good whack on the side of the table. The sound of breaking glass is like a firecracker. All conversation stops for just a second, but everybody is having such a good time, nobody cares that a bottle got broken. My parents don't even look for me. My breath is caught in my mouth; I can't believe no one suspects us. But why would they, the boy is holding the bottle at his side, just below the broken neck, so casual, no one can see what he's done. He sticks his hand sideways through the broken neck and pulls out the pear, wetting his hand.

He licks the pear, then hands it to me, like it was no big deal. Like he'll do anything for me. I hold the slippery pear in my hand.

He licks his knuckles. There's blood on his hand. I pull his hand toward my mouth and lick his wound. The blood mixed with the brandy is making me drunk.

Who am I? I wonder, watching myself lick this boy's fingers, noticing the dirt beneath his nails and not caring. Who is this girl? I don't recognize her.

I slowly start walking backward away from the crowd, drawing him toward the wine racks that touch the ceiling. I need to catch my breath, but mostly I need to get out of my parents' line of vision, because I know that I'm about to have my first kiss, finally my first real kiss, and it's with a Frenchman.

"So you are American, yes?" the boy asks, wiping his cut hand against his pants leg. He's checking out my legs and my Levi's, which I guess give me away.

"*Oui,*" I say. The pear in my hand feels like a grenade. Suddenly, I feel like he's wearing those glasses they advertise in the back of comic books that let guys see through your clothes.

"So you speak French, yes?" he asks, brushing his hair out of his eyes in a kind of bored, cool way.

"*Un peu,*" I say, holding my finger and thumb apart. I

want to seem cute, not too smart, not too weird. That turns boys off. But I want to speak more French, not only because the language is so romantic, but because it would be part of the foreign experience; still, he has to speak really slowly for me to understand what he's saying.

He leans toward me and picks up some strands of my hair, and he smells them with his eyes half closed. I'm not sure what that's about, but I'm glad I just washed it last night. Then he whispers in my ear something I can't understand. The scar intersecting his eyebrow looks like a road between two fields—maybe it was a dog bite, maybe he fell off his bicycle. I laugh out of nervousness, or maybe it's excitement. He steps closer to me and puts his hand on my shoulder like he's feeling the fabric of my shirt. I lean toward him, then back off. He's so tall I'm going to have to stand on tiptoe to kiss him.

Even though we're back behind the casks, I'm still anxious about getting caught. My parents would put me under hotel arrest, or rental car arrest—either way, they'd never set me free in France again. Plus it's not that romantic. I want to be outside in the pear grove. I want him to throw me down on the grass and kiss me. I put up my hand to warn him, not here, not now, but he pulls his hand away from my shoulder and his eyes cloud up, like I'm rejecting him, but I'm not.

"*Non, non,*" I say, and I make a grab for his hand because I'm afraid he's just going to walk away, and I don't want him to. I don't want him to leave. I want to talk. I just want to hold his hand first. I want to stroll through the trees as the sun is setting and share this pear. I close my eyes and try to come up with the proper words to say, "Let's go somewhere else, back outside."

When I open my eyes again he's staring at me, the muscles at the corner of his mouth sort of slack, his eyes sort of unfocused like he can't see me anymore. I can tell he thinks I don't want him to kiss me, but I do. I do want him to, I think. I love the pear he gave me. Then he says something that sounds hurt or angry and sort of hunches his shoulders and drops his head. For a minute he does nothing, then he sticks his foot out and rubs the toe of his black loafer up the back of my leg. I don't know what to think, I can't think. I know I don't want him to leave. He keeps rubbing his toe into the socket behind my knee. Back and forth. It's wrong, I know, but it's also weirdly good. I can feel my whole face turning red. He stops, and for a second I think maybe he's about to apologize, but he doesn't. He just stands there staring at me, but not really at me, more like right through me. I stare hard into his eyes, looking for the boy he was earlier, trying to bring him back. His eyelids start to droop, then he's doing something at his crotch, yanking his hand back and forth like he's trying to start up a chain saw. I don't want to look, or I don't want him to see me looking. But then his pants are unzipped and he's pulling and shaking his thing at me like it's angry, or like it's trying to escape, and I can't look away. I mean, I just stare at it, like I'm hypnotized. It's weird but I like it a little. I am making this happen, I think. He can't help himself. Does this mean he likes me? I can't believe it. It isn't until he cums on the top of my foot that I realize how stupid I've been. I don't know what I'm supposed to do.

Cry, scream, laugh? I know I should laugh. This is a bad joke, but I can't laugh. I don't make a sound.

He grabs his thing and stuffs it back into his fly, which is gaping open like his mouth, zips up, and then walks quickly away from me. He doesn't smile or say good-bye, he just leaves. His cum drips down between my toes. I swear it smells like boiled chicken. Why was it that so many things that were supposed to be exotic or special were all just another lousy form of chicken?

The boy walks fast back out into the main part of the cave, head down, and no one even seems to see him, and then he's gone. Peering through the rows of bottles, I see his profile in one of the small cave windows as he heads back toward the orchard. How could I have let this happen?

Maybe I'm just really drunk, and if I just don't look down, if I don't see it, it hasn't really happened. But my foot is slick and cool with cum. I'm still clutching the pear in my hand. It had seemed so precious. It was stupid of me to think of that pear as being like a woman. I drop it, and when it rolls under a cask, I think for a second about rescuing her—it seems mean to leave her—but I don't. I hope she rots there.

I kick off my sandal and drag my foot back and forth across the dirt floor of the cave until my foot is dirty and it burns. I pour the rest of the eau-de-vie on my foot; it tingles like medicine. Then I shove my foot back into my sandal and head for the door, my face turned to the ground. I don't want my parents to see me, see the look I must have on my face.

My mantra surfaces in my mind, "Pouilly-Fumé, Chardonnay, Pouilly-Fuissé, Sancerre," but it seems dumb now. They're just words.

For a second I wonder if he's outside waiting for me, and my heart beats faster. But outside the sun is just starting to set, blazing orange, smearing the sky with streaks of pink and purple, the way my mother's lipstick bleeds into her dinner napkin, and the boy is gone.

I crawl into the backseat of Josephine and sit there numbly working the door lock. I want to go home now. How could I be so stupid? I slump down in the seat and roll onto my stomach, the way I slept as a baby. I can just imagine my parents' patient smiles that say, *share*, but mean *but don't hurt us. Lie to us. Don't tell us anything that will get you in trouble.* Worse than their anger would be them feeling sorry for me.

I am sitting up, resting my head on the window, by the time my parents and Dee show up. My stomach feels sour and queasy from drinking. My mouth is so dry, it's like I've eaten cat litter.

"Jesus, how long have you been out here?" my father grouses, sliding into the driver's seat. He stows his camera bag in the backseat at my feet. He must be out of film.

"I don't know, a little while," I mumble.

"We were looking for you," my mother says. "We were worried."

"Sorry," I say.

"Are you all right, honey?" my mother asks, cocking her head like she can see me better this way, like she's peering through a keyhole in an invisible door. She leans over the seat and puts the back of her hand to my head, her eyes searching mine for clues.

"Sweetheart?"

My father checks me out in the mirror. A long hard stare. I can't meet his eye.

"I feel sort of sick, I guess." Holding my stomach, like if I move my arms something will spill out of me, something I didn't know I could lose.

"Why didn't you come get us?" she asks like she feels bad for being so mean to me earlier. My father pops his sunglasses in the glove compartment. He rubs his fists into his eye sockets, looking tired and annoyed. My mother hands him two aspirin, and he swallows them without water.

"Let's get on the road, then," he says, and starts up the car. "We're behind schedule."

Dee says, "You can put your head in my lap if you want to. It's okay."

"I'm okay," I lie, and close my eyes.

"I promise I won't touch you or anything," Dee says, and it's almost enough to make me cry again. She has no idea how much I would like that, and how I can't let her.

I lean my head against the window, willing myself to sleep. I watch the landscape through my lashes, green, black, brown, it's all a blur. I can't tell what's fence and what's tree. My father told me once as we walked through the woods behind our house that I didn't need to be scared of snakes. As long as you saw them first you had the upper hand. "Snakes see the world as either tree or food. If you move, you're food, if you don't, you're a tree." My father thinks the world is this simple. Things are magic or true, food or tree. Never both. Dee is humming to herself and flipping through our rock 'n' roll magazine.

"I like Keith Moon too," she says to me, but I pretend I'm sleeping. She pulls my feet into her lap and pets them. "I'm sorry I called you a sexpot," she whispers.

"Mom," Dee calls quietly, "I think she's asleep," and points at me.

"Dee, honey, did you see Evie drinking wine?" Dee shakes her head no, her forehead creasing with worry. She can't imagine why you'd want to do that.

"Don't worry," my mother says, and pats Dee's leg. "She's okay. Everything's just fine."

I try to force myself down into sleep, into that place you come up from feeling somehow cleaned, but I can't. I see the boy's face, I see my father's eyes watching me, watching me walk backward into the dark with that boy.

I am still awake when we reach the hotel. My father goes in to register, leaving us in the car. My mother watches me in her side mirror. Her smile is soft, like she's watching a baby sleep. When my father returns, she whispers to him, "Should we wake her up, Chas?"

My father shakes his head. I wonder how long they will leave me here in the car, in this parking lot. Fine, leave me here like a pile of dirty laundry, I don't care.

I keep my eyes squeezed shut, then I feel my car door open. Through my lashes I see my father standing there, the sun blotted out by his body, his arms hanging limp at his side. Then he kneels down and leans inside the car. I try not to cry, or move, or do anything that might tell him I'm pretending, that all I want is for him to touch my skin, to hold me. Then I feel my father wrap one arm around my shoulders and pull me into his chest. He slides his other arm under my legs. His knees buckle slightly as he lifts me up. His breath is heavy and wine-scented. I let my head fall against his shoulder and I stay asleep in his arms.

NOVICE

BITCH

"Want a treat?" my mother asks, but before I can even open my mouth, Sunny slips a hot-dog-shaped dog yummie between her teeth, bends down, and scoops Waffles up off the kitchen floor. Waffles obediently bites down on the tiny weenie and for a second, nose to nose, they kiss.

"Well, that is completely revolting," I say.

My mother raises an eyebrow, and I wait for her to share some inane dog factoid with me, like how a dog's mouth is cleaner than a human's, but she doesn't, instead she sighs.

Sunny is the wounded mother persecuted by a selfish ungrateful daughter. Mildred Pierce of Park Avenue.

"Dogs are easy. They listen, Mary Beth. They respond to kindness," my mother says, stroking Waffles as she peruses the day's schedule for the Westminster Dog Show. My mother is such a drama queen.

"Poor Sunny," I say. "How do you ever stand it?"

She won't even look at me. She absolutely detests it when I call her by her first name, but I cannot help it, sometimes it just slips out.

Waffles is a King Charles spaniel, the dog most favored by the royal family of Spain and immortalized in the court paintings of Goya. They were lap dogs, canine napkins for their owners to wipe their greasy hands on during banquets. I think this is why my mother bought him, even though he is not a show dog. Sunny still has delusions of grandeur, of the old days when she had a buzzer under the dining-room table that she would push with her foot when she wanted the cook to serve the next course, the old days when my father would instruct the pilot to land the company plane so my mother could pee on terra firma. Now, at forty-eight, my mother is a divorcée in a dim little two-bedroom apartment at Eighty-first and Park that the two of us have shared for the last four years. Sunny is one of those blazered geeks you see trotting poodles in formation, bribing them with liver snaps to stand still on a table while some stranger gropes their withers. She would never have done this if my father hadn't left her for a twenty-five-year-old, forcing her to find something to do in order to make a living. She should thank him; after all, she is always saying, "Dog training is the first thing I've ever done for myself, and it's the first thing I've ever been really really good at it." I am supposed to disagree with her, say she is a great mother. Ha.

Today Mom is showing Mr. Jeffrey, one of her prize dogs. This pug could *make* her.

"Puppy Class, Novice Bitch, Best of Breed..." my mother mutters to herself as she takes down her favorite cereal bowl. I like to say *novice bitch*. It's like a bitch in training.

On this big day Mom's preparing her breakfast of champions—she weighs what looks like a cup of gravel on her trusty diet scale, pours some blue milk over it, then digs in, her chewing sounding like a wood chipper.

When she finishes she puts her bowl on the floor, where Waffles hoovers up the last bit of milk.

"Did you eat anything, Mary Beth?" she asks, peering over her reading glasses so she can actually see me. "Breakfast is the most important meal of the day. Are you getting taller, or is that hemline inching up?" She frowns, and two wrinkles in her forehead cross like swords on a family crest. "I'd like to hear what the sisters have to say about that." Sacred Virgin Academy is supposed to be the strictest of the socially elite Catholic girls' schools in the city, a place where girls from good families can go to have the inner wayward slut disciplined out. I've been going there since I was three. My parents weren't taking any chances. On the way home from school we roll up the waists of our blue skirts to make them minis, stuff our ties in our bags, ditch the ugly navy blazers, push down our socks, undo an extra button on our white blouses to show off cleavage and, in my case, a little gold crucifix with a ruby in the center, caught between my tits. Could you die?

"I ate already."

"What did you eat?" she asks suspiciously.

"I had a donut and milk." I just love watching my mother's face scrunch up in disgust.

As usual, I absolutely could not sleep. I lay in bed fiddling with my crucifix—my father gave it to me for my confirmation—but I just could not lie still, so I got up. Anyway, it was already six, a slit of yellow light catching fire at the bottom of my shade. Sometimes I like to get up really early and just throw a coat over my pajamas, then stroll up Lexington Avenue. It is completely deserted and eerie like a movie set, not a soul around except for recovering alcoholics riding their bikes to AA meetings and doormen hosing off the sidewalks. It is like I own the entire world. At the Korean market I bought a chocolate donut, a carton of Quik, and a pack of Marlboro Lights. I really was not hungry, the cigarette was okay, but that's about all. And of course, about twenty minutes later when I was in the shower I threw it all up. As I was kneeling there trying to push my vomit down the drain, I almost started to cry, which I absolutely never do. I can go months and months without crying. But getting sick like that, it bugged me for some reason. It never had before.

Two years ago, when I was fourteen my mother taught me how to throw up. She'd come home from a New York Kennel Club meeting and found me sprawled and groaning on the family-room floor, skirt unbuttoned, legs akimbo, wallowing in a sea of shiny cellophane Little Debbie Snack Cake wrappers. The way Sunny reacted, you'd have thought she'd found me doped up and naked with a Puerto Rican boy.

After nearly making me beg her to make it better, she dragged me to my feet and pushed me into the bathroom. I felt as full as the ticks I used to pull off of Waffles in the country, ticks big and fat as blueberries that I would explode with matches like little blood bombs. I had this marvelous vision of my mother holding my chin as she fed me spoonfuls of sweet pink Pepto-Bismol, then tucking me into her big bed with a glass of ginger ale.

In the bathroom she cranked the sink taps on full blast, little droplets of water spraying out of the bowl, hanging in the air like a fine misting rain.

"Here," she said, getting down on her knees beside the sink, kneeling in front of the toilet the way we kneeled together at Mass.

"Come on," she said gently, and pulled me down beside her. "There's nothing to be afraid of."

I nodded. This was far too weird. I stared at my mother's hand grasping the toilet seat; I couldn't even imagine her touching a toilet. I could see the tiniest little nicks on her knuckles.

"Now, you want that garbage gone, don't you? Because that's what it is right now, just garbage," she said, her voice suddenly hard and purposeful.

I nodded again.

"Gone forever from your body. You want to feel light and clean, don't you?" she said as though she wasn't just teaching me to puke but also offering to wash away my sins.

"Of course you do." She pushed my hair back behind my ears, and into the back of my blouse, split ends tickling my spine. "For safety's sake," she said.

"Just these two fingers," she directed, holding up her first and middle fingers pressed together. "That's good."

So I opened my mouth, leaned over the toilet, and stuck my fingers in my mouth. I felt that little pendulum of pink flesh in the back of my throat brush the back of my hand. I gagged, of course, but nothing happened. I was failing her. Hail Mary, I prayed.

"Here, let me help you," she said, and took my hand and guided it into my mouth, my teeth scraping the top of my hand. She didn't even seem to see me; she was biting her lip, deep in concentration, as she pushed my hand further and further until both of my fingers were well down my throat, the tips of my fingers touching my windpipe. She held my hand there, even as I started to gag, my stomach leaping like a trampoline, tears bouncing into my eyes. She let go just in time and everything came up—bright yellow Fritos, my garish hot lunch of sloppy joe and fries, chocolate milk, and the barely digested Little Debbies, the cream still visible. My back arched like a cat as I heaved again, this time just at the smell of it.

"Don't worry, it gets easier," my mother said, then stood up and straightened her skirt. "You did very well, dear. I'm proud of you." She bent down and patted my head, then turned the tap down to a trickle. I laid my head on the toilet seat and listened to the water run. I watched my mother walk away, her greyhound legs moving with purpose, high heels clicking on the tile floor. I studied her tight calves, the muscles massed in a ball, permanently shortened by a life in high heels, so that now it hurt her to walk in flats.

That was the closest we have ever been. That was our big connection. She wanted to help me, and I think I loved her then. I think purging is the only thing Sunny has taught me other than how to respond to a formal party invitation and when and where you can wear white shoes. It is so annoying, but almost every time I make myself throw up, I think of her—if just for a split second. Sometimes I think, See, take that, I am not fat, and I am not a child. I can take care of myself. Sometimes I think, I don't want to be you. I want to be just the opposite of you.

This morning when I threw up in the shower I did not think of her, I thought of Dr. Andrews. I had a three o'clock appointment. What was I going to wear?

"You're in bed," Sunny says, stating the obvious.

"I'm sick," I say, and curl up like a shrimp.

"It's that donut," she says. "Good Lord, Mary Beth, do you have any idea how many calories are in a chocolate donut? Do you? They are the atom bomb of the food world," she says, her eyes flitting around the room like a weapons inspector searching for warheads: an arsenal of candy corn, an underwear drawer mined with Tastycakes.

"I don't know about that," I say, rolling onto my back so I can see her upside down, "but in yesterday's *Post* it reported that a recent study found the aroma of donuts to be the single most arousing scent to men."

"Oh, that's nice, Mary Beth, that's a very nice way to talk to your mother."

"Mmmm. Dunkin' Munchkins."

"Fine. I don't want to hear you complain about not having a boyfriend." If only she knew. I would bet money that I have slept with more guys than my mother *ever* did.

"I cannot get over you, Sunny. Here I am near death's door and you are on me about my weight," I say. "I have been vomiting for days. Days."

"I'm just trying to help you," she replies, then pulls out her compact and vigorously powders her nose. "Beauty is power, dear. You better learn it now." She crayons on a bit of shell-pink lipstick, a shade she's been wearing since her debutante days.

"I know, *Mother*," I say, trying to sound forlorn, like she is always right and I am always wrong. I do not want to fight anymore today. I just want her to leave. I struggle to sit up and hunch my shoulders so I look completely pathetic.

"Do you need me to write you a note?" she asks.

I nod.

"Fine," she says as she puts on her blazer and straightens her lapels. She runs her hands quickly up the length of each leg, checking her stockings for ladders.

"If you need me you know where I'll be," she says, and gives me a little half hug. Mother-daughter photo op.

"Oh, I love my sweet baby," she coos, ambushing Waffles as he licks his groin in my bedroom doorway. She cradles him in her arms and kisses him on the belly. She shuts my door, and then a second later opens it. "Dear, do you think you will be able to use those tickets for the dog show?"

"I don't know," I say, annoyed. I am sick after all.

"You know, it would be nice if you took the smallest interest in what I do," she says.

I say nothing. What can I say?

"Well," she sighs, "that's the best ticket in town today, and believe me, some people would give their eyeteeth to be there. It's a big day. Mr. Jeffrey . . . Best of Breed . . ." she says as though this will entice me.

I shrug.

"If his owner calls, could you please tell her I'm already at the Garden, and tell her to keep the dirty laundry off the floor. I tell you, if that dog eats one more sock, saints protect us," she says, crossing herself and closing the door behind her with a ladylike slam.

I flip on the TV and have a smoke. Then I go into the kitchen and open the fridge. There's a wallet-sized studio portrait of Mr. Jeffrey on the door. A pug in profile in front of a blue satin curtain. It looks like a school photo. All he needs is a bow tie. What a runt. I think about taking a little nip of my mother's frozen Stoli, but I don't. My stomach hurts, but it is a good hurt; the insistent hunger pangs remind me that I have control. In one way, I am pure. Still, my heart is absolutely pounding, like a ball-peen hammer on steel.

I pinch a Valium from Sunny's medicine cabinet and think about calling Phillip, but he's at work. Yesterday morning I'd stopped by his apartment at seven. As I was tiptoeing out of the apartment, my mother called sleepily from her bedroom, "Grab a banana."

I had to crack up.

At first he was mad that I'd just stopped by, as he always was, but once he had me tied up to his Ikea bed frame, in my school uniform, white cotton panties at my ankles, he was happy. Afterward, after he'd modestly stepped back into the boxers he'd left like a pair of fireman's boots by the bed, after he'd showered and I'd wiped myself with his lame bondage gear—four Brooks Brothers silk neckties—I sat him down and told him I was pregnant, and he was mad again. He started to completely freak out. "You're seventeen—for Christ's sake!" he said, as though I had to be reminded. Tears came into his eyes. He said, "I hate this. I really really hate this."

"Me too. I've never been in this situation before, I'm lost. I don't know what to do!" I wonder if, like my father's, the tips of my ears turn red when I lie.

Phillip did know what to do. He figured it all out like the businessman he was—he was so good at figuring out profits and risks. I would get an abortion. There was no other choice.

Of course, just being a kid I don't have that kind of cash, even if my dad is rich. Phillip was good about that; there'd be no going dutch, no way. We walked together to the cash machine, but not holding hands. It was so odd to be on the street with him in the daylight, him all grown-up in his Wall Street costume—a dark gray Brooks Brothers suit and black tasseled loafers—and me in my hideous blue uniform. As we walked I started lagging behind him. I wanted him to slow down and walk with me, talk to me, but he was cruising. At one point, I let him cross the street without me, the traffic rushing through the space between us. I stood there with a girl in a uniform similar to mine, but she was maybe eleven. She had chubby thighs and her hair was brushed back into a low sophisticated ponytail and fastened with a tortoiseshell clip, the way I bet her mother wore her own hair. She was holding hands with her father and he was tugging on her ponytail and she was laughing like it was the funniest damn thing in the world. I don't remember if my father ever walked me to school. I just don't remember. When the light changed, the two of them literally hopped off the curb and, arm in arm, crossed the street. I thought, That girl has never even given a guy a blow job. She's never had a guy feel her up and tell her, "You are so beautiful."

Across the street, Phillip was glaring at me. Hands on his hips, he barked, "Come on, step it up," just like my father.

At the ATM he inserted his card, then paused for a moment, turning his shoulder to shelter the screen like some kid who thinks you want to cheat off him. God, he had some nerve.

"I've got to make sure I've got enough," he said in a low voice. "Shit," he said. "It's got to be money market."

He sighed, dug into his briefcase, and pulled out a slim black checkbook. Then, right there in the street, he wrote me a check. I held out my Algebra II book and he used it for a desk. His handwriting was shakier than a boy's; *he* needed a Valium.

"Get a good doctor, a reputable man. Do you know what I mean, Mary Beth?"

I nodded, I knew what he meant—someone discreet. I didn't tell him I'd already made an appointment last week.

"This should cover it, don't you think?" he asked me,

and I saw there a glimmer of who we used to be. Me sitting in his lap at Dorian's, the bar where we met. The romantic dinners in expensive restaurants smaller than my living room, the clubbing and staying up until morning doing coke and smoking pot and talking about his dull Ohio childhood. The pressure of his body on top of mine. The time a homeless guy selling roses and giant stuffed chickens out of a shopping cart told him, "That's one beautiful girl, you best hold on to her," and Phillip laughed and said, "Don't I know it, brother."

It was understood that the money was to cover "the procedure," a cab, some flowers for me, maybe a box of chocolates, some bubble bath. He kissed me quickly on the lips, then pulled me to his chest.

"I'm so sorry," he said into my part, holding me tight against his body, like he wanted to hide me inside of him. It felt good to be touched, to be held in place so tightly. Here I was. Then he pulled away and took my chin in one hand. "Take care of yourself," he said, starting to cry again, and that was that.

Well, I was taking care of myself. I was a girl with a check for $2,000. As I caught the bus to school, I wondered how much money a thirty-three-year-old stockbroker made. What would he have had to shell out if he'd wanted to make me an honest woman? Wasn't two months' salary the rule of thumb for what a man was supposed to blow on a girl's engagement ring?

I'd been gypped.

The doorbell rings. I peek through the fish-eye and see Marco, our doorman, standing in the hall, grinning at me.

"Your mother tells me you're sick," he says when I open the door. Marco is nicer to me than any other adult. I think it's because he and his wife can't have kids.

"Here, I thought this might make you feel better. You got a postcard from your father." He holds it up between his fingers like a magician pulling the lucky card you picked out of the pack.

"Oh really," I say, trying to sound bored, then I snap the card out of his fingers and close the door fast.

Marco reads all our mail, and I don't want Marco to tell me what my father has written.

I take it into the bathroom. These days I have to pee constantly. I turn on the tap, even though nobody's home, and go. In Japan they have toilets that when you sit down make the sound of water running so no one can hear you pee. Sunny would love that.

Dad's card is basically a weather report. In Cancun it's sunny and warm. No surprise. I take it into the kitchen and read it again, between the lines, searching for subtext the way the Sisters teach us in English class.

> *Dear Mary Beth,*
>
> *Greetings! Isn't this sunset amazing? The weather has been great, really cooperating. I've been on the golf course every day. Had a super lobster the other night at a restaurant on the beach. You'd love it. How's school?*

Blah blah blah. Like he can't call me up? Like he can't pick up the phone and ask me how I am? I haven't heard his voice in weeks and weeks. I run my finger over his big loopy script, watching my hand move, is that how his hand moves?

Be good, he writes.

Love Dad, he writes.

I throw the card in the trash, then pick it out. I am so weak.

I think about buying myself a beautiful pair of Italian leather boots with his American Express card. He gave me my own charge because he knows how tight-fisted my mother can be.

"I don't want you to do without," he'd said, pressing the card into my hand, like the key to some imaginary city, "but don't abuse it."

Abuse it? That card wanted it.

I like using his card, it's as if he's actually buying me things. Sometimes when I'm feeling blue I'll go shopping. I'll hold up dresses and ask, Would he like this? Would he think this looked pretty on me? Mostly, though, I use his card because it's my right as his daughter; he owed me that leather car coat, he owed me that handbag. Anytime I'm short on a tab, good old Dad steps out of the shadows to help me out. *Here my dear let me get that for you, no no I insist. My treat.* One day after field hockey practice I took the whole team out for sundaes on Dad's card. Did he ever get mad? Not really. He'd just say, "Be careful with that card, honey." Or when we get together for one of our quarterly dinners in the city, he'll say, "That's a pretty skirt, did I buy that?" and for some reason I always lie and say no, even though I absolutely make a point of wearing clothes he's paid for when I see him.

In my room I change out of my uniform and into a pale

blue cashmere sweater my grandmother gave me for Christmas last year, a knee-length blue flowered skirt, and a pair of black ballet flats, both from Mom. It's important, my mother says, to look nice when you go to the doctor. In case, I suppose, you die there.

The clinic's waiting room is full of slick, uncomfortable orange and yellow plastic chairs, bus-station furniture designed to cause discomfort, to make loitering absolutely impossible, as if anybody would want to hang out here. The ceiling is low. Overhead, one of the fluorescent lights has a bad tube. It keeps flickering, providing a kind of disco effect. Inside the light are dead flies, all on their backs, legs up and crossed. How did they get in there in the first place?

In one corner, sort of hiding behind a dark-blue-and-purple silk flower arrangement, sits a lifeguard type, wavy, slightly long blond hair, tan, good teeth. He's holding a Coach Grace Kelly–style purse on his knee, bouncing it the way you do a baby. His eyes are completely bloodshot, probably not from crying, but from pot. Stoned courage. A tall, dark-haired guy in khakis and a navy blazer stands looking at the selection of pamphlets—*So You've Got Genital Herpes, Infants 101,* and *The Truth About Gonorrhea,* which I once thought sounded like a travel brochure for some mysterious and secluded island that doesn't welcome tourists. He is cute. When he sits down across from me and accidentally drops the lavender cardigan he's been clutching, I smile at him, and he looks completely confused. Thank heavens I didn't bring a purse—who would be its faithful guardian? Certainly not the fat man in the shiny green suit dozing beside me, the day's racing form balanced on his knee. I say a Hail Mary out of nervousness. I haven't told a soul, not even my girlfriends know, no one. They wouldn't understand, they are still caught up in making out and dry humping, playing the power game of stopping guys before things go too far. Well, too far is where I live. I think of my mother. What would she say? What would she do if she knew what I had done? I imagine the lightning crack of ice cubes being hurled into a glass. *Slut!* The slosh of vodka as my mother, Athena of the cocktails, prepared to annihilate me. *You are no child of mine!*

A rotund nurse with a mad scramble of red hair and the tiniest mouth I have ever seen shows me into a cool pink room. It is like being inside a cone of cotton candy. I hang up my jean jacket and get undressed. I drop my sweet-sixteen pearl necklace into the toe of my shoe and put on the blue robe, ties in the front. My hands are shaking so badly I can hardly make a knot. The nurse takes my blood pressure. Her hands are cold and soft. She is humming. She makes no small talk. She just smiles at me and hums some tune like a polka. I can't tell what she is thinking. She scribbles down some numbers. I wonder if she has ever had an abortion, if she hates me for doing this.

"Everything normal?" Conversation would be nice.

She hums and nods and then vanishes.

It is positively arctic in here. I stand on tiptoe. I pinch my gut, I am getting fat. I tell myself, No solid food for two days. The Muzak station is playing the hundred-strings version of "Stairway to Heaven." That was my old boyfriend Mi-

chael's and my song. Now Michael, Michael would have come
with me.

I pace for a while. My feet are freezing from the tile
floor, so I finally climb up on the table. It's a huge stainless
steel table, covered with white paper that comes off a giant
roll, the kind you use as a kid in art class. On the ceiling
someone, perhaps the red-haired nurse, has taped a National
Geographic photo of a cool green waterfall buried in the jungle. It looks like a place you would really have to hike to, a
place that is special because so few people have seen it. It is
a lovely distraction. That's what it is, and I laugh out loud;
that's what Phillip called me once, a lovely distraction.

Where *is* Dr. Andrews? Usually he makes an appearance
before the nurses take my blood pressure and temperature. It
is like he is so happy to see me that he can hardly wait until
they are done with me, but today, so far, he is a no-show. It
is prom season, I think, he must be backed up. Out in the
gray-and-green-tiled hall, gleaming silver gurneys are lined up
against the wall, like limousines waiting to spirit girls into
recovery. Recovery is nice. It's quiet, it is like a war hospital
in the movies, rows of white beds, girls lying there, some
weeping, some sleeping. Some girls have IVs trailing from their
arms, some are chatting with their neighbors. I would not be
surprised to see somebody, one day, break out a pack of cards.
Anything for a distraction. Then the nurse comes by with a
tray of cookies and juice. Everybody who can sit up sits up
and takes one. Last time they were butter cookies with the
imprint of a little schoolboy on them. I nibbled off his feet,
then his stomach, and finally I ate his face. By the time you

leave, you have had a nap and your snack, and a nurse has given you a thick sanitary pad, dense and white as a snowbank. Leaving the hospital with this huge pad in your pants it feels like you are a girl again, like it is your first period and your mother won't let you use tampons because they might break your hymen. It is like your virginity has been restored, and you are a good girl all over again.

I wait. I wonder if Dr. Andrews is married. Does he have kids?

I close my eyes and think of him. He's at least six feet six inches tall and thin as a weather vane, his graying hair brushed straight back from his high forehead, and because he uses some kind of pomade, you can always see the furrows from his comb in his hair. He likes to wear those old-fashioned suits with high-waisted gabardine pants, and on the street he wears a marvelous felt fedora, which makes him look like an old movie star. He's from the Midwest, he told me that, and that as a kid he was clumsy and lousy at sports. He grew ten inches his freshman year of college. Sometimes he sounds a little like Jimmy Stewart. I love to hear him say my name.

The first time, he asked me if I wanted a nurse to hold my hand during the procedure. He asked me if there was anyone waiting for me, or should someone call me a cab. I said yes, someone was waiting for me, but I didn't tell him that Michael was loitering outside smoking like a fiend. Neither Michael nor I wanted him to come in. I suppose he could have sat out in the waiting room with all the other guilty-looking sperm dumpers, but it just felt too personal. Still, I didn't want the doctor to think I was a slut, or somebody who nobody cared about.

The second time, he did not ask me if I wanted a hand-holder, instead he told me jokes. *What did the little pig say when he fell down the steps? Oh, my achin' bacon. What did the grape say when it got stepped on? Nothing, it just let out a little wine.* Jokes, I now realize, that were all about pain. Maybe he was afraid that despite the anesthetic, I would be in pain. He didn't want me to be in pain.

The second time, he told me, "Mary Beth, you are a good girl with very bad luck."

I had lied and written on my form that I was using a condom and a sponge, when in truth I was unprepared. It was my first and only date with Paolo, a gorgeous curly-haired Italian waiter from Mezzaluna. We ended up at the Plaza, at Trader Vic's. I took him up to the second floor to show him the ballroom where I had gone to my very first fancy-dress ball. I thought about saying, "Stop it," but it was over so fast, it was like an accident. It didn't seem so bad until he didn't call me, until I saw how he'd torn the hook and eyes out of my bra when he couldn't get it undone, until every time I went into the restaurant he had somebody else wait on me.

I had told Dr. Andrews that I was alone. I did not tell him what happened, although I wanted to tell him, but I would rather he think me mysterious.

Today, who knows, maybe Dr. Andrews will sing "Ol' Man River" to me and accompany himself on harmonica— that would be a nice counterbalance to the drone of machines, the dreadful sucking sounds. Today when Dr. Andrews asks me about the cab, I will say, "Can't you take me with you?" Or, "Maybe you could just drop me on your way home?"

Then we'll ride together in his car. He'll have lemon drops in his glove compartment, plus maps of all the prime foliage states. He'll buy me a tuna melt at the coffee shop. We'll talk. He'll like me. I'll tell him my really dumb knock-knock jokes, and he'll ask me if I want to go to the aquarium this weekend to see the seals, and I'll say yes, yes please.

There's a soft quick rap on the door. I sit up. Dr. Andrews has my file pressed to his chest. He is wearing a dark blue suit today, with a very worn alligator belt. He pinches the bridge of his long nose and rubs his eyes for a moment.

"So, here we are," he says, closing the door behind him. He's been working too hard. "How are we feeling today?" he asks, sitting down hard on the metal stool, his knees sticking out like a praying mantis's, and I believe he cares, but for some reason he's looking not in my eyes, but at my neck, or into my chest.

"Not so hot." I lean over and grab my stomach. Now I do not want to look in his eyes. Something feels wrong.

"Well, I can't say I'm surprised," he says, shaking his head a little. He seems angry. He attempts to rig up a smile, but he cannot sustain it. It collapses in a grimace.

"I'm sorry," he says. He shakes his head, and rubs his eyes again. I suddenly feel sick. I want to say, "It's not my fault that this happened." Instead I just sit there and feel myself shrinking, getting colder and colder, and smaller and smaller.

He picks up a tongue depressor and starts turning it over in his hand like it's some kind of artifact he's never seen before. He is stalling.

"What is it?" My God, maybe I've got cancer or toxic shock or something.

"Mary Beth," he starts slowly, "as your doctor, I have to advise you that despite your age and good health, what you're doing here just isn't advisable for you, you know that, don't you? Do I need to give you the whole your-body-is-a-temple, sanctity-of-life spiel again?" He pauses; he's actually angry at me.

"Well, I wouldn't say my body is exactly a temple, it's more like a roadside shrine," I start to say, but he interrupts me.

"Now come on, cut the rigmarole, this is, what, the third time you've been here in two years, Mary Beth." He stops. I roll my eyes, but I don't mean to. I want to hear the spiel again.

"Darn it all, forget medically—emotionally, psychologically, I'm concerned. You're a smart girl. I . . ." He looks flummoxed. He pops open the file and extracts a pair of tortoiseshell half glasses from his coat pocket.

"You're, what, a senior?" he says. "Do you know where you are going to college?" he asks, squinting over the top of his glasses.

"I don't know, Swarthmore, maybe Princeton."

"Well now, that's a very fine school. Go Tigers!" he says, some color finally coming into his cheeks.

"Go team!" I say, making a triumphant fist. We both laugh, but it's a small, uncomfortable laugh. I hate the way he's looking at me, so disappointed.

"This is the last time, Mary Beth," he says, settling down

at the end of the table. "I'm sorry," he says, and I think he almost means it.

"What do you mean?"

"Mary Beth, I like you. If you were my own daughter this could not sadden me more. Do you understand? I'm going to write you a prescription for the pill, all right?"

"I do not need the pill. I do not want it," I whine. "It is not like I'm really, you know, sexually active or anything," I say.

"This is it," he says, handing me the prescription. "I'm really very sorry."

I dig my fingernails into the palm of my hand. *But I have to see you again*, I think, you can't leave me. But I don't say it. I cannot believe I'm losing him.

I lay down, scoot my butt down the table, and stick my feet into the icy stirrups. The red-haired nurse comes in and lifts my feet out for a moment, then slides two folded-up paper towels into the stirrups, so they aren't so cold and hard. I don't know what to do with this kindness. I cross my arms behind my head like I'm lying out on a tropical beach. I'm casual and cool. Get it out of me, just get it out of me. But when he inserts the speculum and winches me open, when he goes inside me with the tube, my whole body cringes. Before I'd been so relieved, so ready. Out, out, damned spot! Sayonara.

I try to see Dr. Andrews crouched down at the foot of the table, but he is tented by sterilized blue paper, a white mask hiding his lips and nose, his head covered in a blue surgical cap, his eyes behind glasses that reflect the light. He is like a miner, bent over in concentration, prospecting inside me. This is the last time I will see him, and I cannot see him. My hands fly up to cover my face. He never asked me if anyone was coming to get me.

In the recovery room I lie still as a stick and feel the blood leaking out of me, soaking into the pad. I wish I could pray. I swear I feel as though something is wrong with me. Mary, give me a sign, I pray. I feel like a glass jar spidered with cracks, just waiting to shatter. Do I have to break for Mary's goodness to enter me? What has to happen to make me pure?

The room is quiet but for the hum of the fluorescent lights. Most of the others are sleeping, all except for a woman with gray streaks in her dark brown hair who's wiping her eyes on the hem of the sheet and the black girl beside me who has been staring at the ceiling ever since they wheeled her in. Forgive me, I beg. Forgive me.

"Is there someone waiting for you?" the nurse asks me when I refuse my cookies and juice, although I am ravenous. "Someone you can call?"

I think about my father standing in a pool of tree shade practicing his chip shot. His hand reaching out to stroke his chin, my chin. My mother at the Garden, surrounded by a sea of dogs, her hands authoritatively placed on her hips, giving simple, easy-to-understand dog orders: Sit, roll over, beg.

I shake my head. "I've got cab fare," I say, and turn on my side.

At the front desk I pay for the abortion on my father's credit card. I sign my name boldly, and I write on the bottom of the credit card slip, *Weather is here, wish you were beautiful.*

Halfway home I change my mind and ask the cabdriver to take me to Madison Square Garden, though I do not know why exactly. Out the window I look at the girls on the street, girls my age smiling and laughing, talking on pay phones. I wonder who they are, if they are like me.

The last time I was at the Garden was for some ice show with my school. The nuns are crazy about ice shows. Today the ice is covered up, the hardwood floor is down, and they've laid down AstroTurfy carpet, like half these dogs have even ever walked on grass. I cannot see the show area, but over the loudspeaker a man with an English accent is describing the dogs as they enter: "Belvedere, a plucky miniature schnauzer, is a stocky little playmate! This gay, friendly little dog is Salome, she's a Lakeland terrier, we all know what feisty little showboats they are! Look at that saunter! She simply owns the ring!"

I walk slowly up the aisles, half looking for my mother, half staring at the dogs. Some are locked in cages; others, like a black-tongued chow, are being fussed and picked at while they try to nap in their dog beds; then there are those absolutely ridiculous mutts who are unfortunate enough to be tricked out in gear only leather queens and Milquetoasts could appreciate, like the Yorkshire terrier in a studded leather harness and cap behind the wheel of a miniature red sports car, and the teacup Chihuahua in an ascot and monocle curled up in a miniature armchair. They seem sad and bewildered, but maybe it's just me. I mean, maybe it's not such a bad life.

"Princess Cortina D'Empazzo is a saucy Italian greyhound bitch," the disembodied voice booms. "Dogs smile with their tails. Goodness, I think she's flirting with the judge!"

I feel queasy. Where is Sunny? Two aisles over I spot what looks like the pug ghetto. A superbly snooty-looking man with a pencil-thin mustache presses a paisley handkerchief to a pug's snout like it's a child he is imploring to blow its nose. On the next table is another pug who could be Mr. Jeffrey, but to be honest, all those dogs look completely alike to me. Sometimes when I see a picture of my family it's like this, each of us looking like the other, snub-nosed, gray-eyed, and square-jawed, and I think we resemble a subspecies of man: Upper East Side *Preppus erectus*. Overbred and inbred. Linked by our infirmities. One day we'll be just like the pugs, whose noses and eyes constantly leak mucus because years of overbreeding have made their nasal cavities collapse.

"You should be home in bed," I say to myself, and I am right. It is just too bad if Sunny does not believe that I came, not to mention that I came sick! Maybe if Mr. Jeffrey wins, she will forget she even asked me. She would never even miss me. There really is no point in staying.

I make my way toward the exit, past the poodles, the Afghan hounds, the corgis, and the Pekingese. I wonder if I am pale, if I am walking funny, if anyone can tell what I've just done. Hail Mary, I pray.

I am about to leave when I hear "Mary Beth!" and for a moment I freeze, like Mary has actually heard my plea. I turn and see my mother running toward me. She is hunched over, taking mincing little steps, her pink lips pursed in anger. She is furious. She knows exactly where I have been and what I have done. My God, did someone from the clinic call her? Or can she just tell by looking at me? Imagine. Run, I think, run. But I don't move, I close my eyes, and an eerie sense of relief wells up inside me. I never expected this connection from her, and I am surprised that it pleases me. I wait for her to hit me, or start yelling, but when I open my eyes she is just standing in front of me glaring. There is a dog, a pug, Mr. Jeffrey, I presume, tucked inside her blue blazer, secured under her arm like a hairy football.

"Thank God you're here," she says, her whole body trembling; even her perfectly lacquered up-do is shaking a little, like a tiny yellow volcano. I half expect to see steam rise out of it. *Throw a virgin into the volcano! Appease the gods, save yourself!*

"What?" I am confused. Was she worried about me? I feel something in me give way, get soft.

"You won't believe this animal," my mother hisses, and gives the pug a squeeze that makes his already bulbous eyes seem to bulge. I stare at my mother, who is glowering at Mr. Jeffrey, oblivious to me. I do not know which one of them is uglier to me right now. My mother does not know what I have done. She doesn't know shit. How stupid can I be?

"Come with me," she says, and grabs me by the wrist. Before I can protest, she drags me into the women's bathroom. I have no say. What can I say? I have absolutely no idea what is going on. What I *do* know is that taking a contestant off the floor and into a restricted area, like the women's bathroom, is completely against the rules and could get my mother disqualified. I smile just at the thought of my mother getting nailed.

I follow her into the wheelchair stall. She locks the door. She flips down the toilet lid and puts Mr. Jeffrey down. His glossy black marble eyes are bugging out of his head. He is snorting and sniffling like mad. Mr. Jeffrey knows something is up.

"Can you believe it?" Sunny says, like I have any clue as to what is going on. She puts her hands on her hips and stares down at Mr. Jeffrey in her alpha-male power pose. He starts to whine, stamps his little feet, and halfheartedly tries to leap off the toilet, but my mother catches him midflight.

"No way, buster," she says. He squirms in her arms and tries to bolt again, but my mother will not be deterred. I have never seen my mother like this, so take-charge. She presses her hand down on the back of his head. "I need your help, Mary Beth, now. This is serious. I really need you to help me with this," she says, working her hand down his little barrel chest and back to his potbelly, then back to his thumb-sized penis. She begins to palpate his groin, which just seems to increase Mr. Jeffrey's sniffling, his cold dog snot spraying my face.

"I don't think so," I say, crossing my arms over my chest. My heart is slamming against my rib cage. "That puny dog is beyond revolting."

"We have to do this fast. Lord help us," my mother prays. "I know what you did, Mr. Jeffrey," she says in a kind of scary singsong. "I know what you did, you sick little dirty underwear–loving dog, and I'm not going to have you ruin this day for me. Not when we have come so far, Mr. Jeffrey, so far."

"What did he do?" I ask. I am feeling weak and light-headed. What I really want to do is go home and sleep for a week.

"I'll show you," she says, and turns Mr. Jeffrey around

so his butt is facing me. His tail is curled up in a tight curlicue, his puckered and pink little anus quivering. She wedges his head between her legs, then closes her knees on his shoulders so he is held in the vise of her thighs. She starts massaging his belly again, pushing on his sides.

"All right, do you see anything yet?"

"See what? What do you mean?" Mr. Jeffrey is whining and shaking as he lowers his rump down onto the toilet seat. My mother hoists his hips back up.

"Do you see the sock?" she says, her voice starting to break, her tortoiseshell half glasses slipping down her nose.

"You're joking!"

"No, I am not joking. I most certainly am not joking."

She squeezes Mr. Jeffrey again, and he grunts and snuffles, like he is enjoying it. Then he emits a short gusty fart and I see a little something white poke out of his butt. Then the door to the women's room opens and my mother shoots upright, clamping her hand over my mouth. I want to scream, *Hey lady, we've got a pug in here!* but I do not. I am so weak. Once my mother is sure I've got the message, she takes her hand away and starts to pet Mr. Jeffrey, leaving her other hand firmly over his muzzle.

We hear the unbelting of pants, the unzipping, the press of flesh to toilet seat (no paper down, no crouch) which makes my mother wince. Finally there is the sigh, the stream, and the rezipping, the rebelting. Mr. Jeffrey starts to whine. It is time to change my pad; it feels heavy and cold. My mother looks at me, she looks like she could just cry. I could too.

"Are you all right down there?" someone with a pleasantly clipped British accent inquires.

"Oh yes, I'm fine, just a little, you know—female trouble," my mother says, smiling as though the woman can see us. I smile too. Female trouble? That is pretty hilarious.

"Oh right," the woman replies with restrained empathy.

Thank God the woman does not check under the stall. She does, however, take a damnably long time washing her hands, but finally she leaves.

"All right, that's it," my mother says. "Let's do it."

"I can't believe it. This is unreal," I say.

"No, dear, it's very real. Look," she says.

She resecures Mr. Jeffrey between her knees, and there it is. I step back and bang into the stainless steel sanitary-napkin dispenser. My mother raises her head, she actually looks concerned, and in that instant Mr. Jeffrey pulls his head out from between her legs and sinks his teeth right into her forearm.

"Bad dog!" my mother shrieks, and clamps her knees tight on his head. I can see the angry imprint in her skin. Mr. Jeffrey is subdued now, but I am furious. What the hell is wrong with him?

"Grab it, just grab it and pull," my mother hisses, but all I can do is watch tiny beads of blood welling up on my mother's arm. My stomach is singing with hunger pains. My head is in a fog that seems to be creeping into my ears. I can't stand up much longer. All I want to do is to put my head down on the toilet seat and rest, but I don't. Instead I lean down and pinch the slick bit of cloth between my thumb and forefinger and I start to tug. It makes a disgusting sound, like a wet cork being pulled slowly out of a bottle.

"Careful, careful, for heaven's sake, you don't want to

pull out his entire large intestine," Sunny says, trying to peer around to monitor the state of Mr. Jeffrey's asshole. "Oh Lord, please don't let there be bleeding of any sort, none. That would be the end of me."

I pause and close my eyes for a second. Little white fireballs explode behind my eyes. My mother's French twist has come undone; strands of hair stick to her pink lips. She needs me.

I take a deep breath and continue to gently tug on the shit-stained fabric in earnest. It soon becomes clear that what I am extracting from Mr. Jeffrey's ass is not a sock, but a tiny pair of boys' jockey shorts. First the crotch appears, then one stretched-out leg hole and then the other are extruded from the dog's butt. I pull and pull, until the waistband snaps out of his anus and victory is at hand. I stuff the soiled underpants into the sanitary-napkin disposal. My mother slumps in relief against the wall.

"Thank God," she says, and crosses herself.

I feel the room start to tilt and rise up under our feet.

Mr. Jeffrey nuzzles my mother's thigh, licks her arm where he nipped her. She rubs his ears. All is forgiven.

My mother pushes open the stall door. The light in the bathroom is bright. In the mirror, the two of us look roughed up, as though we've been in a rumble. We both start to laugh, I laugh until my sides ache and I have to lean up against the sink to catch my breath.

"Thank you," my mother says, touching my shoulder as if I might be thinking she was talking to somebody else. "Really. That wasn't any fun."

"It's okay," I mumble. I'm embarrassed by her gratitude.

"Oh, look at the time," she says, wiping her eyes. She hoists

Mr. Jeffrey up into her arms. He sits there very straight, looking stoic and human, like a hairy dwarf with dreadful allergies.

"You'll stay, won't you?" my mother asks. She turns on the water and runs her hands under the stream. She splashes a little water on her face, then heads back into the handicapped stall to get a piece of toilet paper. "Please stay, we'll go for ice cream afterward, my treat," she says, like I'm a little kid who can be bribed. She puts Mr. Jeffrey down on the floor, and he immediately begins sniffing at my calves. I wonder if he can smell blood. Does Mr. Jeffrey know what my mother could only imagine in her very worst nightmare? I lean against the stall door and watch my mother blot her face with the tissue, then drop it into the toilet. The tissue floats in the bowl like a paper angel waiting for somebody to pee on it. "Oh, come on, say you'll stay," my mother says. "You'll like it. I know it."

"You don't know what I like," I say in a voice that seems too loud. My head is full of static; my mother's lips are moving, but I cannot hear what she is saying. She reaches out and grabs my arm and it is funny the way she slides to the floor like a rag doll, like I am pushing her down, but I'm not, I do not weigh anything. I am just a kid. For a moment she looks afraid of me, then she pulls me slowly into her lap. We are wedged in tight between the toilet and the wall, my feet sticking out of the stall. My mother smooths my skirt down over my knees. I'm afraid that I am dying, right here on the floor by the toilet. I am bleeding to death. I want to tell my mother something, but I am not sure what it is. I listen to the water running in the toilet. It is so soothing. My mother's breath hums in my ear. I think I hear her say, "I'm here."

TO SMOKE
PERCHANCE
TO DREAM

The first time my father didn't die of cancer I was fifteen, and it was lymphoma, a lump under his left arm. He let me touch it once. It felt like a grape buried below the skin.

In reality it wasn't a grape. It was smaller than a grape.

My father leaned against the kitchen counter and opened a beer using a bottle opener my grandfather had fashioned out of the antler of a deer. There was a slight hiss, then the whoosh as the seal was broken and air filled the space. Then he told my little sister, Dee, and me what the doctor said.

" 'It's a cocktail onion,' that's what the doctor says, 'like for a Gibson,' the doctor says. Then he asks me, 'So, Chas, are you a gin or vodka man?' " My father drinks. "He asked me that," my father said, shaking his head.

"Did you notice his shoes?" my father said to my mother, and made a face like he was in awe of them. "Hand-sewn Italian oxfords."

"Probably," she said, as though this wasn't odd, them talking about shoes at a time like this. She reached out for the beer—my mother never drinks beer—and took a big gulp.

"I liked him," Dad said. "He's supposed to be the big hot shit."

Dee and I couldn't believe it.

"Cancer?" I said. Tears were rolling down my sister's cheeks. In her arms she clutched Twinkle, the stuffed horse she'd slept with every night of her life.

"Cancer?" The word moved out of my mouth like a snake. I had to say it to believe it. I couldn't stop looking at my dad's hair, black as ink, thick and a little wavy. The thought of that hair falling out in clumps, clogging the bathtub drain, covering his pillow, his head bald as a thumb, made me feel like I was going to tip over.

"It's serious, sure, but it's not so big," my father assures us. "Listen, I'm not saying it isn't bad, but it's not that big, and it's lymphoma. If you've got to pick a cancer this is the one to choose. It's the Christmas cancer," he said, taking another sip of beer. "Believe me—in the world of cancer, this honey's a gift."

My mother winced, grabbed the beer out of my father's

hand, and took another sip. She looked so weird with a beer bottle in her hand. "We're going to be okay, girls," she said. Her breath smelled like alcohol.

My father was thirty-nine.

"What can I tell you," Dad said. He shrugged and took another bottle of beer out of the fridge. "I wish I could tell you something that would make it make sense, but there's no answer. It's just dumb luck. Sometimes bad things just happen to people," he said. The beer slipped out of his hand and hit the floor; it started to foam up like it might explode.

"Oh balls," he said, picking it up with two fingers, but instead of dropping it into the sink or popping the top off, my father stormed out onto the deck and pitched the bottle down into the woods, where it smashed against a tree. Glass everywhere. My mother gasped, and covered her eyes. I'd seen Dad do this with empty wine bottles, lobbing them over his shoulder off the deck, in the middle of a party, but it was in celebration. Never like this. When he came back into the kitchen, he looked different. Nobody said one word. Not even my mother, whose eyes were filling up with tears, which, of course, made me and Dee start to bawl again. There was a look in my father's eyes like shock, the look of a man who has always counted himself lucky now being betrayed by the odds. He didn't believe it.

He'd always taught Dee and me to think of ourselves as lucky.

"People who believe they're lucky attract good luck. It's true. Good things come to them. People like to be around people who are lucky," he'd told us. "You make your own luck."

Well, what happened?

"There was a woman there who had a walnut-sized tumor removed from her breast," my mother said, breaking the silence, her voice breathy, as if she couldn't get enough air. I wondered if this was supposed to make us feel better.

Sometimes bad things happened.

"Take a left on Mercury," I said to Scott, pointing to the turn with my cigarette. "Then straight on to the Milky Way!"

He didn't smile or laugh.

I sat there and smoked, thank God for cigarettes. Cigarettes had saved my life. Ever since the cocktail onion I'd started smoking like crazy. It helped. I smoked Salems and Arctic Lights, anything. I held the smoke in my lungs until the skin across my forehead felt as though it was dissolving and my entire face might float free from my skull. The more I smoked, the angrier I'd get, and the stronger I'd feel. "Fuck you," I'd say out loud. "Fuck all of you." A week earlier Dad had checked in to the hospital. The doctor scooped out the onion, gave Dad like five stitches and a bandage, then sent him home with morphine and antibiotics. Gone, gone, gone.

He'd taken a week off from work. He didn't rest, though, he worked in the greenhouse he'd built off the living room last summer. He'd created a fifteen-square-foot facsimile jungle. Crisscrossing overhead were curving branches draped with sphagnum moss and studded with spiny bromeliads. Below were enormous staghorn ferns, elephant ears, and some rabbit's-foot ferns he'd dug up on the Blue Mountain where he'd grown up. Among these plants were half a dozen pots of purple and yellow cattleyas. When he wasn't tending to his new passion for orchids, he was in the basement welding sculptures. He was into giant fish now. Thank God. He'd even sold a piece that he'd entered in an art show as a lark. It was now swimming in somebody's backyard. For years it had been nudes. There was even one of my mother and us, or I assumed it was us, because God knows we never posed for it. It was a woman with two children, who are looking up at her, and she has her hands on the back of their heads like she's trying to get them to hurry up, or else dance. I tried not to look at it too much.

Twenty minutes before, Scott and I'd been making out in one of the half-built houses in a new development near my house, then I freaked out and demanded he take me home. I still had sawdust on my chest and in my hair, like pollen. My lips puffy from kissing.

He was too good for me; he knew it, I knew it. He was using me, and I didn't care. He didn't know it, but I was using him too.

The new development was going up on what used to be farmland, great fields flush with corn and wheat, tomatoes and pumpkins. The houses came in three lame styles of modern. Dad said this way people felt like they were being real individuals, because they could choose—breezeway, no breezeway? Yellow shutters, green shutters?—while also being perfect conformists. It was perfect. Dad took me there sometimes to practice my driving in the cul-de-sacs. I was a crappy driver. These houses made him so nuts that half the time I could be giving somebody a lawn job and he wouldn't even bat an eye.

"Millions of dollars," he would say, and shake his head. "Can you believe it? Ugly as sin. The joker that designed that sucker ought to throw himself off a bridge."

Then he'd say, "Drive. Just drive."

My father didn't know that kids made out here. Or that my friend Michelle and I came here to hang out and smoke, and maybe pass a Michelob if the workmen left any behind. Sometimes we'd just sit in the windows and peel the sun-burned skin off each other's back and watch the lights of our neighborhood come on. We were going to different colleges in the fall. We didn't like to talk about it, or how we knew everything was changing. I hadn't told Michelle about my new roommate Mary Beth from New York City—how she'd called me at ten o'clock at night and joked that she'd been mugged twice but that they'd never gotten her jewelry, how her laugh sounded like the tinkling of a giant chandelier. Mary Beth didn't sound like a teenager at all, she sounded like a grownup—like twenty-five or something. She'd even called me *darling*. It was sort of exciting. I couldn't tell Michelle that. What was the point? It was like cheating on her to even think about another friend right now. It was like putting it in her face. Neither one of us wanted to think about the future right now, we wanted everything to stay just the same.

Scott had chosen a two-story with an atrium, and I'd fol-lowed him in. There was a sink in the foyer. A bathtub sat in the middle of the living-room floor. We got as far as the half-built kitchen, right where the island and stools should go, and then boom. The first kiss was one of those kisses where you don't pull apart even when you're moving to lie down, like your breathing depends on it. Through the roof beams the moon looked like a cat's claw snagged on black cloth, the stars like nail heads pounded into tar paper. I shrugged off my bra—a very frustrating front clasp—before he took his teeth to the snap like a pothead with a potato-chip bag. I could feel the rough grain of the wood against my bare back. He pulled his yellow Izod shirt over his head. One snap, one shrug, and we were skin to skin. I gasped. He was smiling too much. He wanted me. When he went for my Bermudas I sat up.

"You've got to take me home," I said, fishing around in the dark for my bra and shirt. "My dad is going to kill me."

"Now?" he asked in that half-plaintive-half-shocked-how-can-you-do-this-to-me voice only a boy with a boner can muster.

"Now."

"You're joking," he said, and laughed, like he really believed I was going to say, Gotcha, why don't you just whip it out.

"No," I said. "Please, now." He got up, shaking his head like he'd made a mistake bringing me here. He slipped his shirt back on as though it pained him. He didn't say much. I guess he knew about my father.

He didn't look at me once as I guided him through my neighborhood. North Star was built in the late fifties and early sixties during the country's big love affair with the space program, so all the streets were named for planets and constellations. We lived on Pluto Drive. Nobody on Pluto had ever died. Yet.

Lots of other people in our neighborhood had. I thought it was the radon. New Jersey, Pennsylvania, and Delaware made up the "radon panhandle." Others thought it had to do with the chemical companies, Dupont and Hercules. My father worked for Hercules, at one time as a chemist, but we didn't talk about that possibility much. He was in marketing now, so what was he going to do, quit his job?

The youngest person in North Star to get cancer was five-year-old Toby Kittredge. I imagined the leukemia exploding in his body like poisoned corn kernels. Pushing his Tonka dump truck up the aisle of the Red Clay Presbyterian Church, he resembled, with his baby-powder-white skin and bald head, a beatific grinning lightbulb. Twenty-two-year-old Shelby Reid had thought the dull pain in his back was from water polo. He'd never heard of Hodgkin's disease. Two years after his death, his car, a bright blue '79 Corvette Stingray, still sat in his parents' garage gathering dust. Mr. McArthur was the first man I knew to grow alfalfa sprouts in a jar, and his cancer pinballed from his prostate to his liver to his brain until, in the end, he no longer recognized his family. Miss Spruance was famous for her awesome backhand and her petunias, great purple and pink trombone-shaped blossoms. The doctors removed her ovaries. Then her uterus. Then her right breast. Then she told them to stop.

I wondered if God was punishing me for secretly feeling relieved every time somebody else got sick—you know, thinking that their tragedy just improved my family's odds of staying well. There but for the grace of God, and the law of averages, go I. Now, of course, we were like everyone else in the neighborhood. Well, not really, but sort of.

Scott slid his red Firebird into my driveway. It was 2:00 A.M. I leaned over to kiss him good night, and then it started again. It was my fault, he'd have just let me out, I didn't mean for it to happen. I was out of that car, I was, in my mind, but then my body crawled into the backseat. My body lay down and pulled him on top of me. Thinking, Maybe this is it. Maybe this is really a good thing. Maybe it's love. Sometimes, good things come out of nowhere. Maybe he'd be the one. I didn't want him to stop touching me. I just wanted to live in that backseat, with his skin on my skin. I didn't want to think. My body wasn't responding, though; I tried to pinch my nipples to get them hard; I didn't want him to think I wasn't turned on.

At first, the porch light flicked on and off, a lighthouse signal flashing across my bare stomach. Then the house lights went on. Still I didn't move.

I didn't hear the family-room door open or see my father coming. Scott had his tongue in my ear, my eyes were closed, I was disappearing in the kiss. Then I heard my mother yelling, "Chas, get back here. She's right there, you can see the car, she's fine. Now come back!"

Neither Scott nor I had time to move before the car door flew open, night air rushing in as if a seawall had been breached. I screamed and covered myself, like I was being defiled. Dad stood there barefoot in the driveway, in his sky-blue pajamas, glaring into the car. Scott pushed himself up off of me, craning his head up, posed like a seal with a ball on its nose.

"Oh, shit," Scott said. He sounded scared.

"You can't do this to me!" I objected lamely. What could

Dad see? Nothing. I was in my bra, that was like a bathing-suit top. God, I'd worn less in public.

"Inside, *now*," my father thundered at me, slamming the car door. The windows rattled. I swear it. How could he do that with that awful incision under his arm? It was as if he didn't even see Scott. I sat up, pulled my shirt on. For a minute Dad stood still in the driveway, and I thought maybe he was about to come yank me out of the car by the hair and drag me inside. That would be okay. Instead my mother came out, her red kimono flapping behind her like a Chinese dragon, and pulled my father back into the house. "Get inside," she said. "Inside."

"Oh, man," Scott said, rubbing his eyes, as if maybe this had all been a hallucination. "Fuck."

I sat up and kissed him on the mouth, one last time.

"I'm so sorry," I said, but I didn't really mean it. "Really sorry," and got out of the car. I tried not to smile.

Inside I could hear my mother saying, "Now, why did you have to do that?"

I was dumbfounded. My mother, who never ever crossed or even really disagreed with him, even she had had it with my father.

I didn't want to go in. Ever since my mother took this dopey Parent Effectiveness Training Course, to learn "how to talk so your kids will listen," she wanted to discuss things. Feelings. She'd say things like, "I hear you're angry about not being allowed to wear purple lip gloss," and "How does my saying no to letting you stay out past eleven make you feel?"

Our mom wanted to be the perfect parent.

Our dad just figured he was.

I didn't want to go in. They made me insane. Of course I had to—what, I was going to live in the garage?

I sat there for a second and played the whole thing out again in my head. The day he came back from the hospital I had started trying to memorize my father. His forward-leaning walk, the way he stood on one leg when he brushed his teeth, the way he bounced on the balls of his feet to "Brown Sugar," the way he would hold my face in his hands and kiss me. I wanted to build him inside of me, so I could never forget him.

They were both sitting on the edge of the brown nubby couch, not speaking.

"I think you know we're disappointed. Our trust in you has been shaken," my father said. His brown eyes looked black to me, two angry little coals, boring into my head.

"We were worried, it's not like you not to call," my mother said.

"Sorry, Mom," I said. "I should have called. I am really really sorry."

"You know we'll have to discuss this," she said, then, "I don't think Dee needs to know about this." Now I felt dirty.

Dee didn't even know she was pretty yet.

"I lost track of time," I said. "I was with Michelle and then Scott offered to give me a ride home. It was late, I figured you'd be asleep, I didn't want to wake you with a call. There wasn't really a phone, and looking for—"

"Your shirt is inside out," my mother said, getting up from the sofa.

My father got up, and frowned at me. Then, without saying a word, he pulled me roughly toward him, kissed the top of my head, and left me there in the family room. Just me alone.

On the glass coffee table with the *National Geographics* and the *Whole Earth Catalog* were the books about cancer Mom had taken out of the library, which nobody read, because nobody needed to.

Just that morning I asked my mother if her books explained why it was that cancers always came in the shape of fruits and vegetables. Peas and raisins if you're lucky, grapefruits if you're not.

She said, "I would guess it's a little less scary to tell someone they have a green-bean-sized..."

I waited for her to say the word, but she didn't. She said, "Spot."

Spot seemed much more polite than *lump* or *tumor.*

Alone on the sofa, I thought about my father, the way he ripped open the Firebird's door, the way he pounded on the glass, the whole car shaking like it was made of tin, like he could pick it right up and tip me out into his arms. He could catch me in one hand, like King Kong, and carry me away.

My daddy was going to be just fine.

I started smoking in the woods behind our house, in our old broken-down tree house. I sat staring at our house waiting for something to happen, but of course nothing did. Mom had been talking about how we should all have a family meeting to "rap about our feelings." But that never happened either. Sitting there smoking, I imagined generations of my father's family, all smoking, each one of us a smoke ring, a magic trick. We were descended from French horse thieves; we were too mean to die.

I forced myself to really inhale, even though the smoke scorched my throat and pricked my lungs, making me cough until I thought I'd bleed. The coughing hurt, but it was a good hurt, proof that I was doing something—actually taking some action. I smoked, chain-smoked, lighting the next cigarette off the last, sucking on them until they burned down to the filter, until the ash began to singe my fingers.

I knew how angry it would make my father. I knew that if he found out he'd shake me until I couldn't stand, but I didn't care.

A few weeks after his "procedure," there was a follow-up appointment, and the whole family went. The doctors were going to shoot blue dye into my dad's feet so they could see if there might be a papaya pressing on his kidneys, a green bean in the old spleen.

My parents got all dressed up in their conservative clothes, a dark suit and red tie for Dad, a knee-length jean skirt and blazer for Mom, both of them in loafers. Like it mattered how they looked. Like it was a beauty contest or a job interview: *Hey, nice suit, snazzy but respectable, good shoeshine, we're going to let that guy off with lymphoma. But, oh dear, that one there in the pilling sweatsuit and rundown bobos, buddy, prepare yourself for bone-marrow cancer.*

"This is the worst part," my mother whispered to me as we entered the waiting room, trying to find a seat as far away from the others as possible. "The not knowing. We can deal with anything but this not knowing. Shit," she said.

My mother had only recently taken to swearing, and every time a curse came from her lips she still seemed a little surprised, a little repulsed, like she'd spit up a frog.

After Dad was called in, the three of us sat there in the waiting room, sort of holding hands, but it felt queer, and their palms were sweaty and I couldn't sit still, so I walked around. Everywhere you look in those cancer wards it's all painted pale blue or pale coral, and some genius has hung all these impressionist paintings in every crappy hallway, waiting room, and bathroom, you know—in case you get the bright idea of slitting your wrists. It's like oh, don't get depressed, oh look at the smiling ladies in the big flowery hats and all that pretty yellow—see, see, purple, ooh, happy haystacks, ooh happy sailboats, happy damn monkeys on the Grande Jatte. How many times did I have to see that painting? I don't care! And for your information, the light on the cathedral at Notre Dame is not lavender, not peach or violet. I have been there. The cathedral at Notre Dame is covered in pigeon crap.

In the waiting area people were talking, but we didn't share our story. What was there to say? We had a little spot, the doctor dug it out, and now we're fine. No loss of life, some loss of sleep, but that's it. It sure paled in comparison to the young mother jiggling her leg as she read her Bible, her hand on the head of a boy who couldn't have been older than five, and who was wearing a tiny chestnut-colored chemo wig. Or the high-school football coach's tale of an egg-sized tumor that pressed his eyeball right out of his head. "Holy Toledo, I just thought I had the mother of all migraines!" he said to my mother.

"Mmm," she said. "I can imagine."

But, of course, we couldn't really.

We had nothing to compare to the grapefruit-sized tumor scooped from the balls of a silver-haired electrician who told the group he was now learning to dance all those dances he once thought were too ritzy for him. He already had the fox-trot and the cha-cha under his belt.

"So what if no one does them anymore? I want to know them." Then he got up and got a little Dixie cup of coffee from the "courtesy" table. He had an elegant limp.

You just about wanted to scream your head off.

When my father came out, he looked almost surprised to see us sitting there. "Hey sweet babies, why does everybody look so blue?" He kissed my mom. "Let's blow this pop stand."

"So, are you okay?" I asked. Why didn't anybody else ask these questions?

"Of course, baby girl," he said. Dee threw her arms around him.

Of course.

My mother squeezed my hand.

We went to a little restaurant around the corner from the hospital. Even though it was still officially morning—

eleven o'clock—Mom ordered a kir, and Dad had two beers. Dee and I both got Fresca and chocolate mousse. The scan had showed nothing at all, not one little chickpea, not a grain of rice, not even one mustard seed, and so we toasted our good fortune.

Back home I went to my room, grabbed my smokes, and crawled out onto the roof. I needed a cigarette. Just one.

With the exception of his two weeks of not being able to do yard work, which simply made the yard look as if we were on vacation—the grass lush, and a little long—our household manifested none of the telltale signs of illness. No dandelions, no peeling shutters, no drawn blinds or stink of sickness. Everything was going to be fine.

From the roof I could see my dad in the garden. He was supposed to be resting. He was out in the flower bed, surveying what last night's summer wind had wrought. All the plants looked mussed up, the peonies splaying out in all directions, the lilies slightly dynamited. In my father's back jeans pocket were his gardening shears, their blades so sharp they could snip the ears off a dog; in his hand a knife. He leaned against the split-rail fence and watched a Carolina wren light on a pine. Standing there in silvery-green sheep's ear and budding purple irises, he looked content. For one moment. Then, in haste, he began to work, lashing the white trumpet lilies to stakes like Christian martyrs, binding pink heavy-headed peonies resembling drunk girls on the nod to skinny bamboo poles. I watched him work. I should have been helping him, but he didn't need me.

I watched him go in the house. After two more cigarettes, I heard him calling my name.

"Hey, Evie, come here a second—I want to show you something. Something that will make you laugh."

How funny can it be, I thought. I crawled in the window, changed my shirt, quickly pulled out the jar of Skippy I kept hidden in my underwear drawer, and stuck a fingerful in my mouth. (Peanut butter is better at disguising the smell of cigarettes or booze than gum or mints, which are like taking out an advertisement of guilt.)

Downstairs, I felt so confident I kissed my father's cheek.

"Hey, what's all the hubbub, bub?" I said.

"Did you happen to see Superman using the john?" he asked.

"Superman?" This better be good.

"Yeah, Superman, you know, the man of steel, able to leap—hey, Dee, come here for a second, sweetie," he calls, hearing my sister and Mom returning from Dee's riding lesson. Dee comes clomping out into the hall in her riding gear, crisp white shirt, jodhpurs, black velvet hat, her leather crop in hand. Dee wouldn't give him any lip.

"I hit all my jumps," she said. "I didn't miss one, I didn't fly off, nothing."

"I'm so proud," my mother said, putting her hands on Dee's shoulders. "I had to cover my eyes half the time, of course, but she was perfect," my mother said, then noticed we were all standing in the bathroom. "This is no place for a family meeting," she said.

"Look," my father said, lifting the toilet lid.

My mother peered into the bowl, blinked several times, then turned white.

"Oh shit," she said, her hand flying to her mouth in horror.

A bright blue ebullient turd bobs in the water.

"Superman stopped by and he laid cable right here, in our very own bathroom," my father said. We all laughed.

"Ewww," Dee said, and whacked the toilet with her crop. "Get out of here, gross blue poop," she commanded. The crop made a great thwapping sound.

"Jeez Louise, Daddy, I'd hate to see what the Green Lantern would do," I said, and elbowed my father. My mother wrinkled her nose. "You guys."

"That's my girl," my father said, and messed up my hair. I let him.

I looked at him. Shiny black hair, strong chin, his fingernails so clean they seemed white. A little mole on his cheek. Big smile, big smile.

Everything was going to be just fine.

Freshman year my roommate, Mary Beth, tried to teach me how to blow concentric smoke rings. She could blow a link of rings like a silver necklace. It was just one of her many talents, but one of the few that wasn't appreciated solely behind closed doors and in the company of men.

For my birthday she bought an elegant silver cigarette case with another woman's name engraved on the back. It seemed extravagant, and romantic, and I loved it. I smoked clove cigarettes and cowboy killers and Lucky Strikes. Hey, I had a sense of humor. I soon adopted Mary Beth's brand, a tony English smoke that came in a gold box and were Easter-egg colors. We swapped colors—the lavender and robin's-egg blue looked good with Mary Beth's long dark brown hair and olive skin, the pink and mint green complemented my pale skin and blondish brown hair. When people wanted to bum one they got yellow. Regardless of the cigarette, I took each one into my mouth like a talisman. At college I made new friends and didn't tell them about my father's brush with sickness. I met strangers in bars and bus stations and told them everything about the cancer. Painfully, as though I were slowly pulling off a Band-Aid. Occasionally I'd tell a new friend when I was drunk or high, or needed connection, some delicate sympathy. Afterward, I always felt cheap, like I'd failed my father. Like I'd used him to get something I hadn't earned.

I never, ever smoked in front of my parents. They'd have killed me. It was blasphemy.

After a while I forgot. I did. I forgot. It was like people who become religious during finals week, or when there's a car accident. When the trauma passes, you forget. I became a hobby smoker. I was the annoying person who cadged cigarettes at parties, but never bought them. When I remembered Dad's cancer, it was just one of the things that proved my father was stronger and luckier than any mortal man, and certainly stronger and luckier than I'd ever be, convinced as I was that I'd never hit thirty. After two years of living with other people, Mary Beth and I decided to be roommates again senior year. We moved into an off-campus house with four other girls. The spring before my senior year my parents had taken a trip down the Amazon. In addition to the orchid cuttings my father smuggled back in his jeans pockets, he'd brought back a trophy for being the only man on their trip courageous—or stupid—enough to brave the piranhas and swim in the river. It was a fungus on the X ray. An almond-shaped fungus.

Or, it was supposed to be a fungus.

But biopsies don't lie.

"An almond?" I say when my father tells me. My mother is on the extension, I can hear the glug-glug of her pouring wine into a glass.

Mary Beth mouths, "What's up?" I turn around to face the wall.

She tramps into the kitchen and comes back with an Amstel, then packs her little ceramic pot pipe and puts them both at my elbow. She has no idea.

"Is it a smokehouse almond? Jeez, I thought only doctors and dentists got those, and then only at Christmastime. Or is this almond one of those crummy foil-pouch almonds you get on domestic flights?"

"Honey." My mother sounds appalled.

My father laughs. "Good girl," he says. "Well, you know. I'm not sure. But they seem to think they can get it pretty easily. They think they can do something called a surgical cure," he says.

"Cure, yes, cure," I say. "That's what I want to hear, Daddy."

"Well, we'll see," he says. It sounds as though he is chewing pretzels, or ice cubes.

My mother chimes in, "They're very optimistic. It's localized, and there's no reason to think they can't get it all."

"Think of it as pruning," my father says. Then he gets serious. "There's no need to miss school, because I'm going to be fine. Really. Don't do that."

"Listen. I'm coming home," I say, and instinctively reach for the new pack of cigarettes Mary Beth just bought. I tear the filmy cellophane off the package, the slippery plastic clinging to my fingers like a moth.

"You don't need to. We're fine. I mean it, honey. Dr. Butler pulled some strings to get your father into surgery right away. It's just two nights in the hospital. We can handle it."

"Shit, Mother. I'm coming down. Thanksgiving break starts in a week anyway. My tests won't be a problem. I've been studying."

Mary Beth laughs. Mary Beth is also an art history major, and in truth neither she nor I have cracked open a book. We had, however, set up a slide projector in our bedroom that we left on all the time; Michelangelo's *David* loomed up on our wall. One night we got stoned and drew flowers and pirate tattoos on his body as well as the words *I love cheese.* It was funny at the time.

"Okay, then. Take your tests or what have you ..." my father says. I can tell he's pleased that I'm coming.

"Wasn't one cancer enough, Daddy? Is this about keeping up with the Joneses, or what? You trying to set a record? You want a plaque or something?" I say. My voice is steady, but I can't light my cigarette.

"What can I say? I've always been an overachiever."

"So I'll see you Friday night," I say. I really want to take a drag, but I wait. I wait.

"Great," he says, and hangs up the phone before I can even tell him I love him.

I hang up and instantly call Dee at her dorm. It rings and rings. A girl with a lisping southern accent answers the phone. I can't talk to a stranger. I hang up.

Mary Beth sits down next to me on the sofa.

"Oh darling. Fuck, and more fuck," she says, and wraps her arms around me. "I am so so sorry."

Even though Mary Beth is my best friend, and even though I trust her, I cannot talk to her. I can't talk to anybody. I even think about calling Michelle. She knew my dad, but I can't. If I say it, it makes it true, and I don't want to say it. I want Dee, and just like that, the phone rings again. Dee's voice is scratchy and hoarse as if she has been screaming. "I can't believe it," she weeps. "This isn't fair. What are we going to do?"

"It'll be all right," I say, like I've practiced it a hundred times.

"We need a plan," she says. "What if he dies?" Her voice is small and desperate. She just can't let it go. "It's almost Thanksgiving," she says. "God, it's so unfair."

"For Christ's sake, he's not going to die," I say, making it sound like a joke. I roll my eyes, as though she could see me. "Dee, do you really think Daddy would die without seeing us get married? Come on—think about it. Use your head. Just the sheer curiosity of it will keep him alive for decades," I say, twisting the phone cord around my finger until my fingertip is purple and numb. "The what-if-the-guy-isn't-good-enough-for-my-princess thing. You know Dad."

She doesn't say anything.

"He couldn't stand it."

I can just see Dee in her freshman dorm room, her single bed scattered with stuffed animals, an "autograph hound" covered in the autographs of friends from high school. She is probably wearing torn blue jeans and one of my father's old pullover sweaters that we inherit from him when they get holes in the elbows. He always seems a little surprised at how much we covet this clothing. I pick at what was once just a loose thread, but which is now a hole in a forest green hand-me-down, and worry it like a sore.

"You don't know he's not going to die," she cries softly into the phone. "I'm going home. I don't care about my finals."

"You should care, Dee, you're going to fail out if you don't . . . He's going to be fine. For Christ's sake—this is our father you're talking about here. Tell me, how's school?" I say, trying to distract her. "Are you still trying to decide between the nice guy from Virginia and that rogue from Tennessee?"

When I hang up, Mary Beth is good about not making me talk about it. She lights my cigarette, then makes me a bed on the sofa.

"I should study," I say, but we both know it's hopeless.

"Oh please," she says, flipping through the channels until she finds a 1930s black-and-white movie, *Topper*. We watch for a few minutes and I can feel her staring at me, gauging my reaction to see if a dashing couple who die in a car crash and come back as ghosts is benign enough. She flips to a rerun of *The Muppet Show*.

"You're in Kermit's hands," she says. "That's almost as good as God's."

Later she brings me poor-boy soup—chicken bouillon with carrot wheels and egg noodles. For dessert there's a bowl of fudge ripple ice cream with a pale blue tranquilizer perched on top like a cherry.

"I thought about hiding it inside like the baby Jesus in an Epiphany cake, but it seemed a waste. They are so pretty."

Mary Beth is always generous with her drugs, but the big blue Xanaxes are her favorites, she treasures them. I feel honored.

"Isn't that how you get dogs to take their medicine, stick it in their food?" I say.

She pets my head. "Swallow."

As I lie in bed that night my lungs ache, but I light another cigarette. I notice how the slender tube juts from my fingers like a mutated digit. I inhale deeply, feel my lungs seize. I wonder if this is what my father feels? Or if he really feels nothing at all. Maybe it's just too frightening to feel. I imagine the cancer amassing in my father's lungs like a clump of purple grapes, becoming so heavy it pulls the lung down, and I can't breathe.

That night when the phone rings at midnight, I pick it up and carry it back to my bed. When I lift the receiver and don't hear anything I know for sure it is Dee. I cradle the phone to my cheek, and we both lie there in silence until we fall asleep.

When I wake up the next morning I call home, just to check in. My father answers the phone, something he very rarely does. He hates wasting time on the phone.

"Hey, Puss," he says, sounding chipper.

"Hey, Dad," I say. "How is it going there?"

"Fine, fine. Mom and I were just talking, planning a trip. Your mother has this idea about Borneo," he says, like nothing has happened. "It's the orangutans," he says.

"No way. It's the hair," I say. "She's got that wildwoman of Borneo look going on."

"Hey, did I ever tell you about all those car accidents your mom and I saw driving in the Indonesian countryside? It was something to see. Everywhere, up and down the highways—if you could call them that—you'd see crashes, fender benders, what have you, and the people involved, the driver, the passengers, all of them would be lying there together beside the road taking a nap."

"You mean it *looked* like they were napping, like when we were driving through Ireland and Dee and I would spot a sheep lying, sort of pushed off to the side of the road, and you'd tell us it was just *napping*?"

It's so easy to forget that anything is wrong.

"No, these folks were sleeping. You see, the Indonesians hate confrontation, so in times of stress they just tune out, fall asleep. It's easier."

"Makes sense," I say, wondering if Mary Beth could set me up with mondo mood stabilizers before I left for home. "Like fainting goats," I say. "Look dead and no one will eat you. I lobby for changing the family crest so it features a fainting goat."

"Did you know in Japan people die every day without ever knowing they were sick because their doctors couldn't bring themselves to tell their patients they were dying?" my father says.

"That's cheery."

"Just thought you'd be interested to know that."

They have to saw through my father's ribs to get at the tumor. Once they open him up, they lop off the bottom of his pale pink lung, which I now imagine being like a soft starfish struggling to regenerate itself in the cave of his ribs. Which, of course, isn't possible. When I see him I'm going to say, "So, one lung is shorter than the other—it won't affect your dancing." Ha ha.

On the train the smoking car is blue with smoke. Even the goddamn people look blue. I almost don't sit in it because it seems sad and pitiful, but who am I kidding? I draw the smoke into my mouth, down into my lungs, which seem to inflate as though they were elastic, swelling to meet the heat of my breath. For the last fifteen minutes I ride between the cars. It's freezing cold but I have to clear my head and air my sorry self out.

My mother waves to me as I walk toward her on the train platform. She's got her hair down, and she's wearing a green-and-gold batik dress, some funky wrap number from the seventies, and an armful of gold bangles. That dress, I now remember, is one of my father's favorites. She doesn't want me to be afraid.

I wish I'd dressed up, but I, of course, look like a college student. Khakis, pink button-down Tretorns, jeans jacket. A sweatshirt tied around my waist to hide my butt.

"How was the ride?" my mother asks, running her hand along my cheek. I'm startled to see my father's gold wedding band on her thumb.

"I'm great," I say, and grab her hand between mine, holding it still for a minute. The ring looks huge to me, like hardware, like the anklets people on bail are forced to wear so the state can monitor their movements. It's like he's gone already.

"Oh, that. He couldn't wear it during surgery," my mother explains. "Goodness, you smell like smoke," she says, touching my chin-length hair, which I've been streaking with peroxide whenever I get depressed.

"Pretty," she says absently. It isn't.

"You know that smell makes me sick, now?" she says. "I can't help it. I can't even stand to ride in Judy's and Betty's cars. I can't help it. It makes me so angry. Chas doesn't even smoke. He has probably, in his whole life, smoked, in total, one pack of cigarettes."

"It makes no sense," I say, thinking how strange it sounds when my mother refers to my father by his first name when talking to me. I like it better when she calls him "your father."

"I can't stand anyone these days," my mother says, opening her car door with such ferocity it dings the door of the BMW next to us, but she doesn't seem to notice. "I'm so angry I hate it."

"I think it's appropriate," I say.

"Well, I don't like it," she says softly, staring into space for a moment before she starts the car.

"Would yoga help, or something like that?"

She sort of laughs. "It's been years. I'd break in two," she says, then turns to me. "Weren't there any nonsmoking seats on the train?"

"No," I lie. "I promise I'll boil myself when we get home." I feel like I've injured her.

"Good," she says. "I don't think your father should have to breathe that in. He's got to be careful, you know."

Before we go into the hospital we sit in the car and put on lipstick; I borrow some of Mom's Chanel No. 5 and put it on my wrists, behind my ears. It's not like I expected to see my father sitting outside the hospital on a suitcase, checking his watch, like where are my womenfolk? But I didn't expect to see him still in bed, in one of those awful hospital robes that force you to look at skin you never wanted to see. I didn't expect him to look so sullen, to barely smile when I kiss him and say, "So we're here to spring you, Big Daddy."

My mother kisses him too. "Here," she says, and slides his wedding ring off her finger. He shakes it in his hand, then slips it on without a word.

"Come on," she says. "Let's get you home."

The whole ride home he swears and clutches at the door handle like he's in agony.

"Are you *trying* to hurt me?" he says, holding on to his side as she takes a turn, not too fast—maybe she's a little keyed up, but it's not so bad.

He stomps on the floorboard again.

"You can stop doing that. I had that brake taken out," she says in a snippy voice I don't think I've ever heard before. When we pull into the driveway, he shakes off her attempt to help him into the house. He moves slowly, staggering into the house like a cowboy in a bad western who's just gotten shot full of lead.

"Oh Jesus," my mother says, her voice catching. She believes he's hamming it up.

My mother has rearranged the living room for convalescence. My father won't be able to take the stairs, so she has rented a hospital bed, one with all the levers and cranks. The mattress looks like a huge white life raft. She has turned the velvet-covered love seat around so that it is facing the hospital bed, and made it up for herself to sleep on.

When he stands by the big bed, trying to get up onto it without killing himself, I have to look away. My mother offers to help, but he just waves her away. I don't know why he's so pissed off.

I don't know what to do with myself. I think about calling Mary Beth, or Dee, but I'm too tired to make words. Mom will call Dee. Mary Beth is probably out, or asleep. I wonder where my mother has stashed the tranquilizers her friends have been dropping by wrapped in tinfoil, along with casseroles and potted plants.

We are home only a half hour before my father begins clawing at his chest. "I can't breathe," he gasps. "Oh Christ, I can't catch my breath." I'm sure he's dying. He should never have left the hospital. His face turns a sickly gray, his eyes widen with fear.

"Call them," he wheezes. "Call the hospital." My mother, trying to appear calm, she doesn't start to run until she leaves the living room.

"It's okay, it's going to be okay," I say, talking into his chest. My own breathing is quickening. I don't want to be alone with him. I don't know what to do. I try to remember my health-class CPR lessons. I stare at his sternum, that's where I press my hands if he starts to die. Pray I don't break the rest of his ribs. When my mother comes back she looks relieved, as though my father has been overacting all along. Like he's been faking the whole thing. "It's okay, honey," she says, and adjusts the pillows behind his head. "It's normal."

"What?" he says a little too loudly, like he can't hear her over his panting. "Normal!"

"Lie back," she says gently. "It's just a little asthma, probably from the cat hair. I vacuumed, but..." She hands him the Primatene mist inhaler they sent along with the medication. "Here," she says. "It will pass."

My father glowers at us. "You don't understand."

We don't. We won't. For the first time ever I think my father is afraid. He tries to roll over so we can't see his eyes, but he can't, so he closes them. I want to touch him, but I don't dare. My mother sits in a chair by the side of his bed; her hands clasp and unclasp the silver bedrail. She smooths the sheets with her hand, rubs her mouth with the back of her hand, then clasps the bedrail again.

Before my mother leaves to go run errands—wine, morphine, ice cream—she changes the dressing on my father's back. It's like a science project, or a horror movie. I'm curious. How bad is it? I have to see what they've done to him.

"Damn it," he says as she pulls off the gauze, streaked with yellow and red. Not pus and blood, yellow and red. Mondrian colors.

"Ooh, that's really nice, Dad," I say, and look away.

"What?" I am surprised at how alarmed he sounds.

"Don't move," my mother says.

"Oh, it's just a really great tattoo. Betty Boop, I'd never have figured."

He kind of laughs, but stops. It hurts.

There's a deep red C-shaped incision on the tender skin

between his shoulder blades. It looks like they've split his skin with the ragged edge of an aluminum can, his skin puckering thick and pink against the stitches. It could make you sick if you were weak.

My mother lays new gauze over the incision, then tapes it down, in a really big square.

"There, that's going to make it all better," she says, patting it. "Just like new."

I'm sitting on the couch in the living room staring into the greenhouse. At some point he'll come in here, and it won't be like I'm following him, right? He'll just appear. I was here first.

"Evie," I hear him call from the kitchen. "I need a little help here," he says, sounding frustrated, like I should have offered to do whatever it was he wanted, I shouldn't have to be asked.

"Sure," I say. "Of course, anything." I'm jumpy, we are all jumpy. Everything is going to be fine, but still. He hurts.

"It's this freaking hair," he says. "It's itching like a sonofabitch."

Oh God, anything but that.

"Okay," I say, "you need a towel, shampoo, what else? Anything else from upstairs I can get you?"

"No. I need you to do it." He points to the sink. He leans with his arms apart against the counter, wincing. He has only taken half of his morphine, for fear of getting addicted.

"Sure," I say, "of course." I can never refuse him; this is

a reward after all. He chose me. My mother would be too rough. I understand. I can scarcely breathe.

He tries to fold his collar inside his shirt, but his hands are shaking. So I do it, I can't remember the last time I touched my father's neck. His hair is dirty, waxy. Falling into locks, it exudes an animal muskiness. I can see bloody holes in his scalp where he's dug in his nails.

I turn on the taps and test the water on the inside of my wrist. He nods. I make sure it is lukewarm, baby-bathing water.

"Did you get the stuff?" he asks.

"Yeah man, I got the good shit," I say in this corny Cheech Marin stoner voice. "Herbal Essence, your favorite." He doesn't smile. I reach for his arm and try to lead him to the sink.

"I can do it myself," he says, sounding tired and embarrassed. He bends slowly at the waist and leans toward the sink, then grabs at his side. He hovers, bent over, inches from the spigot, in pain. Without asking, I put my hand on the back of his head, and guide him under the water. My hand is shaking.

"It's okay," I say.

"Slow down," he says. "For Christ's sake, there's no rush," he says. "Take it easy."

I don't wait for his entire head to get wet. I pour shampoo into my hand and rub it into his scalp, gently, but quickly. I don't like having my hands on his skull like that. It's too close. I am scared of hurting him. I keep checking to make sure the lather doesn't run down his cheek and into his eyes. How long do I have to do this? It is good not to see his face, to have his head covered in white lather. I want to forget what I'm doing. I should have put on the radio. I hate this.

I let the water pour over the back of his head. As soon as it runs clear I turn off the water. He lets me guide him backward, his eyes shut, his hair dripping wet.

I wrap his head up in a clean white towel. I don't look at his face when he straightens up. He takes off the towel and mops the water from his face, then shakes his head, the way he does when he comes out of the ocean.

I think he might say thank you, or anything, but he doesn't. He holds the towel over his face.

"Is that better?" I ask. Never again. Never again.

"Mmm," he says. "When did your mother say she'd be back?"

Dad is in bed before my mother gets back. I'd brought him water, watching as he took his morphine, this time the full dose.

I am out on the back deck, which my father built two summers ago, every board and every nail his. It's getting cold out. I am spying on him through the French doors. It isn't like I expect him, now that he's alone, to do a soft-shoe, but I did think it possible to catch him getting out of bed, or turning over, or smiling. But all he does is lie there, so still it's scary. I hear Mom pull into the driveway, hear the side door slam. Then she tiptoes into the living room. She stands there for a second, then, still in her coat, she curls up beside my father in her little bed on the love seat, and closes her eyes. Neither of them is sleeping, but it's a nice picture if you don't look too hard.

Outside it's dusk, the sky low and gray, descending on us, like the top of a box being pushed shut. Everything green seems nearly black. The air feels thick. The earth is folding up around us. It's brighter here than it used to be. It never gets as dark as it once did. North Star used to be the only development out here; overnight, it seems everything has changed, new developments have spread out all around us, on all sides. The lights from the new houses killing the stars. Inside, I watch my father's chest rising and falling, rising and falling; he is trying to breathe very carefully. Trying to breathe without disturbing the stitches. I think he's counting his breaths, like he could save them up, as if at any minute they might stop. I try to breathe in rhythm with my father, matching his breath with mine, like this will reveal some mystery of feeling. Get up, I think, but he doesn't. He won't. I tap a cigarette out of the pack and strike a match.

I remember feeling that first tumor under my father's arm. How it moved under the skin, under my finger, like something alive.

I inhale deeply. It doesn't hurt. I exhale. I watch my breath turn silver.

My father, he isn't coming out here.

USE ME

His wife had ice-cream-cone breasts and was given to fits of crying, which she did alone and in the shower. He would stand in the hallway smoking and listening to her sob, waiting for a pause. Then he'd go in and piss, flush the toilet, and send a surge of hot water raining down onto her naked body. She'd scream and curse him, hurl soap and maybe a back scrubber at him. He'd strip, step into the shower, pull her down on the porcelain, and hold her, then fuck her. Then they'd sleep hard, and when they woke, he'd dress her. He would forbid her to wear panties. Then he'd take her out for a rare steak and eat her potatoes.

Michael Morris didn't tell me this; I knew this because I read it in his books, and his books were the truth, not even thinly veiled. He'd admitted as much. He said, "I write the truth." I read his stories with greedy fascination. In fact, I think he was the only writer who I could truthfully say I'd read everything he'd ever written. Okay, I didn't get to read as much as I wanted to or should. And it wasn't just that he was our college's one star. It was the way he described the senseless brutality he had inflicted on women, especially his wife, Janice. The deep indifference seemed nearly inhuman, and it fascinated me. I read his books because I was hungry for the ugly details of human nature, his nature, my nature, so skillfully rendered it seemed almost poetic. And yet even as I was thinking he was a bastard, I felt deeply attracted to this loathsome man, who seemed to be saying, See how you are exactly like me. You won't admit it, but you are.

Perhaps in some ways he was right, but he was offering his life as art. I wasn't taking anything he didn't mean for me to have, so I seized his stories, combing them for his violence. It wasn't only a voyeuristic thrill or a vicarious pleasure, but absolution from my own small crimes of deceit. I had to admire the way he depicted himself as a creep. He wasn't making any apologies for his behavior; he was just telling the truth, and I respected that. How many people really tell the truth?

Michael Morris said, "My wife is beautiful, and smart, and a better human being than I am." And no one doubted that, except maybe the bit about her being so smart. I heard him say on a talk show, "My life is full of real-life pain and drama. Why should I, if I don't need to, make anything up? After all, I own my life." Because he believed he owned his wife, he plucked out her soul and used it as paint. He dragged her onto the page and shackled her spread-eagle with precise iron-clad punctuation and clear piercing description, right down to the dark hair that curled around her nipples. She was the harping, myopic wife who couldn't intuit the way her husband needed her to be, and thus couldn't understand the sensitive-husband character. She was the wife who woke up in the middle of the night, alone, choking and unable to breathe. Her husband was gone—either out drinking with his "buddies" or, as the case was this time, hunched over his typewriter. "Copying my body, my face, my everything onto the page while I slept," her character laments in one story. "He was robbing me of my self."

He and Janice lived on the far outskirts of town in a large modern house that was mostly glass, in stark contrast to the old gingerbread-style Victorians that dominate our small university town. He used to teach the occasional Honors English class at the university, where I was finishing my senior year, majoring in art history and painting. Now he just did one reading a year, but his presence lingered in the air like the funny, nearly infinitesimal burning smell of electricity after a lightning strike. One of the girls in my off-campus house worked in the English department; she came home full of delicious rumors and innuendo about the intense, dark-eyed man who had sex in cars with various young coeds. It was legend that he was involved with a beautiful Lebanese freedom fighter who wore a bullet that had passed through her body on a chain around her neck, and that his wife had once tried to kill herself in the brand-new Mercedes he'd bought with the advance money for a screenplay he'd sold. She tried to asphyxiate herself in their garage, with the radio on some country-and-western station. That's why he said he didn't believe she meant to kill herself, because she put the radio on a station that she didn't even listen to. The music, he said, was for cheap dramatic effect.

Now the rumor was that he and Janice were divorcing. The split was almost devoid of drama—that must have killed him. He would have to pay her alimony. It would be a lot. She would make him pay that way. Still, the only possessions she wanted were the Oriental rugs. He owed her the rugs. They had bought them on their honeymoon, the last time he was decent to her. Now, he was so sorry, he was crying in restaurants. Torn apart, that's how he was supposed to be feeling. I liked imagining him crying. Ruining perfectly good meals all over town. His head in his hands, weeping into cold soup.

He was throwing himself into touring and promoting his new book to take his mind off it. His first stop was the university. I wanted to see him, I wanted to get a real look at him. I wanted permission to stare. I wanted to hear his words from his mouth, instead of in my own head. I wanted to watch him be Michael Morris. That was why I was in the amphitheater that night for his reading. I'd asked Mary Beth to come with me, then I changed my mind. I lied and told her I was going to the library instead, it wasn't like she'd ever check.

Mary Beth was a voluptuous brunette. She'd had the same haircut since high school, long with bangs that hung just over large cool grayish blue eyes, and a quick laugh. She had the confident air of a girl who had brothers. Older brothers, but she hadn't. It was embarrassing, but I didn't want the competition, and I didn't want anyone to see me getting all tongue-tied if I got a chance to meet him. I snagged a seat in the middle near the front so I could see, and so I was also in his line of vision. Perhaps he would notice the way I was sitting: both legs tucked under me, my arms hugging my body, head tilted, and eyes fixed on him like a scope.

I would nod. I understood.

I would be lying if I said I hadn't imagined appearing in one of his books. Michael Morris noticed small things about people they never noticed about themselves. He saw every-thing—every nuance. What could he tell me about me? I thought about my boyfriend, a political-science major, who was now at his fraternity house getting stoned and listening to the Grateful Dead or watching baseball with the brothers. He was sweet, but I knew he didn't know my dress size, and probably couldn't remember what my favorite color was. Not that it really mattered. I'd asked him to join me tonight, fully confident that he'd politely decline. Readings bored him, and anyway, he hated Michael Morris. "He's a jerk," he said. "He's a jerk who says he's a jerk and that is supposed to make everything okay. I don't buy it. Frankly, I don't see how you can like him."

Maybe that was the problem.

In the fluorescent light of the auditorium I was surprised to see how old Michael Morris looked. He was old enough to be my father. Hell, my father looked younger and better than Michael Morris. Maybe it was the unflattering light, but the lines in his face looked drawn as though with Magic Marker, and wiry, steel-colored strands of gray ran rampant through his black hair. He wasn't unattractive. He was attractive in a coarse, slightly scary way. He was taller than I had imagined. That was nice. His body was long, the muscle compacted on the bone. His hands looked meaty and enormous. I imagined his palms damp from clutching what I thought was probably a flask of Irish whiskey in his coat pocket.

He was much more handsome than his jacket photos, which seemed to present him either looking dark and guilty, as though he'd been caught in the act of masturbation, or intense, gaunt, and unshaven, suggesting imprisonment in the jail of his own mind. He was pacing back and forth in front of the stage as though he was psyching himself into being the great author, Michael Morris. He mounted the stage deliberately, and strode to the podium as though it was magnetized. He put on his reading glasses, and without saying a word of greeting or introduction, he began to read a story concerning a professor's fear that his student lover, who in his presence couldn't help chewing her lips until they bled, would kill herself for him. The second story was about a man who quarrels bitterly with his brother and then tries to rape his brother's wife to get back at him. He read slowly, deliberately shaping each word. Then he finished and stalked off the stage. No question-and-answer period. No "Thank you for coming." Wham, bam, thank you, ma'am.

• • •

Afterward there was a reception; half the audience, apparently repulsed, lit out. The other half were mostly students, like me, and some artsy-looking middle-aged people from town. After tossing back a glass of cheap white wine, I decided to go home. This was crazy. There was no need to meet him. I'd seen him. Heard him. That was what mattered. I wished I'd eaten something before the reading. I was starting to feel a little buzzed. Why shouldn't I meet Michael Morris? After all, I knew all about him. He didn't know anything about me. I could be anybody.

With this in mind, I walked right up to him and introduced myself.

"Hi," I said. "I'm Evelyn Wakefield."

His hand was large and cool, and he held on to mine for a beat too long. Holding it firmly, not limply or by the fingers the way some men shake your hand, as though they were shaking the hand of a child's stuffed animal; he pressed my hand between his palms.

"Evelyn," he said, savoring my name wetly, chewing on it. "Ev-el-lyn." He held it in his mouth like a piece of meat he wasn't ready to swallow. "Evelyn." He offered it like a prize on his tongue.

"It's Evie, actually," I said. So much for my cool and detached Evelyn persona. God, I hated it when I was such an Evie.

"Eh-vee," he said. "Not Eve-ee?"

"You've got it," I said.

"No hard E?"

"No hard E."

"Better still."

"People mispronounce it all the time," I said, like I was apologizing.

"I'm pleased to know you, Evie." He was the first person in a long time who seemed to truly mean it. There was this pause. God, but I hate a pause.

"Your books are . . . well, just amazing," I stammered. In one instant I'd gone from how-do-you-do to slobbering dope.

"Really? Well, thank you, Evie," he said, sounding a little surprised, but pleased. Certainly pleased. A little bit of wine splashed on my shoe. A brief half smile pulled up his lips, like he could tell I was nervous. He enjoyed having this effect on women.

He hadn't taken his eyes off my face for a moment. He really looked at me. He stepped closer. His breath was warm on my face and smelled faintly of bourbon. He had the deep creases around his eyes of a man who, no matter what the weather, drives fast and with the window down just to feel the rush of wind on his face, the confirmation of hurtling forward. Escape.

"Listen," he said, running his hand over his mouth, absently feeling his lips. "There are people here I have to talk to, boring shit, but maybe we could get together later, get a group together?" Then he added, "It'll be a party."

"All right," I said a little breathlessly, surprised and pleased at his invitation, but hoping I didn't look it. He studied me for a moment more, then turned away to find himself immediately chest to chest with another man, an overly tan

man with liquid-blue eyes who half hugged Michael and whispered in his ear, causing him to laugh and shake his head, then
he disappeared back into the crowd.

Wait, did he say he wanted me to get a group together?
No, he must have said *I'll,* or *we'll,* meaning perhaps him and
some of his friends, maybe other famous writer friends. He
couldn't mean *me,* who did I know that he'd want to talk to?
Did he mean for me to round up some other students, some
other women? Well, I *wasn't* going to. What if he didn't come
back, and I'd arranged for a bunch of us to go out with him?
That would be embarrassing. And anyway, I knew hardly a
soul at the reading, and I wasn't about to share Michael Morris
with a bunch of sensitive, earnest English major types with
their long hair and flowy skirts all trying to engage him in
pseudo-lit-crit chat. No way. Maybe it would be a big noisy
affair with lots of interesting strangers, the people who pop-
ulated his books: intellectual men with clean fingernails and
dirty souls, crazy women who drank too much and took pills.
I spotted him undulating through a throng of women wearing
different shades of brown, lavender and cream. Poets. They
alone kept the makers of purple ink in business. He stopped
and talked to a young woman with strawberry-blonde hair and
a gold nose ring. Her whole body washed in pale freckles. He
talked to her for what seemed to me a long time. Was she an
old lover? A student? He laughed. She laughed and waved
flirtingly at him as she moved away. Was she going to meet
up with us at the bar? I wondered, would there be other young
women like me there? Was I behaving like some groupie?
Maybe this was just some cattle call, and he'd choose the
prettiest one to sit close beside him. Why hadn't he just asked

me to go alone with him? Not that I would. I wouldn't. But it was like I wasn't enough. If the way he was working the room was any indication, the party would be huge. I made my way back to the bar, taking care to pass through his line of vision so he wouldn't forget about me. Wouldn't forget that he had invited me along. His gray silk shirt was sticking to the middle of his back, but still he seemed to move easily in his skin, like a big cat, prowling around the crowd shaking hands, clapping men on the shoulders, and laughing loudly.

The crowd was thinning out, but I didn't see him any-where. I picked at the top of my plastic wineglass and thought about leaving. What mattered was I met him. He might not have meant it about the drink anyway, and I wasn't going to stay here and wait for him, only for him to forget me. Maybe I had misunderstood. Perhaps he meant, if I can get a group together we'll all go out and have a drink. I knew he was in pain over his wife leaving. I was sure of that, the way he got so close to me so quickly, like he just wanted to be near a woman. I thought about calling my boyfriend. I'd take over Chinese food and some rum raisin ice cream. His favorite. Then later we'd have comfortable, familiar, forgettable sex. First, though, I'd tell him about Michael Morris and how he wanted me to go out for a drink with him, but I didn't go. Instead I came to his apartment. Because I missed him. Because that's the kind of girl I am. That would be the hard part, saying why I missed him. That part I couldn't do. I couldn't go to his place. It wouldn't work. I know me. He'd seem dull and immature in comparison to Michael Morris, and for no good reason I'd hate him and I'd leave him in a bad mood, such a bad distracted frustrated mood I wouldn't even kiss him good-bye. I didn't want to play out that scene. I should just quickly and invisibly disappear into the night. Go home and write my paper on why the Madonna's face, so perfectly symmetrical, is so often green in Renaissance paintings. Go home and hang with Mary Beth. After all, soon we'd graduate. God I hated that thought. I'd miss her.

Then I felt Michael Morris's hand on my shoulder, his fingertips pressed down into my clavicle like a claim. "Looks like it's just us two. It's a work night," he said, rolling his eyes. "I trust that this isn't a problem," he said as though if it were a problem, he didn't want to hear about it.

"Perfect," I said in a voice lower than my own.

In the dim light of the bar his eyes were intensely brown, like something melted down—maybe the leather interior of an expensive car or a dense cube of black hash. Something foreign. His eyes were darkly oily like that. Slowly they glided in his sockets as he traced my body in front of him, rolling up languorously to smile at the buxom Latino hostess, who smiled back, like they knew each other. "We want to sit out back, in your garden," he said, his gaze moving down her face and over her breasts.

He ordered a double Jack Daniel's. Up. "Get whatever you want," he said. I ordered a white wine spritzer.

"I thought only suburban ladies in espadrilles drank those."

I wrinkled my nose. "Well, I guess I'm proof that's not true." His remark, of course, tapped into all my insecurities. I was a suburban girl, I did once wear espadrilles.

The waitress, a bored-looking beauty, narrowed her eyes at me. "Can I see some ID?"

I fumbled in my purse for my wallet, pulling it out upside down so my change clattered on the floor and my credit cards shot out across the table. My driver's license was AWOL in the murky nether regions of my bag. I could feel my cheeks burning.

"You're of age, right?" she said, annoyed. Michael grinned, he was flattered by the question, which just enhanced his virility. The waitress walked away.

"You *are* of age, aren't you, Evie?" Michael asked, his eyes glittering.

"Ha, ha," I said, wishing my drink would arrive quickly. I hadn't noticed earlier, but on Michael's left eyelid he had a small mole. It kept his lid from fitting snugly back in the socket; it snagged, then relented. I'd never noticed it in any of his jacket photos. I tried to recall the various poses he was in. Was that side always facing away from the camera? It was amusing to think he was that vain.

"You smoke?" he said, shaking the pack with expert casualness so one cigarette poked out.

"Sure," I said, even though I'd quit.

He lit the cigarette for me, drawing the smoke into his lungs. He handed it to me, his fingers touching mine, the filter moist. He lit his own and inhaled. He took a drag and sat back in his chair, rubbing his thumbprint slowly over the filter of the cigarette in tiny circles like he was thumbing a nipple, making soft circles over and over again after each inhale.

"You smoke grass?"

"Sometimes."

"I was getting high before you were even born." He smiled and picked a piece of tobacco off his lip.

"So?" I leaned into the table a little so that my blouse parted and he could see the tops of my breasts. I felt like I was channeling Mary Beth. I never talked like this. I liked it. I liked it a lot.

"You want to get high later? I've got some Thai stick in the car. It's great shit. Nothing compared to the stuff I used to smoke with Ginsberg at Berkeley, but it's good shit. If you can handle it. If you want to," he said, sipping his drink, looking up at me from under hooded lids.

"Good to know," I said, my mind conjuring up fanciful images of Michael Morris and Allen Ginsberg lounging on Indian pillows, passing a hookah, and rapping about Chinese poetry.

"You know you are pretty, don't you?" he said. "I'll bet men give you things, don't they? You've got that kind of face. The kind of face you give flowers to." He kind of laughed.

He pulled his chair closer, as though I were a fire he was warming himself in front of, gazing at my body. I could feel the back of my neck becoming damp with perspiration. I wished I were on fire, then I could beat him back. I would be provocative and exciting, with the power to destroy him a little bit, the power to make a mark on him.

"Tell me about Evie," he said. I was silent. It had been a long time since someone had asked me such an up-front question about myself. I didn't know how to react. Was he just making small talk? Everything I knew about him made me believe that he was incapable of it. I had to choose carefully. What did I want him to know about me? How would he use it? I stalled. "Be more specific. What do you want to know about me?"

"The Evie no one knows. The one you don't talk about."

"Well"—I leaned back into the deep wicker chair and, slipping off my black sandals, tucked my feet underneath me— "what makes you think there is anything to tell? Maybe I just am, as I am." He frowned slightly, then narrowed his eyes as if he was sizing me up. I smiled back at him. This was fun. I wouldn't give anything away.

"Come on, just between you and me," he said, "a pretty girl like you must have lots of stories. Come on."

"Maybe," I said.

The famous Michael Morris wanted something Morris-esque from me. He wanted something raw and personal— maybe even sexual—something I was ashamed of, perhaps. He laced his fingers together, steepling his forefingers, and brought them up to his lips so that it appeared he was kissing the barrel of a gun. He was greedy. My first impulse was to tell him not about me, but about my boyfriend. How he wouldn't go down on me, how he ate his food off his plate in a counterclockwise motion, and how he didn't remember the name of the woman he lost his virginity to. Or to steal from Mary Beth. I could say I'd had three abortions, that I might be pregnant right now. But those stories didn't belong to me, and I sensed that wasn't what Michael Morris wanted. He wanted something of mine. He'd know if I lied.

I would be lying if I said that I hadn't fantasized about appearing in one of his books. I imagined how he would see me. I would be young, my blonde bob would be long and red with a shine like patent leather. He'd mention my breasts, which were really nothing special, comparing them to dollops of fresh white cream. My legs, elongated, would cut through space like scissors. I would be smart, but not too smart. I would be naive. Maybe he'd widen the gap in my front teeth. He would rewrite all his parts so he was obviously the one with the upper hand, and invent poetic dialogue fraught with tense and subtle metaphor. In that way I was sure he wasn't honest. But I would be different. Like a man, I'd have him, and I would leave him. He would put me on the page, but I'd live outside it. I'd live longer than he.

Every time readers entered my page I would breathe, I would move, I would reach my arms out to them. I'd never die. He could make me immortal—if I was willing to play the game.

"All right," he said, and ran his tongue over his lips. "Tell me what you've heard about me." He smiled, running his finger along the wet rim of his glass so that it sang into his hand. "Go on. I want to know. I know you all talk about me."

"Well, I'm in the art school, not the English department," I said, waiting to see if this information disappointed him. If he'd taken me out just because he assumed I was an English major. If that was the turn-on.

"Ah, a painter, I bet."

"That's funny, how did you know?" Perhaps there was some kind of connection between us. All right, it wasn't hard to guess painter; maybe I reeked of turpentine and I didn't even know it. I was also more into drawing, and art history, but still. I'd love to be a painter. I just wasn't as good as I wanted to be. I lacked the necessary passion.

"So, of course, nobody in your department even knows who I am," he said, sounding amused.

"No, no, that's not true. It's just, well, you know what they say. You don't need me to tell you." I was afraid this might be the wrong way to respond, but he smiled, arching an eyebrow as if to concede the point. He knew what the stories were. I wondered if at some point he had stopped simply living and had started concentrating on making the myth of Michael Morris.

"Maybe you'd like to do me sometime. My portrait. I could sit for you," he said, turning into profile to tease me. He showed me the side that hid the mole on his eyelid.

I thought about having sex with him. He'd crush me. He'd call me *little girl,* and I'd get wet. He'd enclose my breast in his fist, owning it, grabbing it like some golden apple. He'd spread my legs wide and bury himself deep inside me. He'd want me to wrap my legs around his head, or stand on my hands. He'd want me on top, touching myself. He'd want drama. He'd want gymnastics. He wouldn't ask if I minded if he smoked in bed. He'd sleep deeply and with his mouth open. In the morning, after he'd showered and taken care of his body's needs, then he'd think about me. Good or bad? Maybe with his pen in hand, or his dick, or maybe not at all. Maybe he wouldn't think of me at all. I'd be just one in a string of women all blurring together. Fur, and legs, and the occasional quick glass of juice or coffee, drunk over the kitchen sink as they exchanged terse pleasantries. Have you seen my necktie? Will you call me? Someone he'd remember until the next girl appeared, and even then my face would be hazy, my name and my body lost. I couldn't stand that idea.

"You got a lover?" he asked me, running the length of his index finger back and forth across his lips.

"Excuse me?"

"You heard me. How many?"

"One," I said. He smiled like he already knew what I was going to say. Still, I didn't think that one should pose any obstacle to us getting to know each other. In fact, it might turn him on. I wasn't sure. I could always deny it later. And I liked the way he said *lover* instead of *boyfriend*. It seemed to suggest that you might have a relationship with another person, male or female, simply for the sexual pleasure of it. No dinner in front of the TV, no talking about religion or your parents, just sex. Just great sex.

"Why isn't he here with you tonight? Doesn't he like my work? Or did you lose him after the reading?" He grinned at me.

"He's sick," I lied.

"Would you marry him?" he asked, letting the smoke slowly crawl out of his mouth.

"Maybe," I lied.

"If you got pregnant you'd marry him, wouldn't you? Even if you weren't sure you loved him."

"No, of course not." I hated that I was blushing. Hated that he assumed I was the sort of woman who wouldn't marry for love, but because of a social stigma. He was saying I was uptight, old-fashioned, a prude.

"You can tell me." He leaned into the table. "You could have an abortion. Would you do that?" He lit another cigarette with the still-glowing tip of the last one, and stared at me as though he really expected me to answer him civilly.

"That is none of your business," I snapped. I thought about Mary Beth at home in the dorm. I wondered what she would do right now. Would she laugh? Throw a drink in his face? Grab his dick? I did know she'd be surprised to see me here with Michael Morris. She probably wouldn't believe it when I told her, if I told her. I knew she'd be amused. Even though I'd lied and told her I wasn't going to the reading.

"Sorry," he said, holding up his hands like he meant no harm. "I didn't realize it was such a touchy subject. No big deal. I just thought we were having a conversation."

"We were talking about love, not abortion."

"Right, love," he snorted, and took a long drag on his cigarette. "Liking the same foods, the same sex—that isn't love." He leaned across the table toward me. "What could you know about love? You are a child." He made his voice soft and knowing. "I know you. As beautiful as you are, and as special. I know you." His arms encircled the table, holding on to it, as if to say, This table here is all that is between us and I have it in my arms. This little thing is all that divides us from being one.

"I'm sorry about you and your wife," I said.

He stopped and looked solemn for an instant, then he said, "I did love her, the bitch. No one wants to believe that." He laughed. "But that's a closed chapter."

"That's horrible," I said, expecting him to respond, but he didn't. "How can you say that?" I asked.

He shrugged. "You want me to say it's some way it isn't."

"You really hurt her. You did. How could you write all

that stuff knowing it would cause her pain?" I asked him, half disgusted, half curious. I didn't want to believe he set out to damage her. I wanted to believe he set out to damage her.

"I didn't hurt her. She *let* it hurt her; that's different," he explained, and paused dramatically as though waiting for it to sink in, as though I *should* understand the difference, and if I didn't, I needed to.

He looked odd sitting in the deep, high-backed white wicker chair. His eyes unblinking, his chest lurched forward and curled over the table, slightly hunched, like he was going to ask me for a favor and he didn't want anyone to hear, or he was going to beg for something horrible, something he needed to save his life, and he didn't want to have to ask. He made me feel that if I were a real woman I'd know what it was. I'd know, and because he was an artist I'd offer it.

He stood up halfway and pulled his chair around the table closer to my side.

"I can't hear you with all the noise," he said. "I can't hear you," he said, pressing his ear into my lips as I said, "I'll speak louder."

His eyes were half closed. His head rising up close to my shoulder. Almost resting there like some big, dangerous baby. He ordered two more drinks. I switched to Jack Daniel's. He smiled as I took my first sip of it and flinched.

"I'm comfortable talking about myself, because I'm a writer," he said, wrapping his arm around the back of my chair. "You're a painter. What do you paint? Do you do self-portraits ever, nudes, what?"

I struggled. I couldn't think clearly with his body so close to mine. "Sure."

"Which—nudes or self-portraits, or both at the same time?"

"Both, I guess. I'm having some trouble right now." I blushed.

I was pretty in my self-portraits. I lied, making myself skinnier than I really was, taller. My breasts high and small. I couldn't paint myself as I really looked. It was embarrassing. I just couldn't. I tried to be honest, I did, but then I just stopped trying; it was humiliating. I never showed those paintings. I was vain, deeply vain, and not a good enough painter to hide it, or exploit it.

His eyes lit up. "Tell me. You don't know, maybe I could help."

"No." I couldn't remember the last time I had said no to someone.

He shook his head. "It's unfair that you know all about me and all I know about you, *Evie*, is that you *paint*." He spit out the word *paint* as though it were too sweet, or rancid. As though I were no different from some little old lady doing paint-by-numbers watercolors of Scottie dogs and windmills.

"Come on, tell me a story, give me something," he said, squeezing my shoulder for a moment. "Here, tell me about your first hickey, prom, learning to ice-skate. Your nose job. Losing your virginity. Tell me that one."

"I didn't have a nose job." I laughed. My nose was one of my few gifts of nature.

"Come on, that perfect little nose. How much did Daddy spend? You can tell me. I won't tell. Lots of girls get them for their sweet sixteen, or their bat mitzvah."

"It's mine," I said, "and I'm a Presbyterian."

"Why are you lying to me?" he snapped.

"I'm not," I insisted, uncomfortable with the rough edge on his voice. He studied my face hard, as though his eyes could burn off any deception I might attempt.

"Good," he said, sliding his hand into the top of his shirt and running his palm slowly over his chest, his fingers fluffing up the black and silver hairs.

"Why don't you tell me about the new book," I said, trying to change the subject. His face hardened.

"They hate me," he barked. "Reviewers. Everybody. Especially the women. They think I'm a misogynist, because I tell it like it is. I don't understand it. If anyone ever loved women, it is me!"

He pounded his hands on the table, nearly upsetting his drink. People at nearby tables murmured. I imagined them whispering, "See that couple? That is the famous writer. Yes, that one. Who's the girl? I bet they're lovers." Their attention, coupled with the drinks, made me want to light a cigarette and blow smoke out my nose. It made me want to lean across the table and kiss him hard on the mouth. A middle-aged couple turned their heads, pretending to look over our heads at something in the distance, but I knew it was us they were looking at. It proved his point, people were against him— against him, and now, by association, me.

I sipped my whiskey. It didn't hurt this time, but warmed my mouth and flooded my body with a pleasurable heat. He reached over and grabbed my hand. "You believe me, don't you?" he asked, his fingers pressed into my palm. He looked younger in the candlelit darkness. It softened his knobbed cheekbones and made his mouth seem thick and lush. I was beginning to surrender inches of myself to him. I let him caress my palm. Then the inside of my arm up to the elbow. He traced a blue vein that ran up and disappeared into my sleeve. I shivered. I could see the soft white skin where his wedding band used to be. It looked like new skin, as though when he had removed the ring he had worn for years, his skin had been torn off with it. This pale naked groove made him seem even more attractive to me. Overhead, stars were sprinkled like tiny pins in a map showing where the bombs are buried—where soon everything would never again be like it was. He whispered in my ear, his lips moving against my lobe, "You know you are sexy."

"Not necessarily," I replied, shaking my head, enjoying the rattle of his words in my skull. I was stimulated by them—*You, are, sexy.*

"How do *you* see me?" I asked, leaning toward him so he could get a better look in the candlelight. "I mean, how do I appear to you?" I pushed the hair back and away from my shoulders, holding on to a strand of it that I brushed back and forth over my mouth.

He looked at me for a minute and licked his lips. "I don't know if you really want me to tell you," he said, raising an eyebrow.

"I do," I said, and squeezed his fingers.

"Later," he said.

"Promise?"

He was the kind of man who liked to make a woman beg. He was the kind of man who wanted to do things you'd never let another man do to your body, like it was his right. Then he'd want you to tell him how you felt. In detail, so he owned it.

I might let him.

He reached out slowly and took my hair in his hands, cupping it, weighing it. I tried to move my chair back a little, but my hair snagged painfully between his fingers. He dragged the knotted hair through his fingers, and I yelped.

"I'm going to take a leak." He stood up leisurely and stretched. "Don't you go anywhere."

My scalp felt seared. It seemed like everyone around me had started talking all at once, moving their heads in minute fractions, like they were listening to signals from the heavens emanating from those silver pinpoints. I rubbed my fingers against the soft indents of my temples. I believed he had pulled my hair on purpose. He thought he could do whatever he wanted with me. I thought about leaving right then. I imagined him coming back to the table thinking maybe I was hiding from him, playing a little game. He'd get down on his hands and knees, get mud on his trousers looking for me. He'd get hard thinking about me half undressed in the bushes waiting for him to discover me crouching in the dirt. Not finding me, he'd think, "That impulsive, mysterious woman has eluded me, and now I'll never possess her."

Or, he'd think, "What a stupid little cunt. Silly thing got scared and ran away; couldn't even say good-bye." That's what he would think.

I gnawed hard on an ice cube. I didn't even hear him return to the table.

"Evie," he said, softly prodding my ribs with his forefinger. "Evie," he said. "Where are you?" He crossed his arms against his chest and sank down into his chair. "Are you thinking about what you're going to tell your friends about tonight? I know how women talk. I don't mind." He rubbed my shoulder.

"I'm here," I said curtly. "And I don't talk that way." He looked a little surprised.

"I'm sorry," I said. "I guess I'm fading."

He rubbed a few strands of my hair between his fingers. "No you're not. I can still see you. I can," he said, gently shoving his hand up under my hair, grasping the nape of my neck with his thick fingers. "I can still feel you." I smiled unsteadily. I wondered how he saw me. Would he tell me? Would he lie? His hand tightened on the back of my head.

"You are lovely. Did you know," he said, and paused as if to tease me, "that I have a photographic memory? I remember the body of every woman I've ever fucked." His hand fell to my shoulder. He ran his fingers down my arm, brushing lightly against my breast. "Every curve. Every muscle . . ." He pulled my hand to his mouth and kissed my knuckles; his tongue pressed itself between my spread fingers.

I pulled my hand away and down into my lap. Then I started to stand up. I didn't think I could do this. Could I? What would the story be? What would my story be? There was no story. He had written this story a hundred times.

"You can't go," he whispered as he grabbed my wrist. "I want to make love to you. Have one more drink. We'll go someplace. I need you."

"I can't." I tried to shake my hand loose.

His face was cold, half angry, half sad, like he didn't

know what to do. "Fine," he said. "You disappoint me," he said. "I thought you were different. I thought you were more than this," he said with a short harsh laugh.

The couple sitting one table over stopped talking and listened for a moment. I could see the light vanishing from his eyes as though there were lamps being pulled back inside him. The front of his face was dark, and empty, and ugly. No one said anything. I was different. I would tell him something. I could tell him something he didn't know. Something I'd never read in his books. Something he'd want, something he'd like and need. He actually looked small sitting there next to me, turning his hands over and over in his lap. So I threw him a bone.

"Okay," I said. His face softened. He opened his mouth slightly, then curved his body intimately around my chair. He wanted my secret. He wanted to ensure that I gave it to him, that he heard it all, and that it was for his ears alone. I sucked down the last little bit of liquor lingering in the bottom of my glass, swallowing it like the tail end of the evening.

"I give up," I said. I took a deep breath, and with my eyes fixed on the candle's flame I told him this: "I've got lousy rhythm. I can't slow-dance. I try to lead. It drives men, especially my father nuts. I've got to close my eyes and give myself over, literally safety-pin myself like a scarf to my partner and let him move me. I'm lousy in bed because of this. It's true. I'm a terrible lover. I'm afraid to lose the power of being the one who's acted upon, the passive one, the one who doesn't risk anything except perhaps my lover's disappointment, and I worry about that. Of course I worry about disappointing. You see, I'm not like other women. I can't become some character,

I can't forget myself and become somebody else during sex. I can only be myself, and I guess I'm not comfortable with that. That's why I don't want to take control, why I want to be taken. I'm afraid to straddle a man and ride him because I can't get into any kind of rhythm and stay there without becoming incredibly self-conscious. I can't play it out, steady, steady, to the point of ejaculation, I've never been able to come like that on top, I can't stay wet. I just panic and roll onto my back, even though I know I'm supposed to want it on top like that— in a position to rule, I know it's supposed to empower me, and turn me on, but I just can't do it. Maybe I'm just afraid that if I take control, if I am secure enough to let myself go, I might find out something about myself that I don't want to know. If I let go, I might be consumed by my desires. I'm afraid of what I might want. What I might need. What it might do to me. Who I might become."

I blurted out all of this. My heart was pounding in my mouth. I stared down into my lap, fixating on my hands lying flat and still over my crotch. I couldn't look up at him. I could feel his breath on my cheek as he leaned into my body. His breathing sounded shallow, and uneven.

"Is that true?" he asked. His voice was throaty and deep. I looked up at him. His lips were slightly parted and his pupils looked large and limpid. I had him.

"What do you think?" I said, my voice steady.

"I don't know. Is it?" He couldn't stand not knowing if I was, or was not, telling him the truth, and he needed to know.

"Why would it matter?" I said, and he just looked at me, like nothing else did matter. I smiled at him, and shrugged. I wasn't about to tell. I curled up in my chair and gazed up at the stars, then back at him until he shifted his eyes to the ground. He put his hands on his knees and breathed in deeply, looking as though I had shoved him hard in the chest.

"She left me," he said, lifting his head up slowly.

"I know," I said. I didn't want to hear the things I'd already read, hear the things I already knew. "Everyone knows that," I said, shaking a cigarette out of his pack. If my father knew the way I was smoking. He stared at me as I tamped the tobacco down into the tip and, leaning across the table, lit it from the candle. His eyes looked flat and black, like he wanted me to just listen to him.

"She was fucking my brother," he said. "My only brother, who I slept in the same room with for fifteen years. Thanksgiving. Hanukkah. Fucking Arbor Day. Two long years I sat there, like an idiot eating their shit while they snuck off and fucked in the bathroom on holidays, fucking behind my back while I slept. My brother and my wife. It's over, they say. The fucking bastards. But, but, that's not why she left me. She tells me, 'That's not why I left you. I am only telling you this so you hear it from me.' My brother, he doesn't say anything. He won't even look at me. I hit the bastard. I beat his head in . . . I beat his head in and all he does is stand there and fucking sob."

I didn't want to look at him. His face was dripping with tears, his mouth open and ragged. I stood up and slipped into my coat. "You can't leave Michael Morris," he cried out, and grasped at my arm. He sprang to his feet, he stuck his hands deep into his pockets, he yanked out a wad of dollar bills and

threw them at the table. He grabbed my elbow. I stopped. I
didn't move. I didn't run. I just let him keep talking.

"Come on, come on, you can't leave me. I've got my car
here," he pleaded. "You can't just leave me like this, baby. I'm
destroyed. I'm destroyed. I need you. You can make it better."
He pulled me toward him, wrapping his arms around me; he
clenched me to his chest. I could feel the coldness of his
belt buckle against the back of my hand. "Come on," he said.
"Use me."

THE GARDEN

OF EDEN

The first thing Evie's father did upon arriving in Amsterdam was tighten the hinges on her bedroom door. "You could have done that yourself, honey," he said, as though home repair was at the top of Evie's "to do" list.

When Evie's first priority really was what to wear to greet her father who had decided to "swing by" for a visit after finishing up some business he had in London. I could hardly believe the way she'd torn apart our closet, finally settling on my black Azzedine Alaïa dress, my Tiffany pearls, and a cunning little pair of alligator sling backs. I hardly recognized her, seeing that as of late she had been favoring old lace slips, fishnets, and combat boots. But tonight she looked like a future trophy wife. If you didn't look too close. She had managed to scour off her black nail polish, but there were still faint traces of violet in her newly bleached white hair. Her father was, after all, still recovering from some awful surgery—not that you could tell—but still, one might assume he could only stand so much.

No, truth be told, the perfect outfit was second on Evie's list of things to do. Her first priority was to get her new boyfriend, Billy, out of the flat before Daddy arrived. Billy was a ridiculous punk rocker she met at the Van Gogh Museum—he was shoplifting postcards, *Van Gogh's Room at Arles* (decorating tips, no doubt)—from the gift shop where she worked. She was afraid she was falling in love with him. *Quel* romance.

"I can't believe it," she would wail over and over again, usually after spotting some particularly cute guy. "It's over. God, this can't be. How did this happen? How could I fall in love?"

"I tried to convince you to get the shot," I'd joke, and flash her my shoulder. "A simple inoculation against commitment."

"No, really, I'm doomed."

"So can I assume Billy won't be joining you and the family for the holidays?"

At this, Evie went absolutely pale. "That isn't even funny, and don't you say a word. Daddy would hate Billy. He has no job, he barely speaks to his own family, and he's a musician, which is just fine in the abstract—you know, my father has that whole, want-to-be-a-rock-star-in-another-life thing—but see, Billy isn't dreaming. He's not going to be some CPA who plays guitar on weekends in some hobby cover band with a bunch of balding armchair outlaws. He really wants to make it." She paused. "And he'll tell my father that."

I can't help myself; I laugh, just a little. It's not that I don't believe her, she's told me stories of how her father used to torture her boyfriends—it's just that Evie is starting to sound just like Billy with all of his eat-the-rich silliness and not wanting to be with anybody who doesn't "burn." It used to be that Evie and I sounded alike, almost like sisters, everybody said so. I can't tell you how many times people still confuse us on the phone.

I didn't believe for one minute this thing with Billy would last. I mean, really. It wasn't just that he looked like a sixteen-year-old delinquent, what with his black sticking-up hair (he styled it with Elmer's, I swear), his holey black jeans and ripped T-shirts, and that silly wallet on a chain thing, which was an utter joke. Who would want to steal a wallet that had absolutely no cash in it? This little *affaire d'amour* wouldn't last because I knew my best friend, and I knew that what really mattered to her was the chase, and she had him. For heaven's sake she had him every single night it seemed. Believe me, I wouldn't introduce Billy Lang to my father either, but then again my father hadn't met any of my boyfriends since he picked me up at tennis camp and I introduced him to Russell Cole. Russell was sixteen and I was thirteen. All my father said on the drive home was, "Is that the Coles of Boston or Savannah?"

I had to confess I had no idea. To me he was just foxy Russell with the nice butt and the fast hands.

Which isn't to say my father doesn't know men I've dated, he just doesn't know that he knows them, it would be awkward, to say the least.

Oh, sometimes when he is feeling particularly fatherly, say, after he's gotten my AmEx bill, he'll ask, "So, any prospects?" But this could mean anything, right? I cannot imagine he really expects me to tell him anything. And I wouldn't.

It seemed every time my mother called me at college she managed to work "So, have you met any nice young men? Have you been dating?" into the conversation. Always in this chirpy Ann Landers voice; that is, until she got tired of listening to me roar with laughter. It's best that I keep my private life private. I just know Sunny would find fault with any man I brought home. Ever since my father left her, or rather *us*, as she prefers to put it, she's maintained, "You can't trust men. Of course they make wonderful escorts, and one couldn't live in a world without men, but on a cold winter night I'd rather the company of a dog."

"Really?" I say. "You'd rather a dog in your bed than a man? Oh, Sunny...."

This of course just frosts her. I can't help myself. I love my mother, but she's just so easy to torment.

By the time Evie has opened and poured the red wine her father brought, her father has finished fixing the hinges, and is surveying the rest of our apartment like a contractor. Evie still hasn't opened the gift he brought, it's just sitting in the middle of the table, driving me nuts with curiosity. My father's graduation gift to me was the summer rental of this flat in Amsterdam—not exactly easy to wrap, but a very good gift.

"Hey, puss," Evie's father says, "do you, by any chance, still have that toolbox I gave you?"

The phone rings and Evie shoots me this look like don't you dare. "Let the machine get it," she says. I know she thinks it's Billy. We don't even have a machine. I wonder for half a second if it might be Gerhard, but I don't care if he calls or not.

"Of course I have it," she says. "Some girls have hope chests, I have a toolbox." She keeps it under her bed. Her father gave her the toolbox when she went off to college, you know, a go-forth-and-be-independent gesture. She's got one of everything in there; we used to use the pointy screwdriver to open cans of condensed milk when we were in our Turkish coffee drinking stage.

Toolbox in hand, her father repairs the latch in the bathroom—"Just a little wood putty and a screw"—and by the time he's finished his second glass of wine he's patched and rewoven our windowscreen. "That hole will get bigger and bigger until one morning you wake up with a pigeon in your bed, or a squirrel."

I had to bite my tongue so I wouldn't say, "Or worse, a Lang." But I wouldn't do that to Evie, not in a million years, even just teasing. We don't make each other feel bad. Some nights we lie in the dark and just talk and talk, having these conversations where you find yourself saying things you didn't even know you thought, confiding stuff you would only tell somebody after you'd slept with them.

I don't tell her that I think Billy is a big poser—after all the boy went to Brown and he lives in a squat and plays in a band called the Seven Plagues that, incidentally, only has three people in it. I figure that they're still auditioning for lice, pestilence, and locust, and oh, yes, a bass player who can turn water into blood. To me Billy is just another one of those once-preppy boys who, because he has a cock ring in his sock drawer, now thinks he is living on the edge.

But because Evie is my best friend I never complain about how Billy and his roommate, Franz, the drummer for the Seven Plagues, just drop by unannounced at all hours of the day and night. I don't dwell on the fact that Franz throws up on people and then steals their wallets. A common pickpocket.

Billy insists that Franz is a revolutionary. "He's just re-acting to the wholesale destruction and commodification of his city. Tourism has turned his homeland into a gaudy sexual theme park. It has no soul anymore. Franz is an artist, man."

Franz is also the band's manager. His vomiting has paid for amps, a new drum kit, and more. I had a little scandal with Franz once. Evie dragged me to a Seven Plagues "show," which was really just the boys jumping up and down in a smoky little club, screaming like lunatics. Afterward, the boys were understandably thirsty and in need of forgetfulness, so we all went drinking. At some point during the evening Evie and Billy peeled off, and I found myself alone with Franz, going in and out of bars looking for a place that sold decent hash. We were just strolling along when all of a sudden Franz stops and throws up all over some guy in a Planet Hollywood jacket. Unbelievable. It was horrifying but very funny. Of course the man froze, and for a split second I was certain he was going to throw up too. The trick, Franz told me later, was to hit your mark square in the back so they can't see too much of the vomit, but can absolutely smell it. Otherwise, you run the definite risk of them throwing up on you. Which is truly disgusting. The trick was to boot just enough to allow you license to touch them, and rifle their clothing—understandably, they desperately want you to wipe your vomit off them. You could even be a little rough, all in the interest of sanitation. I never even saw Franz lift the billfold, but the rest of the night drinks were on him.

Later at a bar he'd said, "You know, a pretty girl like you could make a nice chunk of change . . . you could lift their fucking contact lenses."

For half a second, with his hand on the inside of my thigh, I thought about it. A barfing Bonnie and Clyde but with good sex. Me, a former debutante. I loved it! Just the fact that he even considered it was charming.

Back at the apartment I made him take a bath. I did. I filled the tub up so high it was positively sloshing over and I got in with him. We laid in that tub for a long time, not even talking. I did make him use soap and brush his teeth with his finger.

The next morning it was sort of cute, the four of us getting up together in the apartment, calling in sick to work, eating pancakes Billy made. It was sweet.

Anyway, now I am seeing Gerhard. Gerhard is an art dealer. He has a real job. Evie hates hates hates him. She thinks he should call me ten times a day and tell me how fabulous I am. She thinks he doesn't appreciate me. I can just tell.

Evie's father finishes fixing the hole in the screen, and sinks down into the cushions of our badly stuffed couch. He doesn't even ask what happened to the screen. I guess he doesn't want to know. I wonder if Evie would tell him that she kicked it in the other night at two A.M. when we found ourselves locked out.

Even though I was absolutely exhausted I'd dragged Evie out for a drink. She was in a blue funk. I'd staggered home from my job at a small private art gallery, where I was basically paid to sit there, hand out price lists, and cross and uncross my legs, to find her curled up in the armchair eating Cocoa Puffs, listening to that god awful mopey music (I swear that played backward, those Cure lyrics say, Make yourself hideous), and cutting her hair. These days the look was Tinker Bell by way of Attica. It was because of Billy that she'd cut off perfectly nice light brown hair, bleached it golf ball white and streaked it purple. It was because of him that she'd started tricking herself out like some street urchin. The metamorphosis was certainly not lost on her father. When Evie opened the door the poor man looked stunned, though he held his tongue admirably. "Wow," he said, "tell me about the hair."

Evie said, "Do you like it?"

He said, "Do *you* like it?"

The very picture of parental diplomacy. I just cannot imagine.

In any case, Ev was depressed because last week, while Billy was off playing screeching guitar and nowhere to be found, she had a scandal with one of her art student boys. One with green striped hair and a pierced lip, a budding abstract expressionist, I believe. Maybe, just maybe, she touched his peepee.

Evie thinks it is perfectly acceptable to get completely naked with a man and then say, "Oh let's just kiss." It's true. More than once I have heard her out in the living room talking some guy out of date-raping her on the sofa. Forget being a painter, she ought to work at the United Nations. Of course, I knew she was upset, but I just couldn't let her get all tied in knots over this silly little fling.

"Blame it on the make-out sweater," I said. The make-out sweater was a white angora sweater, so impossibly soft it felt like fur. Boys couldn't keep their hands off it, and once they petted, they were powerless. All my roommates wanted to borrow it in college. It had an incredible track record.

"Yeah, right," she sighed. "That damn sweater."

"It's past tense, darling," I said. "You did nothing wrong. You and Billy are just dating, after all," I reminded her. "Anyway, Billy didn't call. He hasn't called in two days." I stopped myself from saying anything else, but it was hard.

Evie took it all in. First she looked just pained and then she looked grateful, so absolved it was almost sad. I have never understood the need to inflict guilt on one's self.

"If I get off this sofa," she said, "will you buy me a mai tai?"

How could I say no?

Arm in arm we strolled along the canals, checking out the hookers disguised as female tourists milling around as though lost (who can resist a lady in distress?), vinyl flight bags hanging from their shoulders, stuffed, no doubt, with Jesus dildos and nipple clamps. After a few beers and a little space cake we bought ice cream cones and tried to find our way back home. Amsterdam is a fabulous city to get lost in. We'd follow what seemed a familiar canal until we were hopelessly turned around, and then we'd backtrack; at the time it seemed a great adventure. Some sailors ready to ship out the next morning on leave actually attempted to waylay us for a nightcap, but by this time we were too happy holding hands and singing that silly children's song, *"They all went down to Amsterdam, they all went down to Amsterdam, Amster, Amster, shh, shh, shh . . ."*

Back home we soon realized neither of us had keys, so we climbed up the fire escape and Evie kicked the screen in. It's an absolute miracle we didn't fall to our deaths. I always forget how nice and homey and sweet it feels when Evie and I come together, just us two. Like girls. Evie put on water for pasta, then fell asleep on the kitchen floor. I made a risotto, then woke her up, and we ate it in my bed with the TV on.

"Amster, Amster, shh, shh, shh," we sang, flipping channels.

It was just like old times. I hated thinking that one day we wouldn't do this.

She got under the covers. "Tell me again," she said as she was falling asleep. "One more time."

"You did nothing wrong," I said, and tucked her in.

Things felt so incredibly comfortable, and safe, and easy, that I considered telling her about what had happened with Gerhard—why he hadn't called me in days and why I was jumping out of my skin whenever the phone rang. It was bothering me and I hated being bothered.

I wanted to tell her that Gerhard had invited one of his

friends to watch us having sex, but I knew she would just die. I nearly died, at first. It wasn't like he said, "Hey do you mind if my friend watches?" Of course if he had, I'd have said, "Are you out of your mind? What do you think I am?" And I would have missed out. Evie would freak if I told her the whole thing turned me on more than it did him.

It sounds completely unbelievable to say it just happened, but it did. We were in the back room of the gallery—we often had sex there, there was a four-poster bed, and a gorgeous Tuscan-tiled bathroom. But I suppose I should have guessed something was up by the way Gerhard was actually moving around. Usually I was on top, but that night it was one minute on my back, legs in the air, then he wanted me up against the wall, then doggie style. Then, at some point, I turned my head and there was Peter, this sculptor friend of his that he represents, sitting in a chair inside the doorway. I never even heard him come in. I had no clue how long he'd been sitting there. I started to pull away, of course, but then I saw how Peter was looking at me, how into it he was getting, and I thought, I will never be this young again. It's Amsterdam. Nothing that happens here counts.

Ultimately I don't think Gerhard even came, I think he faked it, but I did. I did and it was amazing. I never imagined I could do such a thing.

And I never imagined that I'd want two men at one time. That I'd be looking at Peter looking at me while Gerhard was inside me, and I'd wish that Peter's cock was in my mouth. Who could imagine that? But I did.

That night I could have done anything. Gerhard knew it, Peter knew it. Maybe they'd talked about it earlier, maybe the

plan had been all along for the three of us to have sex. I don't
know. It doesn't matter. I just know that while it was happening I felt good. For the first time there was enough,
like everything I wanted or needed was being taken of. I was
filled up.

I know it should have made me sick, but it didn't. It
didn't. It was like something just opened up inside me. It was
good, believe me. But I could never tell anybody, not even in
confession. I could never tell Evie. Not that I was ashamed. I
wasn't. I just knew I couldn't make her or anybody else understand that the thought of having sex with just one man
seemed boring now. And the thought that I would never ever
have sex in front of another person again, that prospect made
me unreasonably sad.

Evie and her father are sitting together on the sofa, he's
telling her about some dinner party he and her mom threw
recently. Her sister came down and they roasted a suckling
pig, and there was dancing in the backyard—a real suburban
bash. Evie's head is tilted, she's listening and laughing at all
the right times, they look so Hallmark it's just amazing. I
excuse myself to no one in particular, they're too caught up
even to notice, and go into my room to smoke a cigarette and
change. I wouldn't smoke in front of Evie's father, absolutely
not. I still cannot get over how Jackie Onassis was never ever
photographed smoking. She never smoked in public. No one
outside her inner circle even knew she smoked. I can't decide
if it shows incredible restraint, or incredible self-consciousness.
Instead of the long black skirt and fitted jacket I'd picked out

earlier, I decide to be festive, why not, and go for the Nicole Miller cocktail dress—low cut, off the shoulder—after all I am not the daughter. I am a person.

The walls of this apartment are like tissue, this is how I know that Billy told Evie he loves her and wants her to move in with him—into his squat—how ghastly is that? Squat. Classy with a K. Just the word squat implies public defecation and people sitting back on their heels staring into sooty little pits where they roast pigeons. Because the walls are so thin I could hear the silence that followed his invitation, but I don't know, perhaps she whispered her answer.

Because the walls are so thin I can plainly hear Evie and her father arguing in the living room.

"Listen, I'd be lying if I said I wasn't a little scared," her father says, his voice rising.

"I don't want to hear it," Evie says, like she's joking, but she's obviously not.

"You asked."

Evie doesn't say anything. The big problem with eavesdropping is that you can't see anything. It is such a tease.

"You asked if I felt good, if I was a hundred percent, and I'm answering you honestly."

"Okay, okay, enough honesty," she says. "But you're fine, you said so, you said the doctor said everything is fine. Right?"

"For now, yes. I have no reason to think otherwise, but..."

"Mary Beth," Evie calls out, I hear her standing up. "Hurry up, or we're going to be late."

I wait a second, best not to appear like I've been spying.

In the living room her father is at the far end of the couch doodling on the back of a magazine. He looks annoyed.

"I'm ready," I say. She is looking at me to save her. "You're right, we best go if we're going to make our eight o'clock," I say, tapping the spot on my wrist where a watch would be if I could ever hold on to one.

"Is this the restaurant you were talking about taking your father to?" Evie asks, and as soon as the question is out of her mouth I can tell she regrets it. Obviously she thinks my father not visiting bothers me, but it doesn't. The restaurant is beautiful—intimate tables, big flower arrangements, oil paintings, a few lesser Cezanne charcoals. Evie and her father choose to sit with their backs to the terrace; I get the view.

"My father just got remarried," I explain, "for the third time. And can you imagine, my new twenty-three-year-old stepmother doesn't want to spend her honeymoon in Amsterdam with her husband's twenty-one-year-old kid?"

"Oh," her father says, not like a word, just the sound, as if the idea of a twenty-three-year-old wife hit him in the stomach like a fastball. I can't really remember what Evie's mom looks like—pretty, I thought, but I'm not sure. She's certainly no twenty-three-year-old.

Her father moves the knot in his Ferragamo tie. Lovely. As though he'd never thought of dallying with younger women. They all do. When I was a child my father's passion was baby-sitters. Once, when my mother was at Canyon Ranch, he actually had one of them dress up as the tooth fairy and slip money under my pillow. She reeked of Gilbey's. To be fair, he figured I was asleep, but really.

Everybody has something.

"You know what's rich?" I say. "Megan, and I, that's my new stepmother's name, we used to date the same guy at Andover—Chip Barton—he's into bonds now, lives in *Darien*."

"My God," Evie said. "Are you joking?" I hadn't mentioned the part about Chip before. I really just remembered it myself.

"I know. Couldn't you just die?"

"So." Evie's father turns to her. "Have you been able to find time to draw?"

He's uncomfortable I can tell. I hadn't figured him for the puritanical type. Maybe it's that he doesn't look old and stuffy. He's tan, his dark hair is a little longer than the norm and just touched with silver, so he looks like a liberal politician or an aging actor who still wants to get the girl. He coughs, and for a long second we all just sit there.

"Yes, some, not much," she says. "You know I've been working a lot at the museum, it's inspiring, and of course terrifying to be surrounded by such amazing work."

"She ought to work, she's good," I say.

Her father smiles at me, "We think so, but you know, we're prejudiced."

"I still have trouble with hands. Everybody has to keep their hands in their pockets or behind their backs; anxious people in china shops," she says, "that's my speciality," and with that she elbows her wineglass off the table and on to the floor.

"Don't worry," I say, "it just increases the value of the

rug." This is what Evie says every time anyone spills something on our floor. It occurs to me, judging by her father's smile, that he is the source of this saying.

By the time dessert is served—chocolate decadence and crème brûlée—we are all toasted. Not on purpose of course, but we do seem to go through a lot of wine very quickly. It's that kind of night. It becomes clear that Evie is drunk when she nearly falls off her high heels (my shoes) on her way to the ladies room. While she is in the loo her father and I look out at the city below us, there is a pack of Christian missionaries—mostly teenage boys in cheap blue suits—trooping over to the Red Light district to spread the good word.

"Jeez, if anybody is converted down there, I'll never forgive myself for forgetting my camera," her father says, "Damn it anyhow—watch, we're going to see a mass baptism in that canal."

Left alone with Evie's father, I suddenly feel a little shy. Before I know it Evie is tottering across the restaurant toward us, with her hands slightly out at her side like a tightrope walker. As soon as he sees her, Evie's father starts to stand up like he wants to rescue her, but it's obviously a matter of dignity, and so we both just watch, and sigh with relief when she finally plops down in her seat.

"I can't believe I didn't bring my camera," he says again.

"Oh, Daddy," Evie says.

"Hey, you'll be happy you have those slides one day," he says. "The memories . . ."

"No, no, no memories. Now, I don't want to talk about it," she says.

"I was talking about taking pictures," he says, "honey."

It's clear that he doesn't think it's appropriate to have this conversation in front of me. Thankfully, the waiter appears at his side. "Sir," he says, "would you or your wife care for a cognac?"

"Excuse me?"

"Your wife," the waiter repeats, nodding at me. I start to laugh, but I catch myself when I see the look of shock on Evie's face.

"Oh, no," her father protests. "This is not my wife."

"Ah, too bad," the waiter says, then with a shrug, he turns and saunters away, not the tiniest bit embarrassed by his faux pas.

"What a cretin," her father says. "I ought to . . ."

He won't. I've seen my father reduce waiters to tears, and Evie's father just isn't the type.

"How ridiculous," I say, but it isn't. It isn't ridiculous at all. "Did you see that dreadful caterpillar mustache?"

Evie reaches over and takes a sip of her father's wine. She glances at me, then looks away. It's awkward, it shouldn't be. It should be funny, but for some reason it's not, or at least not now. Surely one day, if we ever speak of it again, we'll laugh.

"Well then," Evie says, a smile frosted onto her face, "let's get out of here, shall we?"

Evie holds tight to her father's arm as we walk back toward the apartment, maybe it's the wine, or maybe it's the shoes, or maybe she thinks I might try to steal him. If I was another kind of girl, I might be hurt, but I'm not. I'm not. I just feel like telling her, fathers like me. Just now, I am re-membering how as a little girl I got invited along on more of my friends' family vacations than anyone else. Cancun, Gstaad, Hilton Head. The fathers were always nice to me. I laughed at their jokes, and they bought me lift tickets. I told them they were getting too skinny, and I got an all-day pass to Disneyland. I liked fathers and fathers like me. Why had this never occurred to me before?

Maybe I get a little lost in this thought and take a wrong turn, or maybe it's just that we were all looped, but before I know it were right smack in the center of the Red Light district. Not that it matters, after all, one shouldn't come to Amsterdam and miss out on this wonder, but for half a second I felt a little uncomfortable, and then I thought it's just that Evie was uncomfortable. The only one who appeared com-fortable was her father. I liked this. We were alike, both of us liked adventure.

The buildings in the Red Light district seem closer to-gether than in any other part of the city, like they can't help crawling on each other. Their facades are absolutely gray, al-most papery-looking, the result of pollution and perhaps all those postcoital smokes; the floors and floors of heavily cur-tained windows lit up with yellow light make it feel like a hive. There's an undeniable heat in the air, an illicit buzz that draws you in regardless of how uptight you are.

Evie's father had untangled himself from her grasp and was now walking ahead of us. If you had noticed Evie staring at him, frowning and hobbling to keep up with him you'd never even guess that he was her father. He could have been any man.

Tourists moved silently across the bridges of the canal, peering into windows, slowing, but not daring to stop, to commit, or appear to bargain shop; after all one never knew what fantasy might appear just around the corner. A thirty-year-old shaved angel in red leather, an unbelievably obese young girl in a see-through teddy. It is all so cinematic.

As we walk deeper into the center, more women began to appear in the doorways, lounging against the walls, like baseball players in a dugout, perhaps talking shop and sizing up the crowd, or exchanging stories about their kids, how they weren't invited to speak at their kids' Career Day. It's strange but they seemed so comfortable, superior in some way to the rest of us.

Behind us in the distance I could swear I heard the far off sounds of those boys praying, a dull and distant howling, following us, their coyote yelps of conversion echoing in the canyon of streets. You'd think they'd just give up.

I hurry to catch up with Evie's father. My shoes are so slippery it's like I'm skating on the cobblestones, for an instant I reach out and take his arm, he seems surprised, but he doesn't pull away.

"Look," I say, and point up at one of the yellow and gray windows above us, the large liquid outlines of women luring men to their quarters thrown up on the walls. A shadow of a woman taking off a man's coat looms above us, his hands moving like bats, swooping onto her breasts, then he wraps his arms around her hips.

You can't not watch. There it is, it is impossible to look away, but of course I barely have his attention before Evie interrupts.

"Dad," she says incredulously. Her father is mesmerized by the couple's shadows, spread out on the wall, getting huge and hazy, becoming a dark indistinct mass as they move away from the window. "I can't believe you."

"I'm fading," she says. "Let's go back, okay? We can have a nightcap at our place."

"All right, honey," her father says. He's obviously annoyed. We were just starting to have fun. "It's been a long night, I guess. Jesus, I'm all turned around here. Can you get us out of here, Mary Beth?"

"Of course," I say.

Even though I was supposed to be leading, her father hurries ahead of us, taking in all the sights. Gerhard always had to walk slightly ahead of me too, and it made me crazy. Would it kill a man to walk beside me?

I wonder what Gerhard would do if he happened on me here with Evie's father. Maybe he would make a scene or follow us. He would be jealous. I knew Chas Wakefield would protect me, he'd put his arm around me and tell Gerhard to fuck off. He wouldn't ask any questions, he would just defend my honor. He wouldn't let anything happen to me.

"God, I hate this place," Evie says, hurrying to sidle up alongside me. "Men ruin everything."

"Oh, right," I say. "You really know."

"What?" she says.

"That Billy, he's really a fabulous catch, huh?"

"What's wrong with you?" she says in a low, don't-you-dare voice.

"Come on, Ev, you've got to admire the girls' spirit," I say loudly.

"Absolutely," Evie's father says, sounding for one sick second like my own father.

"Why don't you just call Billy and have him pick you up?" I say. "Oh, darn he doesn't have a phone. How would you live without a phone?"

"What are you talking about?" she says. I am about to ask her when was she going to tell me she was moving out, but I notice that Evie's father is getting too far ahead of us.

"Oh god," I begin to moan, bending over at the waist, clutching my stomach. "Owww," I moan again, but louder.

"Jesus," Evie said. "Do you think you're going to be sick?"

I don't answer her. I moan again, holding tight to my middle. I don't even lift my head until I see the tips of her father's shoes.

"I just need a moment," I say, so stoic. Concern flickers in his eyes.

"Jesus, are you all right?" He reaches out and touches my shoulder. I nod up at him. He cares. "Maybe we should get a cab, or..."

"No, I'm fine," I insist. "Really."

"Can you walk?" he says.

"Oh, absolutely," I say.

He takes off his suit jacket. "Here," he says, handing it to me like a rescue blanket.

"No," I say.

"Please," he says. "I insist."

"I'm better now," I say, slipping my arms into the slippery silk-lined sleeves, which are still warm.

Evie wraps her arms around her, like she's cold, but it's a warm night. She just doesn't want me to have anything.

"All right, buckle up kiddos," I say. "It's going to be a bumpy night."

Despite feeling a little drunk and light-headed I set off quickly toward the short cut, an escape route Franz once showed me, a dark and twisting alleyway. Chas is close on my heels as I take off down an unlit and slanting side street, turning the corners quickly. It's far too narrow for cars and barely wide enough for two to stand abreast. It's an adventure. I bet he is loving this. Even though I can't see, I plunge ahead madly, arms out testing the dark, then I stumble, stretching out my arms, bracing myself for the fall, but I recover my balance. I think I hear my name being called. The alley makes a T and I take the left. I can hear Chas close behind me now, he is also moving fast, hurtling along like he can't stop himself, like it's a game. I hear him stop at the T. I wait, trying not to breathe too hard, pressed up against the wall. My heart is pounding like I'm afraid, but nothing is wrong. I don't need protection.

Chas peers around the corner, and seeing me, grins. He collapses against the wall across from me, and leans there, eyes closed, panting and out of breath, half-smiling, half-embarrassed, as if he is asking me to be patient with him, as if this sort of thing never happens. I move over to his side, I turn my head toward him, both of us resting against the wall. I swear I can hear the echo of those evangelizing boys baying at the moon. Who among them could resist a girl like me who wants just one thing? As her father struggles to catch his breath, his eyes find mine, and there I see that eagerness, that same blank and grasping desire I've seen in so many men's eyes.

I watch as my hand moves to touch his chest, as if to stop him.

SISTERS
OF THE
SOUND

A nun peered at me through the hedge as I rang the bell of the convent for the second time. I sat on my suitcase and wiped the sweat from my lip. I wondered how many other pregnant women had sought refuge at the Sisters of Saint Genevieve's convent. How many of them had been desperate enough to lie to the Mother Superior, as I had on the telephone, professing to be a Catholic? When in fact I was a Presbyterian interloper who'd just recently embraced Catholicism because I was desperate for religious rules and rituals that imparted meaning to life's suffering. I'd sought out this holy place because surely if God existed, he was here.

Even though Mary Beth and I weren't as close since Billy and I got married two years ago—she was the maid of honor—she was still the first friend I'd reach out to when there was a crisis. Even though I had friends I saw more and spoke to more often, she knew me best. I didn't have to explain anything to her.

Mary Beth had recommended the convent, which accepted paying pilgrims as lodgers. The fashion magazine where she was an editor had recently done a photo shoot there.

"It's an austere spiritual fortress," she assured me. "A perfect escape from loving husbands and sick fathers."

"I'm not sure."

"I can get you into the Golden Door if you'd rather, darling," she offered. But I knew the convent was the answer.

In reality, the convent, snuggled down among pink dogwoods and wild rosebushes, resembled a cheerful little Bavarian-style castle, as likely to be inhabited by a pack of singing dwarves as the faithful and pious brides of Christ.

As I rang the bell again, I could feel the baby moving inside me, wedging toes and fingers between my ribs, dancing on my kidneys. I wondered if when my father lay in bed awake, he could feel the cancer inside him, if he could ever feel it growing. If he ever had any affection for it.

Although my father hadn't said he disapproved of me taking off for the convent, he clearly didn't understand the need or the inclination to go directly to God and beg for his divine assistance. For fourteen years and two stays of remission, our family's way of coping with my father's illness had

always been an unholy amalgam of defiance and denial, suf-
fused with the belief that my father had the power to save
himself, and us, too. He always had, until nine months ago.
It was the inoperable part of this lung cancer that scared us,
that scared me into getting pregnant. I feared that one day
my father's pain would eventually outweigh his love for my
mother and sister and me. He'd give in and give up. So, self-
ishly, I tried bribing him with a baby. A baby we barely
spoke of.

"A convent, huh?" he'd replied when I told him my plan,
offering no hint as to whether my sudden embracing of
Sunday-school-style religion, the gaudy show of penitence, the
white gloves and panty hose, amused or comforted him.

"I think so, I think it seems—"

"Is it pretty?"

"Pretty?"

I coughed. I'd recently developed a strange cough my
doctor could find no cause for.

"What's the architecture like? It's on the Sound, you say?"

"Yes, I think so—but I'm going there to, you know . . .
I don't imagine there will be time for—"

"Take advantage of the water," he said.

Since my father had a lung removed some seven years
before, he'd taken up swimming and scuba diving, which
seemed to me not only reckless, but as if he was flashing the
bird at God, saying, "Go ahead, take me apart in bits and
pieces, but you can't stop me." Seeing him working out in the
yard without a shirt on, his torso mapped with scars of tumor
excavations, it was easy to think of them as war wounds, a
keloid diary of adventures.

Waiting outside the convent's front door, I said a quick prayer.

Help me, Father, to understand your plan. Help me, God, please, save my father.

From here I could see the blue of the Sound stretching to the horizon. I glanced quickly back at the hedge to see if the nun was still lurking, but she'd vanished. Perhaps I had imagined her. Perhaps the pregnancy and the heat had caused me to hallucinate a nun with—I thought—a butterfly net. I knocked, no one answered. I knocked again. Then I saw the nuns, at least a dozen of them, their moth-gray habits whipping in the wind, black-and-white veils blown stiffly back from their heads like flags as they tramped over the lip of the cliff, a column of sturdy, industrious ants approaching the convent like God's army. They marched in two straight lines past me without even a glance, their heads bowed, their hair discreetly concealed by wimples, their fingers polishing rosaries, intent on their prayers. Up close, they were not the dowdy, carbuncular, cow-faced lot I'd expected. Most of them were young, their faces unlined, unblemished except by a faint mustache here and there, and one lazy eye. One sister, with skin white as chalk, was unmistakably a redhead; another had a mole on her lip, bright and big as a ladybug.

According to the brochure, the nuns of Saint Genevieve hailed from Italy, Mexico, India, Spain, and Guatemala. Deep in prayer, they filed by with their heads bowed, all except one sister, the nun I could have sworn only moments earlier was spying on me, a pretty Indian nun who now boldly sought out my gaze, her large, dark-lashed green eyes framed by high, arching brows that threatened to meet over the bridge of her nose. Her gaze moved down my body to my swollen abdomen, and then to my left hand, which, because of swelling, was bare of its wedding ring. She imagined, no doubt, that I was a single mother, my no-good lover on the lam, or a born-again Christian carrying my rapist's child, or maybe that I'd been recently, tragically, widowed. Surely some sordid story had brought me here. In reality how dull my tragedy was. At least she and her sisters could understand my desire for celibacy. I wanted to tell them how my husband seduced me against my wishes, over and over again. The back of the neck, the back of the knee. I was helpless.

"I need you," Billy would breathe into my hair. "I need us," he'd say, holding me as close as one can hold a pregnant woman. "This is too fucking scary, all this grown-up stuff," he'd say, sucking on my earlobe. If I didn't believe him, I needed only to check the recycling bin: half-gallons of scotch and whiskey, a silver sack of beer cans.

As the pregnancy progressed, I'd imagined he would become less and less interested in sex, but I was wrong. "I had no idea pregnancy would be so erotic," he'd say, kissing my belly. "Maybe it's not all bad."

There are women who would want this, would kill to have a husband ambushing them in the shower, in the closet, in the kitchen, in the car, but I am not one of them. I am ashamed to say there were orgasms, big ones, that came all in a rush, like somebody cutting open a sack of candy. But it wasn't me, it was just my body. The nuns would support and value my quest for celibacy. They'd understand that being touched by Billy could ignite a panic in me akin to being held underwater. That even with his tongue in my mouth, all I could think about was my father.

The Indian sister smiled beneficently, as though she could read my mind, her teeth as shiny and white as the mother-of-pearl rosary beads she clicked between her fingers like dice. Perhaps it was the heat, but I felt as if I might faint. I started to tremble, my whole body vibrating like a blade of grass being blown between God's thumbs. I studied her small, square, mannish hands. Three of the fingernails on her left hand were bruised a dull blue-black and appeared ready to drop off. I wondered if she had done it herself, an act of obeisance, or if she'd slammed her hand in a drawer. Perhaps she'd willfully battered her hand with a stone, or bludgeoned her fingers with a hammer. Just as I'd attempted to curry God's favor by getting pregnant. Perhaps the way to his heart was mortification of the flesh, but really, how much more mortified could I get?

Mother Saint Agnes stepped out of the formation and introduced herself with a curt nod and a handshake worthy of a Teamster. Happily, she wrested my bag out of my hands. We entered the building and, taking the stairs at a clip, she led me up two flights of steps to the top floor of the convent. The guest rooms were there, far away from the mysterious quarters where the nuns bathed and slept.

I'd hoped for a drafty stone room with a cold slate floor that would make my knees ache, a hulking crucifix looming over me as it strained on a tenuous-looking wire, and lots of gilt icons depicting saints and martyrs ecstatic on skewers and burning at stakes. Instead, my pale blue guest bedroom was carpeted with beige shag and filled with light from a bay window that overlooked the water. The walls were adorned solely with a large carved sandalwood rosary and an oil painting of Christ, the romantic, sexy, long-haired rock 'n' roll savior version, flashing his wounds. I'd hoped for a thinning-hair, gangrenous, suffering Christ, a savior swollen and poisoned by my sins. I was surprised that the nuns preferred the handsome Jesus. Didn't that conjure erotic musings that might prove distressing? Or was he hanging there to remind us pilgrims that we were base, celibate in neither flesh nor spirit? Months ago, I might have been subtly turned on by the Jim Morrison Christ—guiltily getting my jeans down around my ankles in two seconds flat, and collapsing in a self-pleasuring stupor on the bed—but not now. Certainly not now.

It was clear that I would need the spiritual guidance of the Sisters of Saint Genevieve. Especially Sister Corrina, the nun with the blackened fingernails. She must be the most devout. She would be one to blow in God's ear for me.

That evening, along with two other guests, I was invited to attend Vespers in the convent's pleasantly dark and narrow white marble chapel. This church, with its holy reek of incense and burnt wax, its hard mahogany pews with unpadded kneelers, and its forbidding cistern of holy water, lent my suffering focus.

The church of my childhood was a stark cream-and-stone colonial-era church, always a little too cold, but bright with sunlight, like we had nothing to hide. Its high, vaulted ceilings and brass Williamsburg chandeliers, white-shuttered windows exposing blue, green, and yellow stained-glass windows glorifying the disciples, discreet cream-colored cross, and freshly cut white lilies on either side of the pulpit, made it seem as optimistic and unmysterious as a nursery.

Ringing the convent's chapel were ornate stained-glass windows depicting the Annunciation, Crucifixion, and Resurrection in shades of ruby, sapphire, and purple, the bright sunlight casting brilliant kaleidoscopic birthmarks onto the bodies of the parishioners. I kneeled and said my Hail Marys. Still I felt empty, impoverished. I wished I knew more prayers. As I got off my knees and slid back into the pew, bright red lesions of light dappled my arm and a diffuse purple glow bled across my chest and belly. I scooted down the pew toward the stained-glass windows to see if I could attract fractals of gold and green, but all the colors vanished, replaced solely by a tight wavering blue dot on the back of my left hand.

The sisters, led by Mother Saint Agnes, padded in and took seats at the front of the church, then, in unison, got down on their knees and began to pray. I craned to see Sister Corrina, but her head was bowed, her face obscured by the veil. I lost interest once the priest, silver-haired and beatific as an oatmeal salesman, appeared in his purple-and-gold robes. He trundled up into the pulpit and towered over the lectern. In a deep and resonant baritone he began to recite the Mass, half in Latin, half in Italian. I felt myself relax into the pew.

I felt certain that God was listening.

After the service, Mother Saint Agnes herded me into a bright wood-paneled dining room. Instead of eating with the sisters, as I had hoped, I would take all my meals with two other pilgrims, plump middle-aged women in dark blue pantsuits and white pointy-toed sneakers who worked as librarians at an all-girls college. Hanging around both of their necks like skeleton keys were matching oversize sterling silver crucifixes.

"Hello," I said, sliding into the seat across from them.

The women both greeted me with pleasant nods, but spoke not at all.

"So," I said. Again they smiled. They'd obviously taken a vow of silence for their visit, but I couldn't stop myself. I was floundering.

"Well," I said. "So . . ."

The pilgrims averted their eyes, staring into their pink lamb chops, as though trying to spare me further embarrassment.

Still, even in their silence they seemed to communicate with each other. A raised eyebrow was rewarded with the salt dish, a shrugged shoulder offered the end of a tapioca pudding. Staring at my reflection in the back of my soupspoon, I felt more alone than I had in months. I pressed my palms against my belly, searching for the round moon of the baby's butt, but even it was ignoring me.

That night I snuck downstairs and called Billy on the pay phone.

"Hey, am I ever glad you called. I don't want you to freak out or anything, but I forgot to pay the phone bill so I'm only getting incoming."

"What!"

"Don't. It's taken care of, I hocked some old Miles Davis on vinyl, doubles, don't worry, nothing good. Nothing valuable."

"I can't believe it," I said, but of course I could. We'd been without phone and lights before. Still. "We're going to have a baby, Billy. Are you planning to just run down to St. Marks Place and sell records every time we need diapers?"

"Relax. I took care of it," he said, sounding defensive. "And, you'll be happy to know, I've got a lead on some soul-numbing studio work—it's incidental music for a soap opera. Aren't you proud?"

"I'm sorry," I said. "I miss you." I did. Now that he was far away and couldn't get his hands on me, I missed him.

"Are you okay, baby?" he said. "You sound lonely. I could be there in no time. You just say the word.... That's it, I'm going to drive up there and rescue you. If I leave now we can—"

"No. I need to be here. Alone."

"Oh, come on. You just said you missed me." He sounded hurt. "How's Dad? Tell him I got a job, would you?"

"Billy, I have to go."

"Wait, wait, not yet. I can't help it, I keep imagining you in that little black dress thing, you know... What are you wearing right now?"

"Billy." I laughed.

"Are you wearing a bra?"

"I can't believe you. I'm at a convent and you want to talk dirty?"

"And the problem is? I just miss you like crazy."

"I have to go."

"Don't."

"Sweet dreams," I said, and hung up. Although I could still hear his voice coming through the receiver, I cut him off.

What was I thinking, having a baby? Even if I loved this baby. Billy and I couldn't possibly have a baby. Then I thought of my father, my father holding my baby, that baby wrapping its hand around his finger, and things made sense.

The next morning, after Matins, despite the heat and the oppressive humidity and my sore, swollen feet, I strolled the convent grounds, hoping that Mother Saint Agnes—or, better still, Sister Corrina—might approach me and, while attempting not to stare at my pregnant bulge, inquire into the nature of the spiritual crisis that had brought me to the convent. I watched the sisters working in the vegetable garden, bent over in the garden pitching zucchinis as big as small dogs onto the grass, but didn't dare approach. In truth, I didn't like seeing the sisters outside the convent walls. Earlier I'd watched Mother Saint Agnes and a few other nuns pile into a big blue station wagon and drive off into town. I imagined them with windows rolled down and veils blowing, singing along with some Christian rock station. I wanted them inside, under glass, in diligent pursuit of salvation, not groceries and feminine-hygiene products.

I ventured down to the water. A peeling white boathouse filled with rubber rafts and rust-stippled beach chairs, long out of use, perched on the narrow, rocky beach. Off the dock was a rickety metal ladder, corroded badly at the joints, leading down into the water. For half a second, standing there on the dock, sweat dribbling down my spine and under my breasts, I wished I'd packed my bathing suit, but despite what my father suggested, I was here to pray, not swim. I would *not* swim, if only to demonstrate to God, and my father, that I meant business.

Instead I lumbered back up the steep hill to the convent and collapsed into a chaise set up under a maple tree. Sleepy from the heat, I was content to meditate on the grassy hillock that rose up behind the convent, obscuring all but a thin blue slip of the Sound licking the shoreline. Off to the side, Mother Saint Agnes was prowling around the perimeter of the convent, gardening. Every few feet she'd stop and frown and examine the rosebushes and dahlias, her lips moving as if she were praying or perhaps cursing the plague that was destroying her plants. Then she'd draw her veils up tight over her mouth and nose like a desperado, cross herself, and spray the bushes with an old-fashioned tin bug mister. As I drifted off to sleep, I wondered what Billy was doing, if he missed falling asleep with his hand on my stomach. I thought about how it seemed a trick the way the baby was drawn to his touch like a moth, as if even in utero it knew its father.

The following afternoon, I took refuge on the library sofa. Again Mother Saint Agnes was outside studying the ragged chew holes and brown scale that was attacking her bushes, but this time she wasn't treating her plants. Instead, a six-pack dangled from her fingers, and every few feet she'd crouch down and pour some beer into the grass. Or that's what it looked like.

Instead of investigating, I lounged drowsily on the lumpy velvet sofa paging through a gilt-edged tome of saints, too lazy to get up and turn on the light even though the afternoon sun was projecting ominous leaf shapes on the library wall, murderous sword grass and gaping Venus's-flytraps, killers in a botanical horror film. I tried to focus on the saints, the martyrs. I feared that since I'd arrived at the convent three days ago, instead of seeking communion with God in the hopes of saving my father or, at the very least, of understanding why my family was being punished, I was sliding into a kind of surreal stupor, the days flowing into an ocean of sleep. Yes, I prayed, but nothing was changing for the better.

Hope was like poison in my veins. The previous morning I'd stolen five minutes on the sisters' ancient black telephone, only to learn from my mother that my father's white cells were diminishing. As far as she could tell, all he'd eaten in days was Pepperidge Farm cookies and red wine. He refused to drink the canned vitamin shake the doctor recommended.

"He said, 'It tastes like shit. It's for old folks, stroke victims, vegetables.' " My mother laughed uncomfortably. I could hear his voice under hers.

When I asked her to put him on the phone, he'd refused to speak to me.

"It's the radiation treatments, they're making him a little deaf," my mother tried to explain, but I wondered if it wasn't something else. I twisted a lock of hair tight around my swollen pinky. I was growing, every pink and blushing inch of me trumpeted the promise of life, and still I was losing him. I didn't even want this baby.

I was so absorbed in self-pity that I didn't hear anyone enter the library. It wasn't until Sister Corrina's long, dark, oval face appeared above me, hovering against the forest of shadows, that I realized I was being watched. She leaned down and, covering my hand with her own, tilted the book so she could read the title. She was younger than I'd first thought; she was much younger, maybe eighteen, just a girl.

"Hi," I said sheepishly, struggling to sit upright. I felt vulnerable, not to mention unattractive, sprawled on my back, pinned down, as it were, by the weight of the baby. "I'm searching for names."

She nodded, watching with polite curiosity as I attempted to maneuver my body into an upright position. I was surprised at how rough her hand was, how I could smell her perspiration, mingled with dirt from the garden in the weave of her gray habit. I crossed my arms against my balloonish breasts.

"May I?" she asked, flopping down on the sofa beside me before I could answer, the overly soft cushions tipping her body toward mine in a slightly suggestive manner she seemed oblivious to.

"It's nice to have someone to speak English with," she said.

"Good," I said, staring at her blackened fingernails; one of them looked loose enough to tear off with your teeth.

"I learned as a girl," she said with evident pride, "before I joined the order."

"Really?"

"I was only twelve. I knew nothing, but I was called." She sighed.

As she flipped through the book, she caught me staring at her dirty elbows and hands, and blushed.

"I've been in the garden," she explained, "cutting flowers, weeding, but mostly looking for the beetles. I like bugs—it's silly, no?"

"Silly? No, it's not silly," I said. I thought of my father's explanation of why he didn't attend Sunday services. "God listens in the garden as well as in the pew."

"Sometimes," Sister Corrina said, "in the beds, working, I make myself forget I'm looking for them, and then I get the shock, the surprise of them. You understand?" she asked, her brown cheeks flushed scarlet. "I like the little scare of seeing them, you know?"

"You like bugs?" I asked. "You mean like butterflies?" I remembered now the fleeting glimpse I'd caught of her that first day behind the hedge, the flash of the veil, the glint of her net.

"The butterflies, the worms, but the beetles, mostly, the blue and green and black ones, the ones that walk like jewels on legs. The big black ones like armor with large snapping jaws. The moths with wings that look like the eyes of owls, even the ants, the red ones, that bite. I love them all."

"Really?" It seemed so absurd.

"The others think it's silly, or a terrible thing. They crush them under their heels, or flush them down the sink, or—"

"That's awful," I said, though I too found few things more satisfying than the crack of a cockroach under a rolled-up newspaper. I was the killer in the family. Billy was squeamish and too softhearted; even flies he would shoo out the window.

Corrina nodded vigorously. "I catch them, and I gas them, and I pin them down to the boards," she said proudly, then clarified, lest I think her simply murderous. "Just the rare or beautiful ones, ones that look like walking sticks and leaves, or ones with bright wings patterned like snakeskin..." She fumbled for a word, then shrugged. "The others I enjoy. Like a scientist. I like to watch them work, they are so busy. There are no lazy insects."

"You're not afraid of getting stung or bitten, or..."

"The ants sometimes, a little. No bees, though. I leave the bees to the Trappists—the monks love honey. It should be a sin." She trapped a girlish laugh against her lips with her hand.

"It's a passion," I said, then blushed. I couldn't recall ever saying that word out loud before.

"Saint Dominic says, 'He who governs his passions is master of his world. Command them or be enslaved by them,'" she said, folding her hands in her lap.

"I see." This wasn't exactly how I imagined my interaction with the nuns would be. My head felt so wobbly, I feared it could be pinched off like a dead flower. My whole body hummed and buzzed disconcertingly. I coughed.

"Boy or girl?" she asked, leaning closer to me.

"I have no idea." Which was true. I gave little thought to its sex, although in my dreams it was a girl. A girl. A girl like me, worthy of sacrifice.

"So," she said, in the way people do when they have run out of conversation, but still cling to the idea that connection might be possible.

"So." Looking at me in a way that suggested I was to tell her something. Confess something. Before I could speak, she bent her face down close to my belly, resting her ear on my navel, then placed her hand on my lower abdomen. She closed her eyes as though she was listening for the baby, the sound of waves, or a babbling infant song. I couldn't breathe, my heart was afraid even to beat.

"It's a girl, I think," she said finally, and raised her head, but left her hand on my stomach for a moment longer. "Healthy little girl," she said, still gazing at my stomach, transfixed, as if the miracle of birth were in some way more incredible than the miracle of faith.

"I have to go," she said, hopping up off the couch suddenly. The book of saints crashed to the floor, landing in a split. Her cheeks were flushed. "I've been forbidden . . ." she started to say. "Mother Saint Agnes is looking for me," she said, hastily arranging her veil, grinning like an adored but often chastised child. "She's a bloodhound."

A sharp report of footsteps echoed in the outer hallway, and the vestibule was suddenly illuminated as if by a searchlight. Sister Corrina bowed slightly to me, then, under her breath, whispered, "If you like, I can show you the bugs."

I coughed, covering my mouth with two hands, hoping to mask my goofy smile, the blush burning my cheeks.

During Vespers I couldn't help staring at Sister Corrina. I didn't want to be distracted from my prayers, and she, having obviously been scolded by the Mother Superior, never once glanced my way, but still I couldn't stop myself from guiltily sneaking glances at her. I tried to force myself to focus on the pilgrims, the purity of their silvery-white hair, the gentle dusting of dandruff on their shoulders, their mouths slightly agape, ready to digest God's word.

I tried to concentrate on my father and Billy. What was Billy doing? Was he in the studio? Was he lying on the 1950s sofa he'd gotten off the street last week, listening to Bird and

Coltrane? Was he playing his guitar at the kitchen table? Was he thinking of me, missing me, or just the baby?

I remembered a story I'd read in the newspaper a week before, something about how breast milk, or at least that first milk, the colostrum, had been found to have curative powers for cancer patients. I'd read it out loud to Billy at breakfast, watching his face drain of color, as if my hope wore him out.

"Oh," he said. That's all. "Oh." Then he'd pushed his bowl of Cheerios across the table, unfinished.

"Come on," I said, "face it, they're canteens. I could nurse a small starving nation."

He reached out and touched the back of my hand.

"I could be the hero," I said.

It gave me chills just considering what I might do to save my father's life.

Genevieve. I turned the name over in my mind as the priest preached to the Sisters of Saint Genevieve in Italian. If my father was saved, I would name the baby *Genevieve* in thanks. According to the book I'd been reading earlier in the library, Saint Genevieve was the patron saint invoked against plagues and disaster. The name meant "white wave," beautiful irony considering the convent's proximity to such a placid body of water.

Then the priest began to speak in English. Leaning into the pulpit, he seemed to direct his remarks to me alone. "Quoting Jean-Paul Sartre," he said, his blue eyes burning like gas jets, "if there is no God, then everything is permitted."

I sat stunned and motionless, pinned there by his gaze.

If there was no God, there was no hope. Nothing. I shifted uncomfortably in the pew. Surely everyone noticed how he was singling me out. Was he trying to prove to me how tenuous my faith was, how self-serving? Or was he saying that of course there is a God, and nothing is permitted—certainly not my flirtation with Catholicism in the hopes of ingratiating myself to God to save my father, nor my base feelings for young Sister Corrina? I stared at the other congregants. The two silent pilgrims were doused in a clear blue light, the woman in front of me mottled violet; only my body was devoid of any beautiful kaleidoscopic deformity. Pain spiked behind my left eye, a fit of coughing rose up inside me like a storm, and a sick ache moved up my spine, twisting my muscles against the rocks of my vertebrae. The congregation rose for the final benediction.

If there is no God, then everything is permitted. The words pounded behind my eyes as we filed out of the chapel. Head bowed, I hurried down the hall, past a recessed nook housing a small plaster statue of the Virgin Mary clutching baby Jesus to her breast, a cluster of candles lit by people with unanswered prayers burning at her feet.

I dragged myself up the long wooden staircase to my little room, locked the door, and collapsed on the soft bed, my head pounding. Christ stared down at me with sad reproach, as if he'd known all along that I'd fail.

After five hours spent dipping in and out of a sick sleep, the migraine began to ebb and I was able to sit up. Achy and nauseated, I slid off the bed and onto my knees, resting my head against the bed frame. I tried to pray, to focus, but all I could think was, *I can't pray.* I can't pray. I can't pray.

I didn't know what God had heard, if he heard *Save my father* or *Save me*.

I thought about calling home and begging Billy to come get me. I considered calling Mary Beth and telling her she was full of shit, that there was no peace here, no escape. But really I wanted to call my father, even if he couldn't hear me, even if all I could do was hear his voice. I could call and hang up. But I wanted to talk to him, even though I wasn't sure what I'd say. I wanted to apologize to him.

Fumbling in my bag, I located the train schedule, but I was too late. There were no trains into the city until morning. I was trapped.

I thought of Sister Corrina in the library, the indentation her body had left in the cushions, the warm place she had left behind. I wondered how it would be seeing Sister Corrina for the last time, how it would be saying good-bye. I closed my eyes, imagining our hands touching, her lips on my cheek. The blessing she'd give me.

I stared out the window of my room at the Sound, my hips and knees aching under the baby's weight. What did this baby matter? Right now it was nothing more than an intruder. In the gloaming, the water was a polished gray, inhospitable, unyielding, and cold as metal.

The baby inside me pushed off from the floor of my cervix and floated up under my ribs. I sucked in my breath. It was as though I were being turned inside out.

When I woke late the next morning, it was to the sound of the water. Any thoughts of escaping on the 9:05 were vanquished by the sight of early morning light gilding the blue-green water. Sitting on the low stone wall that buttressed the convent, I spotted Mother Saint Agnes stalking around the flower beds, frowning. At first I thought she was going to scold me for missing Matins, then I noticed again the six-pack of Pabst Blue Ribbon. Someone, somewhere, was having a party. She stopped to poke at the eviscerated leaves of a rose-bush and shook her head in dismay. She glanced in my direction and gave me a curt nod, then popped the top of a PBR and drained it into the flower bed. She made her way around the flower beds this way, and after draining the last can, she heaved the empties into a blue trash barrel outside the basement door with distaste. Then she retreated back inside the convent.

I waddled over to the bushes, the smell of beer rising up out of the flower beds. At first the swell of my belly prohibited discovery, then my toes banged into something cool and hard. I took a cautious step back. In the grass was a china teacup filled with beer, and floating in the beer, belly-up, were two flesh-colored, thumb-sized slugs, wallowing drunkenly, their slippery bodies entwined, intoxicated, drowning, oblivious to the danger I might present. Every few feet of the garden ground was planted with these teacup beer traps, the live slugs bobbing like happy hedonists in the foamy ale, the dead slugs sinking to the bottom like a warning.

"Good morning," a voice called. I turned to see Sister Corrina waving to me as she hurried down the cliff side overlooking the water. I raised my hand feebly. The smell of beer, earthy, sweet, and rotten, was nauseating.

"Hello, again," she said, her hands fighting to keep her

veil from blowing across her face and into her mouth. She paused, and then, checking over her shoulder for the Mother Superior, she made a beeline for the basement door. She stopped, her hand resting on the knob.

"Do you want to see?"

"Yes. Sure," I answered quickly. "What exactly?"

She grinned mysteriously.

Just as I was about to follow her, I stopped. Someone was watching us. Moseying through the tall grass were the pilgrims. They stopped for a moment, cocked their white woolly heads in curiosity, then slowly ambled up the cliff to a meditation bench with views of the Sound. Was it luck or God's will that the only witnesses were mute?

"Are you coming?" Sister Corrina called.

"Of course," I said, hurrying after her. *If there is no God, then everything is permitted.*

It took a minute for my eyes to adjust, and for a disorienting few moments I couldn't see Sister Corrina at all. I was unsure of where I was, only that inside it was warm and damp, smelling of dirt and mildew. Then I could make out cans of white paint, Christmas lights, and an ancient push mower. I could see moldy wooden rafters strung with spiderwebs, dust motes captured like tiny swirling hurricanes in the pale, sticky webs, a series of tragic satellite weather photos rendered in spider silk. So accustomed was Sister Corrina to the cryptlike darkness that she seemed oblivious to my blindness.

"Follow me," she called as she disappeared into a darkened corner of the basement. She led me toward a wooden worktable strewn with large spotty glass jars, an assortment of stainless steel tweezers, and a range of tiny hammers.

She flipped on a light, a single yellow bulb that cast a hazy golden aura of light over the muslin tablecloth streaked and splotched with red and brown polka dots. At the back of the table was a row of miniature jelly jars filled with long, thin metal pins, sharp tacks, and what appeared to be elegant carpet staples. There was a clear bottle marked ETHER and a glass decanter of cotton balls that would have been more at home on a lady's dressing table than here among these primitive implements.

"I searched and searched for a long, long time, I never thought I'd see one," Sister Corrina said excitedly. "Never. I'd read about it, I'd hoped, but last night I was outside recovering the shears I'd left by the rosebushes and out of the corner of my eye—that is the way you always see these things, out of only one eye—I saw it on the tree."

She paused, grinning proudly. "I show it to you first." She reached down and took my hand, giving it a long squeeze, then let it go just as quickly. She reached to the back of the table and slid forth a large bell jar. She pushed it toward me so I could see that underneath the glass was a luminescent yellowy-green moth the size of a child's hand dozing on the pillow of an ether-soaked cotton ball. Its sculptured, bow-shaped wings seemed clipped out of felt. The edges of the upper wings were trimmed in a cocoa maroon; the lower wings flared out into delicate points festooned with a violet-and-white dot no animal would confuse with a predator's eye. Its whitish green body was as plump and furry as a small mouse. The thick-lashed antennae fanned out of the head in pinkish-brown fronds. With two hands, she slowly lifted the bell jar. She pinched the moth's soft body between her fingers, then laid it reverently on a square wood platform with canvas stretched and stapled over it.

"Luna moth," she whispered. "They come out at night. So rare. What was God thinking when he made the luna moth? How pleased he must have been, seeing what he'd wrought," she mused as she arranged the moth in the center of the platform with a pair of needle-nosed tweezers. Then she selected a pin and pierced the moth just beneath the head, securing it fast to the board.

I expected blood, but there was none.

I expected some kind of sound, some crack as the carapace was pierced, but there was none.

"You have to have faith," Sister Corrina said, tucking some pins between her lips, which gave her the appearance of a genetic seamstress about to make some transspecies alteration, such as sewing on flippers or adding a tail. Under her breath Sister Corrina said, "Praise be to God," and pushed another pin through the moth's middle, where I imagined the heart and lungs and stomach to be. "And to his Son Jesus, and our Mother Mary," she said, then took up her hammer and tapped the head of each silver pin until it disappeared in the milky-green fur, so the moth seemed to be suspended in space, alive.

"Are you all right?"

"Mmm," I said.

Sister Corrina put down her hammer. "Is it the baby?" she asked, and reached out to cup my abdomen.

"It's my father, he's sick," I heard myself say, feeling her hand pressing hard against the baby, as though this would explain my sudden swoon.

"Very sick?"

"He's dying," I said, words I'd dared not speak to another soul.

"Is he in pain?" she asked, her voice quickening. Then, with her thumb, she pushed two tiny tacks just underneath the body of the moth. I supposed this was so that the weight of the moth's body wouldn't pull it down off the nails and tear the wings.

"Yes, I think so," I said in a barely audible squeak. "No. I know so."

"You're sad," she said, surprised. "Is he sad?"

I shrugged. I didn't have an answer, and it disturbed me. I assumed so. He must be. But I couldn't answer her question. This didn't seem to bother her. She propped the luna moth in its wooden box against the stone wall and admired it.

"I feel as though we're being punished," I said, my throat dry.

"Punished?" she asked curiously, and thought about it as she ran her finger along the rim of the moth's wing, as though the moth could feel it. "Maybe it's a gift from God," she said.

"A gift?"

"Doesn't it make life more beautiful to you?"

"Excuse me?"

"Doesn't it make life seem more precious, more mysterious . . ."

"No. No, it doesn't. It seems awful." I was confused by her reaction, angry. I wanted her to tell me everything was going to be all right, that he would be saved, or he would be going to heaven, or something. Anything. I'd expected comfort, but there was none.

She stared at her moth, then turned to me and touched my face, taking it in her hands. For a moment we just stood there staring awkwardly at each other. Then she shut her eyes, and I believed for a moment she might lay her head on my shoulder, but she inclined her head toward mine, her lips parting. Panic and eagerness flooded my body, but I didn't move. My hands fluttered at my sides. I was afraid if I moved everything would stop. She'd stop.

I thought: I could fall into that mouth. Then I did.

"I just wanted to show you," she whispered in my ear, "there's so much beauty."

My mother answered on the second ring.

"Do you feel better, sweetheart? Is it better at a convent?" she asked. What she meant was *You're not Catholic. Wouldn't your time be better spent here, at home with your father?*

"It's fine," I said. "I need to talk to Dad."

"How's the baby?" she asked. "How is he doing?"

"You really think it's a boy, don't you?"

"Don't you? No—it doesn't matter. It really doesn't matter. I just want you and the baby to be okay. That's all. It's a good thing to think about."

"I need to talk to Dad, okay, Mom?"

"Oh." She sounded surprised, a little hurt. "He's repairing the eaves. I'll get him for you."

"How's his hearing?" I asked, but she'd already put down the phone.

After what seemed like an eternity, he picked up. "Honey," his voice boomed.

"Hi," I said. Even though he was out of breath, I liked hearing his breathing in my ear.

"What?"

"I miss you," I yelled back, my voice ringing in the empty corridors.

"It's gorgeous here," he said. "I've been outside working all day. No shirt. It's hot as hell. I'm going to convince your mom to go swimming with me tonight, take a bottle of wine, maybe the old rope swing down off the bridge."

"Daddy," I said, seeing in my mind my father in his jean shorts, the long, sickle-shaped scars on his tanned back, white in contrast. I couldn't imagine it was safe. "You shouldn't be *swimming*," I said.

"Oh, is that right?" he said angrily.

"Don't," I said. "Please."

There was a pause. I listened to him breathe, his breath rasping and catching. I remembered Sister Corrina's breath on my cheek, my collarbone. Her kiss. The tip of her tongue.

"For God's sake, what should I do?" he said. "Huh? What *should* I do?"

"I miss you," I said.

I could sense him fuming on the other end of the line.

"So, how's that baby doing?" he asked, his voice suddenly full of a strange, unsettling cheer. He almost never asked about the baby. Never. He'd ask how I was feeling, how Billy was bearing up, but not how the baby was. Sometimes I assumed my father didn't ask about the baby because it caused him pain to imagine not witnessing his grandchild's first steps or ever hearing himself called "Grandpa," other times I feared he just couldn't care anymore, that all this was for naught.

I didn't bring it up. I didn't want to. I didn't want to confess that relinquishing the luxury of simply being his daughter and taking up the yoke of motherhood was horrifying to me. That giving life meant little in the face of losing him.

"What's the due date, again?" he asked.

"I'm sorry, Daddy," I said. I didn't want to talk about the baby. "I'm so sorry."

"What are you talking about, honey?"

"I came here to pray, to do something, I don't know what..." I stammered. I was afraid I was going to start crying.

"I never asked you to pray for me, honey," he said. "Forget about it. Listen, I know you love me," he said. "Do me a favor, would you? Enjoy yourself. Take a swim."

"I miss you," I said again, this time quieter.

"Okay, then," he said. "It's settled."

Had I not been starving, I would have stayed in my room, alternately forcing myself to kneel by my bedside, wallowing in guilt and confusion, and stalking back and forth across the room in a dizzying prickly state of desire, unlike any I'd ever experienced—lying down was just an invitation to fantasize about Corrina, slip my hand into my panties, and I didn't want to. No, I wanted to. I couldn't.

Thankfully, I was ravenous. The baby was ravenous. I had to eat. As I approached the dining table, my fellow pilgrims' faces belied nothing sinister or suspicious. Their expressions were masks of peace, as though they'd been rolling in spiritual clover all day. Now they were eating roast beef with baby carrots and parslied potatoes and chewing with somber, bovine placidity. I envied them, and I hated them. I knew they wondered why I was slipping off into the basement with Sister Corrina, why I hadn't attended any services today, although God knows I should have.

I had betrayed my husband.

As I ate, I tried to ignore their stares. I gobbled my food, barely able to catch my breath between bites, and the pilgrims perched nervously on the edge of their chairs, as if ready to bolt, their watery blue eyes widening in horror as I devoured roll after roll wet with butter. Afraid, no doubt, I'd snatch their pudding, or lick their plates. I was voracious. Clearly, nothing was safe around me.

All that anchored me was my migraine, which had come back. My head throbbed in a comforting, strangely pleasant way, a sliver of pain right through my left eye, causing the occasional roman candle of white light to appear in the corner of my vision. A divine intervention.

Later that evening, sitting on the edge of my bed, undressing for sleep, I imagined standing on the creek bank watching my father swim in the dark. I watched him disappear underwater, his body invisible to me, then, just as I began to get frightened, just as I was about to dive in after him, I watched him reappear, suddenly breaking through the water, gasping.

That night I didn't kneel to pray. There was no hope. I didn't ask for miracles, or forgiveness, which perhaps was a miracle. I curled up in bed on my side and prayed the "Now I lay me down to sleep" prayer of my childhood, complete with God-blesses, then tucked my hands securely under my pillow. That was when the baby came alive, paddling and kicking so that my belly looked like a bag in which an animal was trapped. A heel distended the skin below my rib cage. I reached out and pinched it between my thumb and forefinger, holding fast to the tender back of the baby's foot for a moment, feeling the surreal tremble of flesh and bone and muscle. Then it slipped from my grip. I rolled onto my back and palpated my abdomen, searching for some part of my baby to grab on to, something to touch. I feared this was love—a guilty pleasure. I was betraying my father. How could I embrace a future with this child as the sun, and not him?

When I awoke the next morning, my whole body ached, as though during the night unseen forces had been wrestling and tugging on my limbs. I pulled on a sleeveless red cotton dress ticked with black sunflowers that I'd packed on a whim. I hadn't worn it all summer because it clung to my breasts and accentuated my belly, but now I didn't care. I didn't even recognize myself anymore. Quickly I cleaned out my drawers and packed my things away. *If there is no God, then everything is permitted.* I wondered if God had sent Sister Corrina to test me, if he was playing with me like a bug, a potbellied bumblebee, legs bowed and woolly with pollen, wobbling toward the anesthetizing pleasure and forgetfulness of reality's bell jar.

As I zipped up my bag, a finger of sweat traced my spine from neck to tailbone, and my hips ached under my weight. How my hips hurt as they spread, widening like a wishbone. I shoved my feet into tight sandals, my feet and ankles so swollen as to appear boneless. The baby lay low and motionless in my body, still and heavy as a stone.

I had an hour before my taxi picked me up. I dragged my bag downstairs. The convent, though silent, felt ominous, unsafe. My only refuge was the outdoors. I'd lost. I'd accomplished nothing.

Now that I knew about the beer traps it seemed I was destined to step in them. After narrowly avoiding overturning three cups secreted in the grass, their soggy, slumberous occupants lolling like nihilistic sybarites in an alcoholic hot tub, I made it down to the water. There they were, the entire sisterhood, at least a dozen barefoot nuns, some in their gray habits, others in knee-length white T-shirts and footless black tights, huddled together on the dock. It was obvious by the way that they clung to each other, giggling nervously, that few of them could swim. I watched as they strapped on safety-orange life vests and removed their headdresses, bobby pins pinched between their lips, shyly exposing themselves as redheads, blondes, and brunettes.

Mother Saint Agnes lined the sisters up on the dock. One by one the nuns crossed themselves, pinched their noses, and, with extreme reluctance, plopped into the deep, gasping and shrieking as they hit the water, their habits and T-shirts ballooning around them, then slowly deflating, swirling around their waists as they bobbed to the water's surface. The most frightened held fast to the dock like gray barnacles, not trusting God; the others headed for the shallows or treaded water furiously, the Sound churning with the music of their kicks, the slap of their hands beating the water. Overhead a pair of gulls screamed over the shrieks of the sisters. The echo of their laughter imprinted on the air.

I watched Sister Corrina dog-paddle into the eel grass, emerging from the water, her sopping habit hitched up to her knees. I couldn't help staring. Across the width of her thigh was a long gash, fresh and red, as though she'd gartered her leg with barbed wire. She made her way toward me, stopping only for a moment to cocoon herself in a blue beach towel. Under Mother Saint Agnes's gaze, she was tentative, but determined to speak to me.

"So, do you swim?" I asked, my voice wavering, remembering how she'd held my face. I kicked off my sandals, then wished I hadn't, as droplets of water fell from her wet body onto the tops of my feet.

"Swim?" she protested breathlessly. "Oh, no. I can't," she said, staring out at the Sound, her lashes beaded with salt water.

I felt dizzy, holding on tightly to the arms of my lawn chair.

"Are you all right?" she asked.

"I'm not sure."

"You're fine," she said, casting her attention back to the water. "You're going to have a baby."

"You're scared of the water?" I asked. I couldn't imagine she was afraid of anything.

Mother Saint Agnes called out to Sister Corrina, waving her back to the fold.

"You will never be alone," Sister Corrina said. Her hand reached out quickly to touch my hip, then pulled away. I'd wanted her blessing, but it wasn't that sort of touch.

I walked toward the water's edge. The rocks were wet and slippery with algae, and the cold singed the bottoms of my feet.

"What are you doing?" Sister Corrina asked nervously, her teeth tugging hard on the edge of her loose purple nail. "It's not safe," she said, her eyes fixed on my belly, the black sunflowers rippling with the baby's movement.

"It would feel good," I said. "Wouldn't it?"

"No," she said, shaking her head vehemently. "Don't go."

I gasped as the water spread my dress out around my hips and lifted me up.

"You shouldn't be swimming," Sister Corrina said, reaching out to grab my shoulder, to pull me back onshore.

"What should I do?" I said as the current picked me off my feet, pulling me into the heart of the Sound. *"For God's sake, what should I do?"*

WILD

KINGDOM

"Oh, this is silly, isn't it?" my mother said, as she dumped
out some sticky buds on a *Gourmet* magazine she had balanced
on her knees. "*Obviously,* your dad can't smoke," she said, sep-
arating weed from seeds. "Sometimes, though"—she smiled—
"I blow it into his mouth."

Sometimes I blow it into his mouth.

I had no idea, when I asked after the quarter-ounce of
Yellow Man's Paradise that I'd given Dad as a Father's Day
gift, that Mom would tramp upstairs, rifle her underwear

drawer, and return with the dope, stashed in a caviar tin, and some rolling papers.

I had no idea my mother could roll a joint, really roll a joint. I was amazed at her nimble-fingered joint wizardry.

"Should we do it?" Mom asked, waggling the little jar of pot. "Do you want to try some? This stuff, my, it's so strong. We could never, if we lived to be—"

"Sure," I said.

My little sister, Dee, now attorney-at-law, let her jaw drop. Really drop, like in the cartoons. You could have driven a truck into that mouth. Two shots at the bar had only stoked her zeal for truth and justice. Except when it came to speed limits. But something like drugs, that was non-negotiable. I hoped Mom didn't pick up on Dee's shock. I didn't want anything to make her feel bad, or break the spell.

"Huh," Dee said. She didn't want to be left out, but she was floored. Here was our mother, a former leader of the Bluebirds, who used to wash my mouth out with soap for swearing so regularly that all our soap bars bore my tooth marks, not only putting a finishing lick on a fat spliff, but getting our dad stoned. Even at twenty-five, Dee still saw our parents as the gods we imagined them to be as children. She tucked her feet up under her and crossed her arms against her chest, staring at her perfect pedicure, each toenail shiny and pink as the lip of a seashell. She shook her head so her straight corn-colored hair fell across her face, then stared at the unlit joint dangling from my lips with the suspicion of a little sister used to being duped. She acted like I'd planned all this.

I hadn't, but for the first time in a long while I was enjoying myself.

Or rather, I *had* been enjoying myself. Now, Mom and Dee are hiding out in the car and I'm hunting snack food in the smoked-meat-and-motor-oil aisle of the Mobil Convenience Shop. So stoned I am bounding up and down the aisles with the gait and authority of an overblown pool toy, my ass seeming to rise up behind me, threatening to tip me over onto my face.

Home was nice. The three of us lounged out on the back deck in our chaises drinking a nice Sauvignon Blanc. In an imitation of casualness, my mother leaned over the arm of my chair to light the joint. As our arms touched, her hands cupped around the flame, a ripple of excitement spread through my body, a gulping giggly terror. As the flame ignited paper, I imagined we were in a bar, she was the brave soldier, I was the daffy showgirl, and Dee was the inscrutable professor recording our every moment. Our mother was strong, in control, she would always protect us, but what did she want in return? Did she want anything? Anything I could give her?

When Mom handed Dee the joint, she took it, with only a second's hesitation, and toked away. This was our mother, after all. We smoked, and coughed, and smoked, giggling like kids getting away with murder. We had all afternoon to sober up before the men came home. Neither my father nor Billy would ever need to know. I was happy to have them both out of the house, though I was a little jealous that my father had asked Billy to go to the Kentucky Derby party with him. Just because it had been an all-male event for twenty-five years didn't mean I didn't want my father to invite me.

My father, to my surprise, had liked Billy from the beginning, despite the facts that he'd never mowed grass, or been hunting, or seen one ancient ruin. Despite the fact that he was a musician who only worked sporadically doing studio work, despite the fact that I told him I'd fallen in love with Billy at first sight. Unlike with other boys, there had been no initiation, no long silences or trick questions asked under a bamboozlement of alcohol. He'd taught Billy how to rebuild a carburetor and repair a cane chair, and the two of them had rebuilt the back deck and reshingled the roof. Sometimes I felt like my father had just given me to Billy. Really given me away.

But it was good that Billy was going. He could drive, and Dad could drink if he felt like it. It would be good company, and maybe they'd even win some money. It was silly to be jealous.

"So, this party is in Greenville?" my mother had said this morning, emptying the dishwasher, not looking at my father. I'd heard her ask my father a variation of Do You Know Where You Are Going at least three times this morning.

"God damn it, Grace," my father said, shaking his head, then he got distracted by the fact that the cuffs of his khakis were pooling on the tops of his loafers. He'd lost more weight.

Billy came galloping through the kitchen with Annabelle in his arms. He dashed into the living room, tossed her, squealing, onto the sofa, and kissed her baby stomach. When Dee and I were small, we played on that sofa with our father. Every night after dinner we'd beg him to do the Crab. The object was to scare us. Dee and I would play on the sofa as though it were a raft, and my father would lie on the floor pretending to be a giant crab. We'd dangle our legs over the side, and he'd pretend to be asleep, finally when we got bold enough to actually touch our toes to the carpet he'd attempt to grab us by the ankles and drag us down onto the floor and tickle us. We'd scream until we were hoarse.

Last night my father had been been lying on the floor in the living room with Annabelle asleep on his chest, his eyes closed. I couldn't even look at them.

"Check it out," Billy said. "What do you think, is it me, or what?" He had on an old blue-and-green madras jacket of my father's, one he wore in the sixties, and a little panama hat from the same time, both from the attic. My father laughed. "That's the spirit. Hey, listen, they're yours, son. Take 'em."

We all laughed, covering up his words. This was no time to give anything away.

"All righty, I am ready to take somebody's money," Billy said, rubbing his hands together. He picked Annabelle up off the floor and gave her a good-bye kiss. "So, Ev, you're okay with this, me leaving you with the baby?"

"Of course," I said. It was a little humiliating how much better Billy was at being a mommy than me.

"I just gave her a bottle, she's clean, and we've got eye rubbing, so she's probably going to go down soon."

My mother covered her mouth so Billy couldn't see her smile. Nobody had figured Billy would take to fatherhood the way he had. It was the job he was born for. I'd joke that it was because he'd been taking care of me for years, and no one would dispute it.

"Okay, so I've read her the Elizabeth Bishop poems she

likes and that *Goodnight Moon* you put out, but you know, I think she's beyond that. She's very advanced."

"Of course," my father said. "We'd expect nothing less, right? It would be a shame to throw such a beautiful baby back."

"Billy, honey," my mother started, but my dad grabbed him by the arm. "We'll see you later."

Certainly my father would have wanted no part of this dope-smoking escapade. It was a matter of dignity. No matter how sick he was, he was still our father, and in his mind fathers didn't do drugs with their children, regardless of their age. So even though I'd watched him hold the Ziploc up to the light, examining the fat green buds graced with sticky yellow flowers, even though I'd heard him upstairs violently puking, smelled vomit on his breath, watched him refuse my mother's offer to make him anything he wanted—a grilled cheese, a chocolate milk shake—listened to him reply, "I can't, I can't—this freaking nausea is going to kill me," I was to act as though the weed didn't exist, as though none of this was happening.

The only part Dad wanted to discuss was the buy. Mary Beth had made the buy. "Let me, darling," she insisted. "I don't mind. Really." I was relieved. Even though we hadn't spoken in months, probably since she came to see the baby six months ago, she was there for me. She'd offered, knowing of course what a chicken I was. "Tell me again," he'd say, like a little kid eager to hear a tale of derring-do. So, I'd tell him about how Mary Beth had gone on an adventure to a trendy architecture firm in midtown that did a little drug business on the side. Depending on my mood, I sometimes improvised a fire on the subway tracks, a man who could have been an undercover cop following her at a distance.

"They really had a big binder filled with swatches of various strains of marijuana inside?"

"And hash, and Thai stick."

"Thai stick! Amazing."

Here he'd pause. "And they gave her the pot"—a special blend to curb nausea and give you the munchies—"in one of those hard paper tubes architects carry blueprints in.... And nobody suspects a thing—she took the subway, no fear of drug-sniffing dogs..."

"The risks I take for you," I said, even though it was Mary Beth who had, it seemed happily, assumed any risk, not me.

"Amazing," he said.

While we were sitting out on the deck, we heard someone start up a lawn mower, and my mother began to laugh.

"Wouldn't it be funny if the neighbors dropped by, or the lawn boy showed up?"

"Is he cute?" I asked.

"Who?"

"The lawn boy."

"Oh my God," Dee said, scrambling to sit up straight in her chair. "No way. Are you serious?" Then she began to giggle. "Wait, I'm a lawyer. I'll get us off."

"Oh my, this is good, isn't it? I don't think I've laughed like this since, um..." my mother said, wiping her eyes on the sleeve of her linen blouse, her train of thought derailed in smoke.

Nothing could touch us. For the first time since before

Annabelle was born, I felt relaxed. Nothing existed but the puffy white clouds, somersaulting over our heads like fat puppies.

"Look, baby animals," I said. My mouth stretched into a huge, stupid grin. Nothing hurt. We were unreachable. Then the phone rang.

Blame the Shackleford Zoo, aka Wild Animal Drive and Conservation Park, for ruining our afternoon. The party planners they'd employed to choreograph tomorrow night's gala benefit had hit an impasse on table placement, and my mother's presence was requested—no, demanded. The benefit, which would enable the zoo to purchase two adult Borneo orangutans, was my mother's baby. The zoo was deeply in debt, due to low attendance and the fact that the owner, Jip Slingluff, purchased wild animals the way some people bought fancy clothes or stereo equipment. All it took was a photograph of the awesome, highly photogenic, marmalade-colored giants of the ape world, Mr. Ya Ya and Booster, to turn Slingluff's head. Unfortunately, a zoo in Ohio—one with deep pockets and a snappy monorail—was equally in thrall to these gentle beasts. Jip Slingluff believed my mother was his best hope.

Because there are no secrets in a small town, he knew that two years ago, while in Borneo at a game preserve (the last trip my parents had taken, and probably ever would), my mother had had an ecstatic experience while bottle-feeding a baby orangutan orphaned by poachers. As far as I know, it was her first and last epiphany. "It was magical," she'd said, her eyes all moony.

"Magical," my father agreed, but it wasn't the orangutans so much as the rain forest that enthralled my father, the opportunity to discover orchids he'd only ever read about. There were orchids with petals mimicking human flesh, orchids exuding the scent of meat and honey, orchids whose flowers sported petals like long hairy ponytails, and others whose faces looked like wild boars. He wanted them all. My father believed he could induce these highly temperamental plants, which often refused to bloom for periods of nearly a decade, not only to grow but to propagate in his own greenhouse. He was patient. He misted and fertilized, cultivating plants whose leaves were plain, not even slightly decorative, and whose roots grew wormlike out the top of the pots. He clipped and turned them to or from the sun, hoping that sometime years from now they might send up a spike and bloom for a few weeks. Half the time it was impossible to tell if they were alive or dead.

Since my parents' return, they had contributed handsomely to the ApeWatch fund to preserve the orangutans and their habitat, and had become quite chummy with the slightly mad woman who ran the camp in Borneo. A little political wrangling on the part of my mother swung the decision in the favor of Shackleford. Knowing that she thought zoos were depressing and barbaric, I found it hard to understand why she'd taken on this crusade. My father was likewise perplexed, but as usual he was loath to criticize or even ponder my mother's intentions. She was above reason.

"It's your mother's decision," he'd said that morning at breakfast, watching with a kind of sick bemusement as his orange juice sloshed over the rim of the glass he held in his trembling hand.

"It's a distraction." He shrugged.

"Yes," I said, "but—"

"Listen to me, Evelyn, you leave your mother alone," he said, getting up abruptly from the table. "Do you hear me? You leave her alone."

These lightning flashes of anger had become common. They were the weather of our lives. He didn't lash out at my mother and Dee nearly as much as he snapped at me. He knew I could take it.

"Your mother has to go to Shackleford," my very stoned mother said, hanging up the phone in disbelief, her pale blue eyes nearly slits. "Oh my holy, holy, what?" She laughed. "Can you believe it?"

"Cool," I said. "We'll all go. All three, four of us," I said, and headed upstairs.

It is an axiom of parenting that one never wakes up a baby. Never.

But I had no choice. Was I to force my mother out into the cruel, unfriendly, unstoned world with Dee as her navigator? Impossible.

Thankfully, Annabelle was half awake already, lolling in her crib, sucking her fingers, smelling sweetly of talcum and milk. My little lamb was the poster baby for procreation.

It wasn't until I scooped my angel in my arms that she started shrieking.

"Now, now, little pumpkin, don't you cry," I said, embracing her and doing that magical, unique-to-each-child, mother-baby dance, Annabelle's head bobbing as though she were on a pogo stick, her green eyes squirt guns of tears.

"Sweet pumpy," I said. I sniffed her bottom to see if she needed a diaper change. Pumpy? I started to giggle. Shit, I was really baked. God, if Billy were here...I didn't want to even think about it. I lifted my shirt and nudged her to my breast, but she turned away.

Then Annabelle started to holler, to really howl. It was so loud, so shocking, I burst out laughing, bad mother that I am, then I got ahold of myself. Remember, babies are as uncomplicated as animals, I told myself. They are ruled by instinct. I ran down the checklist: boob, refused; diaper, clean; hugs and kisses, administered. And still the tyrant sobbed. How could I let this happen, and at a time like this? Then, out of my fog, it occurred to me—the poor lamb was sick. Yes, of course, sick. I salvaged a bottle of red syrup out of my emergency medical kit. A cure-all elixir for babies' fevers, colds, headaches, teething, runny nose, earaches...I'd discovered it was even good for hangovers. I took out the enclosed dropper, sucked up a good inch of the stuff, pried open my darling's wee mouth, and pumped it in.

"Stop screaming, lamby-poo," I said in the humiliating squeaky-toy singsong genetically programmed into parents because babies respond to the pitch. "Please, peas and carrots, stop all this carrying on, you little monster."

Still she cried. Oh, why aren't babies like tires, something you can submerge in water to determine where the leak is? Then, because some of the medication had dribbled out of her mouth, and because I wanted to be a good mommy, I gave her another dose. Like magic, it shut her up.

I heap the brightly colored bags of pretzels, chips, Cheetos, Fritos, Doritos, and other snack foods ending in *ito* on the counter along with a six-pack of soda, all the while watching myself in the closed-circuit surveillance camera. My father's dark blue cardigan is misbuttoned, my high-tops are untied, the collar of my rumpled white oxford is splotched with red baby medicine. I look hunch-shouldered and disreputable, like a shoplifter or a recently paroled substitute teacher. A fever blister, evidence of my toxic nature, is forming on the top of my lip. I run my hand over my short red pixie, the bangs, which I trimmed this morning with a pair of cuticle scissors, are uneven and too short.

The teenage cashier, his face a buckshot of acne, looks at the junk in awe. "That'll be twenty-five even," he says, and as I dig in my pockets for the money my mother gave me—I'm almost thirty and still my mother treats—I say, "I can't help myself." He nods sadly, like he understands, and hands me the bags. Our fingers touch for one second, and I want to explain that I have to ensure my good mother wants for nothing, plus my little sister, she's got the munchies so bad I fear she might start gnawing on her own limbs. I want to tell him this, but instead I grab the bags from him and call out over my shoulder, "Ciao."

God, I hate that word.

· · ·

In the parking lot I see that my mother is no longer scrunched down in the front seat hiding from the neighbors, but is turned around in the front seat talking to Dee, who is leisurely braiding and unbraiding her hair. She's nodding. I'm sure they are talking about me, and I pause before opening the door.

This is why I don't get high. Paranoia. I always feel like Lassie, a particularly neurotic Lassie, *yap-yap-yapping* like a maniac, while a malevolent thick-skulled Timmy stares back at me blankly, fighting back laughter.

What's that, Lassie? Calm down, girl. Get off the furniture.

Oh, the baby's in the well!

Oh, you think we all want to kill you, how hilarious!

I yank open the car door, hoping to surprise them, but I need only to hear the words *preserve* and *cowboy hats* to know I am safe. My mother is again defending her involvement with the Shackleford Zoo.

"Unfortunately, people don't preserve what they don't understand. People, you know, need to know orangutans don't just exist in Clint Eastwood movies—they aren't supposed to ride motorcycles and wear cowboy hats. It's wrong. Damn it. They belong in the wild. They *are* wild," my mother says. When my mother sees the bags in my arms, the anger vanishes from her voice. "Evie, sweetie, tell me you got me a Tab," she says, reaching for the bags. "Your mother really needs a Tab."

"Tab. Mmm, Tab," Dee says.

"Unlike human beings, animals kill solely to survive, Dee." She pops open a soda. "They kill to protect themselves and they kill so they can eat, they take no pleasure in killing, it's not sport to them the way it is to some humans." She takes a long sip. "*They're* pure."

"Wow," Dee says. "Yeah."

I think of my father, who is living on Linzer cookies and painkillers big as Ping-Pong balls. It makes no sense to me.

"For instance, a lion makes one kill to feed herself and her pride, no more," my mother says. "One kill. Like Evie here, today at the Wiggly Piggly, or what have you—the Mo-bil."

"Is that guy staring at us?" Dee says, and slides down in her seat. "Oh God, we're dead."

I look at Annabelle, slumped in her car seat, her eyelids beginning to flutter. Earlier, after my father forsook my company for the misty privacy of the greenhouse, I'd opened my shirt, thinking it was safe, and started to nurse Annabelle. I've gotten used to the feeling of vertigo that comes over me, but I am still eager to stop. I'm shooting for the six-month mark, which is supposed to ensure no earaches, less of a chance that Annabelle will be morbidly obese, and immunity to a host of childhood ailments. It is twice as long as most of my friends— granted, most of them had to go back to real jobs, whereas I am "freelancing" since quitting the craft museum. I've picked up some stylist work. One day I spent six hours slathering plums and bananas with Vaseline for a photo shoot at *Ladies' Home Journal* on the Wonder of Fruit, and half a day pouring gallons of chocolate syrup into a bathtub to simulate blood for a fashion shoot in *Details* where the men modeled white Armani suits and wielded chain saws.

I am a good mother.

This morning, while I was nursing, Dad slouched into

the kitchen and began rooting through a drawer, a small orchid pot in his hand.

"Ah, jeez," he said upon spotting me at the table, and turned his head quickly, his ears reddening, as though the sight of my naked breast would incinerate him, biting his lip as if I'd tricked him into witnessing this spectacle.

I'd seen this before, this desire to flee the room when I had to nurse Annabelle. At first it seemed old-fashioned, sweet, but now he seemed pissed and it infuriated me.

"You've been swimming in shark-infested waters—on purpose—you've tramped through jungles full of boom slangs and pit vipers and black mambos, and you're going to tell me a little boob freaks you out, Daddy? Come on..."

"Listen, little girl, I'm your father," he said. "Don't you talk to me like that. Don't you ever, ever forget—"

"You know what? Forget it, just forget it," I said. I picked up Annabelle, still suckered to my breast, and brushed past him, stomping up to my room as I'd done a hundred times before after fighting about curfews, drinking, and boys.

"Fuck you," I muttered, loud enough for him to hear, but his hearing is shot from all the radiation treatments.

Given my mother's orangutan obsession, it makes sense that she would want to do whatever she can to help those apes, I suppose, even if it means preserving them in captivity. Considering the way things are with my father, she'll probably never ever go back to Borneo, or anywhere else again. So if Mr. Ya Ya and Booster are going to end up behind bars regardless, well, better they be here in Delaware than Ohio.

What I suppose is most unsettling to me was my mother's idea that the benefit, in her words, "really show animals being animals." At $500 a plate, my mother wanted Hunt Night to raise not only capital, but the consciousness of patrons, turning them on to the realities of holding animals captured in the wild. It seemed punishing to me, an impulse bubbling up out of a dark place in my mother I didn't know existed. Still, I understand it. After all, how surreal it must be for a polar bear to backstroke in a swimming pool, gazing at the tops of buildings, dreaming of arctic skies. How tedious and depressing it must be for a caged snow leopard to meditate daily on the painted scrim of the mysterious and majestic Kilimanjaro hanging behind his cage while dining on boiled chicken and leopard kibble served out of a dog bowl. These wild animals are living life in a diorama. Until Hunt Night. If my mother had been given her way, on Hunt Night the polar bears wouldn't dine on whole kosher turkeys that had been hidden in the rocks, but instead would fish for salmon and seals; the leopard would have its pick of gourmet gazelles; the anaconda would deep-throat a whole live baby goat; and the African lion, in lieu of chainsawed horse meat, would be loosed to stalk and kill real live free-roaming zebras. It would be a real bloodbath. But as my mother had been quick to point out, with a nod to animal-rights activists ("I am one of you," she'd said), it would be a choreographed bloodbath—the proposed animals for sacrifice weren't endangered, and many were older, or diseased. The benefit would be a kind of manufactured natural-selection process. In the zebras' case, well, there had been a glut of zebra births in the spring, and as with calico kittens, the zoo couldn't seem to give them away.

"We'd be doing them a favor," my mother said.

But it was too hard a sell. "Nobody wants reality," my mother sighed. What they wanted was "The Peacable King-dom."

For a while we sit in the parking lot and just feed, silent but for the violent music of mastication, the crunching of chips and the grinding of teeth.

"Wow, Annabelle loves Yodels," Dee says. Her finger, coated with chocolate cake and cream, is stuck in my baby's mouth. "Oh God, did I smoke Thai stick?" she says in a panic. Then she starts to giggle. "Tie stick." She giggles.

"Dee!" I mean to sound outraged—Billy and I swore that no white-sugar poison would touch her baby lips until she was three—but I laugh. Annabelle looks hilarious in her white bunny suit, her chin whiskered with chocolate.

We are a movable feast. My mother pinches the jar of bean dip between her knees, Fritos spilling at her feet, as she weaves into traffic. I turn up the radio and Dee and I sing along with Cheap Trick, *Mommy's all right, Daddy's all right, they just seem a little weird, surrender, surrender, but don't give yourself away,* as we bob along the highway, my mother the captain of our craft. God, I love that song. I roll the window down all the way. It's painfully sunny, and the electric-blue sky is hung with banners of cloud. With my mother at the wheel, the world is an ocean in a teacup.

My mother lifts her tangled mane of blondish-brown curls off her neck. She has started covering the gray. Her nose is sunburned pink from working in my father's garden. It hurts him to bend over. She pounds out the rhythm on the steering wheel.

"Oh, this is better, isn't it?" my mother shouts out the window. "Much, much better!" She turns to me and smiles hopefully. The whites of her eyes are pink, her lips are shiny with coral gloss, but her mouth is open too far, her teeth too visible. I don't recognize this mother.

Annabelle yawns widely, then her head droops to the side and she drifts into a deep sleep. A lovely strand of drool unspools itself from her lips. All I want to do is protect my daughter. She's quiet now, isn't she? Peaceful? She's happy, right? Sometimes, like now, when I look at Annabelle, I love her so much I'm afraid it will swallow me whole.

In the backseat Annabelle snores. Our car gently careens into the median strip, then bounces merrily back into our lane, as though we're riding a rubber raft.

As Ted Nugent launches into the electric-guitar assault of "Cat Scratch Fever," my mother takes a sharp left into the Shackleford Wild Animal Drive and Conservation Park as if she'd forgotten where it was, or maybe we're just going too fast. A green-uniformed guard waves us through. All is right with the world. We are privileged, we are lucky. The kind of people who beat the odds. There, spread out before us, is the faux Okovanga Delta and the Wild Kingdom game drive— it's Botswana by way of Delaware. We barrel up Baboon Alley, our car cloaked in clouds of red dust so I can just barely see the baboons crouching up in the trees.

"Hold on, I'm coming," my mother sings under her

breath, her face dewy with sweat. Speeding is bad karma, but my mother is under the orangutan spell. We're supposed to amble up the road, ten miles an hour or less, spotting the game, the scarlet macaws, who pair for life, perched in tree-tops, the troops of white-faced capuchin monkeys frolicking in the shade, and the baboons who stalk around looking as disgruntled and dazed as spurned lovers, their protruding asses and their exposed pink genitals inviting a backdoor assigna-tion.

"Hello, boys," I call, waving to them. A branch thrown from the treetops glances off our windshield, like a baton tossed by an attention-hungry twirler, but our mother doesn't flinch or even slow down.

"Shit." I sit back in my seat.

"Damn baboons," my mother says. "Dee, is your window up? They're like little kids—they love junk," she says, her eyes trained on the dirt road ahead of us.

Dee locks her door. All of a sudden my mother hits the brakes and the back of the car fishtails, sending a cascade of chips into the front seat, landing in my hair and sliding down my back. The feeling is awful, like roaches. I scream.

The reason for the sudden stop is a family of four in a truck parked in the middle of the dirt road. The baboons are crawling over the truck like they've taken it hostage. Two rakish monkeys sit in the back, lounging like terrorists, their yellow teeth flashing. Then, spotting us, they leap from the truck and sprint toward our car. Someone, me I suppose, yelps.

My mother honks politely, *toot toot*, but the truck doesn't move. They've got a video camera trained on us. I can imagine us ending up on one of those true-horror videos exploiting campers decapitated by grizzlies and deep-sea fisherman zapped into comas by nests of electric eels. We will be the comic relief, stoned chicks teased to frustration by monkeys.

It is my mother who starts making faces at the baboons. She takes off her sunglasses, then scrunches up her nose and bares her teeth. "Come on, girls," she says, sticking out her tongue at a mother baboon with a baby slung across her back like a handbag. I stick out my tongue and let out a halfhearted *nyah nyah nyah*. It's a purely defensive taunt, the kind I am most familiar with.

"Mother," Dee says in her low and reproachful lawyer voice.

"You don't scare me, you big marvelous bully," my mother coos at the baboon mugging in her window. She raps at the window. "You know what, I could kiss you. I could just kiss you, yes, that's right," she says, pressing her lips to the windshield. "Oh, Dee, you aren't afraid of a little old baboon, are you?" my mother says, and hits the horn again.

Dee hiccups.

The biggest male of the troop mounts our front bumper and bounds onto the hood of the car. The Volvo sinks a few inches on its shocks as he marches up the roof. The rest of the troop follows, and in seconds the car is crawling with baboons. Flashes of silver glint in the sun as they rip pieces of chrome from the chassis, stripping the car like chop-shop bandits. Two older capuchin monkeys with faces like Salvation Army nurses peer into the backseat at Dee and Annabelle.

"Mom," Dee shrieks. "Mother!" as if our mom can do anything to stop this.

"Oh God, they're going to flip us." Maybe it's because

I'm high, but I swear I can see the future. "They're going to flip the car," I repeat louder. It's apparent that neither Dee nor my mother knows what I know.

"They want the baby," I say, smacking my palms on the window glass to chase them away. "Oh my God, they want Annabelle."

"Life is just amazing, isn't it?" my mother says, resting her chin on the steering wheel, her watery blue eyes staring blankly into the treetops. "Did I tell you girls that your father believes this is the most beautiful spring he's ever seen? Really. Did I tell you about him saying that even the bark on trees is beautiful to him?"

Dee and I don't say anything.

"I mean, sometimes I just don't know what to tell you girls, and what not to tell you," our mother says, her voice catching.

I reach at my feet for—what? A wrench, a snow scraper? My hand closes around a can, an aerosol can of cheese, and before I can really think that this isn't at all like Macing an attacker—after all, the windows are up, and cheese isn't known for its blinding ability—I shoot a ribbon of nacho spread at the windshield. It adheres stickily to the windows, but the baboons don't react at all. Then, as quickly as they'd appeared, they jump off the car and run skittering for the treetops. Balanced on the back of the largest female is a hijacked hubcap, a big silver bowl that catches the late afternoon light and brightens it.

I stare out the windshield, stuccoed with bright orange snakes of cheese.

"I know I should be angry," my mother whispers, dreamily

watching the baboons tearing up handfuls of grass and throwing them into the hubcap. "But I'm not. I don't know why. You'd think I might be. You'd think I'd be furious. I just can't get angry. Who would I be angry at? Tell me. Your father?"

The truck in front of us peels out, leaving us in a cloud of red dust. My mother turns the key in the ignition and steps on the gas, the car lurching forward as though it had just been too frightened to move.

I reach around the seat and put my hand up to Annabelle's lips, checking her breathing. "Thank God," I say.

"What?" my mother asks, rummaging in her purse for a pack of sugarless gum.

"That didn't just happen," Dee insists. She leans forward wrapping her arms around the headrest of my mother's seat.

"We could have been killed," I say.

"This is bad," Dee says. "Don't even say killed."

"Oh, nonsense," my mother says.

"We could have been scratched," I offer meekly. "You've heard of Ebola, haven't you?"

My mother hits the brakes again; we're all jolted forward.

"Shit. What do you want me to do, Evie?" my mother snaps. "Tell me. Tell me, please"

This kind of outburst is so uncharacteristic that both Dee and I are struck dumb. What I want is my father. That's all. I want *him.*

After a few silent moments, Dee whimpers, "I want to go home." When neither my mother nor I respond, she says, "Tell me that we're not going into that zoo."

"We're already there, you idiot," I snap at her.

"For heaven's sake, girls, stop it. We're fine," my mother

says. She rolls down her window, the hot air blowing her hair back and into her face so she can scarcely see.

In the parking lot I suddenly feel sober. Maybe it's wiping my shameful attempt at self-defense off the inside of the car with aloe baby wipes, or maybe the pot is wearing off, or maybe it's the weight of Annabelle in my arms. It's strange, but for some reason my daughter seems more manageable dressed like a bunny. As I try to slip her into the Snugli baby carrier, she wakes and, wailing, beats at the air with her fists. Her eyes run with angry tears. Please, I think, not now. Dee is still in the car, refusing to leave the backseat, her arms wrapped around her knees, staring out the smeary windows of the car like she's been through some kind of disaster. I let Annabelle scream in the hope that she'll tire herself out. I take off my sweater and wrap it around my sister's shoulders. The sun is skulking behind the trees; the banners of clouds now look like bandages.

"Dee? Hello, Dee. Come in, Dee. Do you hear me?" I shake her gently by the shoulder. Her hair is adorned with long skinny braids like a flower child's.

"What's up with Mom?" she whispers to me, her gaze fearful. "Is she nuts?"

"What do you mean?" I ask, knotting the sweater under her chin. I will entertain no talk of mutiny. No fissures of dissent will be tolerated. *We follow Mom to the death.*

My mother appears at my shoulder. "Is she all right?" she asks.

"She's just fine," I say. I flash my sister a pull-yourself-together look, then grasp my crying Annabelle's limp hand. I make her wave at her grandma, like an infant Miss America. I kiss her sticky fingers. I want to make my mother smile, but she just looks rattled.

"I can take care of this," I say. I root through the diaper bag and locate the sticky bottle of red elixir. I extract a quarter inch, pop the dropper in Annabelle's howling yap, and squeeze.

"Stop it," I coo. "Stop it, you bad, bad little girl, I want no trouble from you, no I don't." I kiss her head, the soft spot on her skull, her fontanelle, covered in sweet baby velvet. I kiss her chocolate-covered cheeks and taste her salty baby tears mingled with icing.

"Dee?" my mother says again, touching Dee's shoulder as though she's not even sure she's alive.

"I'm staying in the car, it's the only rational thing to do in this circumstance," Dee says.

"Well, we'll miss you," my mother says. Then, when Dee doesn't respond, she coos, "It will be five minutes, honey. You can watch the seals. You like the seals. You always have."

"Here," she says, sticking out her hand. "I'll hold your paw."

"All right," Dee says, getting out of the car and taking my mother's hand. "Just don't leave me anywhere."

As we enter the zoo proper we are accosted by a friendly group of giant rodents, or rather college-age volunteers dressed up as a raccoon, a rabbit, a chipmunk, and a beaver. These chipper woodland guides spend their days zealously handing out maps and offering assistance to anyone who might require it. I'm sure we look like we require assistance.

"Cease and desist," Dee says as the beaver approaches us.

Clinging to my mother, she stares down at the filthy matted paw he extends toward us. He smells of cigarettes and Brut cologne. I step up and give him a poke in the chest. "Back off, beaver," I say, as though he were a playground bully.

"There," a muffled voice says defensively, "the ladies' room." He points out the comfort station, then, looking rebuffed and dejected as only a boy in a beaver costume can look, he shuffles off to join his furry friends, who are regarding us with a keen eye, perhaps debating what airborne contagion could cause such red eyes and surliness. Is it possible all three of us could be infected?

The problem, the urgent problem that requires my mother's attention, is the dinner tables. Just how close should the tables be set up to each exhibit? The big-ticket buyers are closest to the lions and elephants, but the question is just how close they should be. A horsey-looking blonde, one of Delaware's greatest natural resources, approaches us decked out in a blue pant suit with gleaming epaulets, an outfit so garish, it must have cost a fortune. "You're here," the woman brays.

"This must violate some kind of animal-rights law," Dee says, hands on her hips. "Eating lamb chops near a lion's den—it's entrapment. You don't know what could happen. Boom."

"Ooh, you make my point perfectly," the woman says. "This is the proximity concern, Grace." The woman lowers her voice and takes my mother's arm in an attempt to draw my mother aside, but Mom won't follow her. "You see, we're not covered for such a thing as dry cleaning," she says, "or what have you."

"Excuse me?" my mother says. I wonder if Misty of Chincoteague can tell my mother is stoned, and if she can, would she tell anybody?

"Animals are messy." The woman laughs. "You see my concern, of course."

"Someone's nice suit might get trashed," my mother says, a slightly malicious tinge to her voice. "Here's an idea, perhaps everyone who paid big money to be up close could get a complimentary slicker, *no*, a *trash bag*, to wear over their clothes—how would that be?"

I know what my mother is thinking. Last Saturday night, while driving crosstown to the University Club for dinner, my father shit himself in his linen suit.

The woman stares down her nose at my mother. "Uh-huh," she says, and glances at her clipboard. "All right, then," she says, setting her equine chin, "I'll be over there with the hot-hors-d'oeuvres people."

My mother just stands there. She looks helpless—my father should be here to help her, to protect her. I wonder if my father is still at the party, sipping juleps, cracking jokes. I wonder if he bet on a winner? Is Billy driving him home; is Daddy sleeping in the car? Or is he at home, calling upstairs and down into the basement, looking for us? Waiting for us, wondering where we are? Wondering why we didn't leave a note?

"Mom," Dee says, "do it for Booster and Mr. Ha Ha."

"Ya Ya," my mother says. "Mr. Ya Ya."

"Ya. Good," Dee says.

My mother calls out to a man in overalls and starts directing him as to where to place the tables. I can tell she wants to get the hell out of here.

"Feel my head," Dee says, leaning heavily against my shoulder. She is cold and clammy, her skin cast with the palest green. Her head looks like a grape.

"You're fine," I say.

"Really?"

"Yes," I snap. "Really."

She lays the back of her hand against her forehead.

"Stop it. Nobody is sick," I say.

"I'm going back to the mother ship," Dee says. "Get it? The car. Mom's car."

"Dee, sweetie," I say, "stay," and because she is my little sister, and because she knows in her heart she'd be abandoning me and our mother, she stays.

My mother is done in ten minutes. In this time Dee and I make the executive decision to pick up beer on the way home. At least a twelve-pack. Maybe some of those Susan Anton cigarillos.

On the way out we pass Little Borneo, the future home of Mr. Ya Ya and Booster. My mother stops cold, and stares through the mesh that is draped over the fifteen-foot-tall cage. Branches are woven through the bars to give the illusion of jungle. In the back there's a little shelter made of bent-over branches, a bed of crushed-down leaves, and, up high, a concrete ledge, the pretend canopy. Everything is ready for the happy couple.

"Will I come here?" my mother asks no one in particular. "Will I ever come here?"

· · ·

On the way home, I keep thinking of my father as he was last weekend, when Billy and I visited. His back was sore, and so he asked me to wash his hair, as I'd once done a long time ago.

"You know, that shower—" he started to say, then stopped.

"No problem," I said. I wanted it to be me leaning his head into the sink, me staring dumbly as the water plastered his hair flat against his skull, me squirting baby shampoo into my hand and freezing for an instant before I dared to touch his head. A shiver of fear, then thrill, that it's me he's asked to wash his hair, me he trusts. We're that close.

I know he asked me because he knew I wanted to do it.

I know he asked me to spare my mother the hurt.

I know he was afraid he'd slip in the tub.

Afraid.

I turned off the tap and handed him a towel. I turned away as he wrapped it up like a turban.

"Lawrence of Suburbia," he'd said, striking a pose, his hand shielding his eyes as though our neighbor's rooftop satellite dish were the burning sun.

My father's car is in the driveway. Billy and my dad are out on the back deck, an empty bottle of Veuve Cliquot upside down in the ice bucket. The table in front of them is littered with red pistachio shells. Their fingertips are stained pink.

"We didn't go," my father fairly crows.

"What?" my mother says. Her eyes light on the champagne. It was supposed to be for pre-dinner cocktails. Every meal is a celebration these days, even though my father doesn't eat much. He does drink though, rolling the empty wine bottles across the dining-room floor. I haven't seen him throw a bottle off the deck since Billy's and my wedding three years ago. Back when we were all happy. I remember him standing there in a tuxedo, making a toast to Billy and me, and then hurling the bottle off the deck and into the woods, where it landed soundlessly. The way they disappeared without a trace, without a sound, made the woods seem like the sea.

"For Christ's sake, that Derby party is just old farts sitting around swapping liver-failure stories—nobody even watches the race anymore," my father says. He gets up, goes to the fridge, and gets a beer for himself and one for Billy, who leans against the railing of the deck like a sailor on leave. Dee had only made it as far as the living-room sofa.

"So what did you do?" I ask Billy.

"We went to a bar," he says. "Watched the race, had a few beers. How's Annabelle?"

"She's asleep in the garage. In the car seat, you know, not in a wheelbarrow or anything. You can go see for yourself. I was just about to bring her in."

"No, no, I'll get her," Billy says. He seems eager to escape.

"So where *was* this bar?" my mother asks, trying to sound nonchalant. She knows they got lost. She knows that my father got confused and didn't know where he was, he got angry and embarrassed and they just gave up.

"It was in Wilmington. You know, we were driving by and we saw this big-screen TV, and anyhow, it seemed like a good idea, so we parked and went in."

"Oh," my mother says, straightening up the counter, which doesn't need straightening.

"Which bar?" I ask. I too was curious.

"Bottoms Up." My father is obviously, cracking up. He tosses a nut into his mouth.

"You're joking," my mother said. "The topless place?"

"They've got a great TV." My father is obviously enjoying himself.

"You're not serious," my mother says, looking horrified. "Oh my God, you are."

Billy walks through the kitchen with Annabelle asleep in his arms. "She's really zonked," he says, hurrying through the kitchen, his head down, avoiding my mother's stare. My stare. I don't know what to think, the idea of my father and husband in a titty bar doesn't make sense. I can't picture it.

"We had a couple beers, we talked—mostly about you, of course . . ." my father says, and laughs again. His cheeks are flushed. I wonder if the cancer is in his brain.

"I'm just surprised," my mother says.

My father offers no explanation, just shrugs.

Mom looks baffled, betrayed even. It's ridiculous. You know what, I'm glad. I am so glad my father spent his afternoon doing what he pleased, I'm glad he blew off the stiffs and glad he felt footloose, like he was getting away with something. I hope he forgot. I don't think about Billy.

"So," my father says. "How was your day, ladies? Do any shoe shopping?"

"Some of us have been working," my mother snaps. "*We* had to go to Shackleford and deal with those idiots who are putting on the benefit," she says. You couldn't tell she was leaving anything out. She's good. Still, she looks wiped out, her eyes tired and bloodshot, her hair on end.

"So I guess I can assume you'll be feeling up to going tomorrow night, huh, Charles?"

"Whatever you like," he says.

He gets up slowly from his chair. "Evie," he says, "come with me into the library, I want to talk to you."

"I'm going to lie down," my mother says, her voice tight. "Then I'll make dinner, but right now, I'm lying down." She marches into the living room and flops down on the sofa across from Dee. Dee is flattened; her arms and legs sprawl out like someone has stepped on her. My mother makes a show of closing her eyes and laying her hand against her forehead. She'll be asleep in minutes.

From the foot of the stairs, I can hear Annabelle making cranky baby noises. I wonder if she's woken herself up, or if Billy woke her. I wonder how long it will be before she is crying again. Then I hear Billy start reading to her, and she is quiet.

The walls of the library are tea-colored and decorated with mounted heads of bucks and does, and loot from my parents' trips abroad. There are bronze statues of Buddha, ebony masks tufted with animal hair and straw, signifying fertility and long life, and an exotic arsenal of handsomely carved Indonesian shields streaked with tree sap, bone spears fashioned from the femurs of cassowary birds, and berry-painted blow darts. If war ever erupted in the suburbs, my parents could kick their neighbors' asses. If it weren't for the banal squeals of a police-drama car chase emanating from the living room, where both my mother and sister now lie fast asleep, you could imagine you were holed up in a tiny game lodge.

My father settles himself down at the end of the brown leather sofa.

"I'm particularly fond of that one," I say, pointing over my father's head to a shield emblazoned with the image of an irate, multifanged, knife-wielding infant.

"Huh, really?" my father says, distracted. It obviously didn't hold the same sway for him.

I sit in the middle of the sofa, close, but not too close to him.

"So," he says, smiling, hands folded in his lap. "I'm concerned, not really, but concerned a little about what you're reading to Annabelle. All this poetry is fine, but kids need stories. Real stories," he said, his eyes bright. I don't know if the gleam is from his foray into jiggle heaven or something else.

"All right," I say. "But I need a drink." He gets up and pours us both port, an old, old Sandeman he'd bought for his and Mom's thirtieth wedding anniversary. There is just a little left.

I crane my neck to stare at the wall behind my father, where our family's personal trophies hang—the bust of a stag, the head of a doe, and racks of antlers. Whenever I'd attack my father and my grandfather, old One-Shot Harry, not only for being brutal cold-blooded Bambi-annihilators, but for using their heads and horns as home decoration, my father would coolly defend himself by insisting, "It's family history." Then he'd say, "These mounted heads aren't simply glorifying the hunter's skill, honey—they're honoring the life of the animal, as well as the battle itself."

I lean my head back and stare up into the skylights my father and Billy put in last summer before Dad's neck and back started to hurt. I shift my gaze. From this vantage it looks like my father has an enormous rack of antlers. His chest seems to heave with the effort of holding them up.

"Indulge me," he says, handing me my drink and sitting down beside me. The port is sweet and plummy; it lies heavy on your tongue, coating your mouth like blood distilled with fire. "This is the story about a man who kills a bear."

"Oh, sure, that's child friendly. I see a pop-up book, with lots of blood. A scratch-and-sniff, like *Pat the Bunny: Slaughter the Bear.*"

"For Christ's sake, can't you just listen, Evie?" he says. "One time."

"By all means," I say, staring out the French doors at the deck and the woods outside.

"Okay, one day this father goes out deer hunting in the forest on the Blue Mountain with some of his buddies. He's out in the forest and somehow he gets separated from them so he's all by himself."

"Wait," I say. "Give me more details."

"Fine, he's a good man, he's got a family, a wife and two daughters."

"And?"

"And what?"

"Does he love them, do they love him, has he ever cheated on his wife, does he secretly love one of his daughters more than the other..."

My father grits his teeth. "This is my story," he says. "Let me tell it."

"Oh, please, go for it." I couldn't stop him.

"Okay, so all of a sudden, it starts to snow, and so he decides to head back. Just then, a huge grizzly bear appears in the pines in front of him. The guy is like, Oh shit. You see, no grizzly bears had been seen on the Blue Mountain in, say, a hundred years. Right then, the bear charges at him, and the man stumbles backward into a ravine, dropping his gun on the way down. Well, it looks pretty bad for him."

"I'll say. This is the part the kids go crazy for, right?"

He ignores me and takes a sip of his port. "When he comes to, he's hurt his leg in the fall, he's lost his gun, his friends don't know where he is so they can't help him, and worst of all, he's pissed off this grizzly bear, who he's sure is still in the area. The father thinks, Oh great, I'm going to die. If the bear doesn't kill me and eat me for supper, I'll starve to death in the woods. He's never been so scared in all his life. He's praying like crazy."

"Really? He suddenly gets religion, huh," I say, but my father barrels on ahead.

"Somehow, though, the father manages to crawl out of the ravine and find shelter under some low-hanging pine branches covered in snow and he builds a fire, which he knows will keep away the animals, and he eats the beef jerky and cookies his *wife* and *daughters* put in his pack, and before you know it, he falls asleep."

"He falls asleep? Doesn't he know he'll freeze to death if he falls asleep? He can't fall asleep, Daddy," I say. "Shouldn't this story at least teach Annabelle survival skills?"

"He knows it, but he can't help it. The guy is in a tremendous amount of pain, and—"

"He can't. For Christs' sake, he should think of his wife and daughters, think of how much they love him. That should keep him awake."

"He's doing what he can," my father says. "So lo and behold, in the morning the hero is still alive! He can't believe it. He thanks God. He somehow manages to crawl up the ravine and finds, as if by miracle, his gun, sticking up out of the low branches of a fir tree, and he starts to make his way home, knowing his wife and daughters are, by now, really, really worried about him. Just then, he hears a sound and turns, and sure enough, it's that damn grizzly bear again."

"Same bear or different bear?"

"Same bear."

"Is that possible?"

"Why not?" my father says. "Just let me finish, all right?" He leans closer to me. "But this time the bear is so close the hero can see his cruel black eyes and razor-sharp yellow teeth. The bear swings at him. The giant paw gashes the father's face. Just as the bear is ready to go in for the kill, the father lifts his gun and, though he can barely stand, he shoots the bear. But it keeps coming at him, so he shoots again and then again, and finally, with the last shot, the bear gives a great bellow and collapses, dead."

My father sucks in his breath, as if he can see the bear staggering and falling into the snow before him. He drinks his port.

"No one can believe how brave and lucky this guy was. Like I said, nobody'd seen a bear, let alone shot one, in these woods for a hundred years," my father says, his voice faltering a little. "Oh man, people remember this and talk about it and talk about it forever," he says, his cheeks all pink, then he pauses. "They say what a great and brave man he was, or whatever. You can make the ending good."

"Oh, am I supposed to write this all down?" I say.

"No," he says. "I will, and I thought I'd do drawings, a little pen-and-ink jobby. Or you could do the drawings. . . . "

He reaches over and grabs my foot for a second, giving it a little shake, the way he used to reach into the backseat when he was driving and grab me around the ankle and give me a squeeze, as if to tell me he hadn't forgotten I was there.

"That's not a bad story, is it? It's pretty good, I think," he says, sounding pleased with himself.

"It's not bad," I say, laying my head on his shoulder. I can smell wood smoke in his sweater and the encroaching tang of something metallic, medicinal.

"Does he apologize to his family for worrying them half to death?"

My father doesn't answer. He frowns for a moment and I wonder if he is in pain. He finishes his port and lowers the glass to the carpet. "You decide."

"You know what, Daddy? I was so afraid that when you were telling the story, you were going to have the ending be, 'And then the hunter died. That's the way these things are. Life is cruel. Nature is merciless and unpredictable.' " I can't catch my breath.

For a long moment, the library is silent, except for the wind pressing against the glass doors. He shrugs, as though the ending is out of his hands.

"Well, you don't know, it could go that way," my father says. He reaches down to pick up his port glass as though he's forgotten it's already empty.

"No," I say. "That's a shitty ending. I mean, I wouldn't tell a kid that story. What kind of story is that?"

My father straightens his back defensively. "It wouldn't mean the man wasn't brave or good, or that he shouldn't be remembered that way, does it?" my father asks. "Hey, we are talking about mortals here."

"He's the hero," I say. "Remember?"

"Yes, but he has to be real, right? Not some kind of—"

"Real doesn't last." My hand is shaking so badly, I'm afraid I'll spill, so I swallow the end of my drink.

"Listen," he says, exasperated. "You take the story, use it. Do with it what you will."

He leans over and takes my hand between his, and for an awkward moment we hold hands on the sofa, his cold hands holding my warm ones.

"It's a gift." He brushes an invisible lock of hair from my forehead. "A good father, a brave hunter out in the wild, come on, that's a character a kid would remember, isn't it?"

"Of course," I say. I don't want to fight.

"It's a good story, don't you think?" he asks me again, his eyes shining. He bends down and picks up the bottle of port. He pours some in his glass, and then mine, saving the last drops for me.

"All right, all right," I say. "It's a good story."

"I know you expect more," he says. "Listen, I would hope having gone through all this for sixteen years that I'd have developed some sense of understanding of either myself or the illness, and it's really disappointing. I don't really have anything to offer you. It's just kind of one of those things that everybody does, and I'm probably going to do it sooner than I should be, and certainly sooner than I would like to."

Slowly he gets up from the sofa, the empty bottle in hand. He kisses the top of my head, then he opens the library doors and steps out onto the deck. I watch as he raises the bottle over his head and flings it off the deck and down into the woods. From the sofa I can hear it land, hear the clink, as it finds its mate in the tall grass.

TRY

AN OUTLINE

I. Finding Out
   A. The Phone Call
   Your father says, "I have some bad news."
   You say, "No."
   You are afraid of this bad news. You've heard bad news
before, and it's never good.
   He says, "I'm afraid so."
   You say, "No, no, no."
   How long can you keep him at bay like this?

"Oh honey," your mother says. Her voice is drunk on tears. Damn her. She always takes his side. Always. Last time this happened it was the same damn thing. What about that surgical cure?

"It's bad," he says. This is how he explained the very first bout of cancer to you fourteen years ago. You were a kid. Bad meant *not good.* It did not mean *death.*

"How bad?" You imagine some pain, some unhappiness, discomfort, but life. Still, you think you feel a small tear, like fabric being ripped inside you.

"I'm probably going to die," your father says. It sounds like a bad movie written in English, translated into Chinese, then into pig Latin.

"It's already metastasized to my spine, and who knows where else," he says. "You know what that means."

"No," you say. But you've already tried this tactic.

B.   What You Do

1.   Refuse to sleep in your bed. Pull out the sofa bed and turn on the TV. Cartoons. It's after midnight. Watch cats being flattened with anvils, a mouse blown apart by a rocket. See them in the next frame, unharmed, not a scratch on them. Watch a bird set an elaborate and comical trap for a coyote, watch it work. Count down the hours until you board your train. Five hours.

2.   Wonder if there are any chimpanzees right now going under the knife in the name of lung-transplant research. Speculate that if your father were the president of the United States, somebody would do a transplant. Wonder if there are

medical mail-order catalogs where you can order lungs, flat and blue and inflatable upon arrival. Fail at strategy. Four hours.

3. Don't take chances. Take another sleeping pill.

4. Embrace unconsciousness.

2. Dealing with the Intruder

A. Wake. Wonder when you fell asleep. Wake with the word *metastasize* on your tongue fizzing in the back of your throat like an aspirin. *Metastasize, metastasize, metastasize, metastasize.* You can't stop it.

B. When you see your father he looks perfectly healthy. "Cough," you say. He shakes his head, then messes up your hair the way he used to when you told him knock-knock jokes. None of this makes sense. Back in those halcyon days of Dixie riddle cups and book reports, when you and Dad camped out every school night at the dining-room table bent over homework, he'd say, "Okay, you've got a problem. Try an outline, break it down into things you can handle. Then attack it."

When will you learn?

Introduce the option of a second opinion.

"I saw them myself, Evie," your father says as though the cancer cells were UFOs. Your father has a Ph.D. in chemistry, he believes in the power of science, he believes in his doctors. Don't rock his faith. Remember that somewhere you read that a good mental attitude is the most important weapon in the battle against disease. What the hell were you thinking by trying to get him to question his own doctor? Why not just tie his hands behind his back and push him down a flight of stairs?

Ask yourself whether you would rather have him alive and in pain for five years, or alive and pain free for one. Go for five. You are so selfish.

When you see him out watering his orchids in the greenhouse and dancing to "Jumping Jack Flash," using the hose as a microphone, realize there's been some kind of terrible, hilarious mistake. One day you'll laugh about it. *Remember that mix-up with the X rays, how we thought Dad was dying but it was actually somebody else! That was rich.*

When your father flies into a rage at your confession that you will feel lost without him, and yells at you that you better start taking your life seriously, stop wasting time, and start saving for your future, think it's the cancer talking, not him.

Think, You can't make me. Guess you'll just have to stick around. Hold my hand.

Don't say this. He looks mad enough to hit you.

When your father gets angry, back down. Talk calmly, like he's a man on a ledge about to jump; he holds his life in his hands.

The customer/dying man is always right. *Here's your paper hat and yellow blazer, welcome to suffering school!*

When he starts to tell you the story of The Bad News, how his doctor of fourteen years said, "Everything looks great. You look healthy. Seven years no cancer, that's what we call a surgical cure. Let's just pop this chest X ray up on the screen to make sure . . . ," close your eyes. When he says, "And there they were, millions of tiny cancer cells everywhere, filling my lungs, and the doctor said to me, 'Jeez, I hate to tell you this, Chas, but you're going to die. I'm so sorry,' " don't tell him he's told you this story already three times before. Wonder if he's saying it because he doesn't believe it. Does he really need to keep hearing it? Do you?

"The doctor was so upset," your mother adds. "He really likes your father."

"Well, of course he does," you say. Hate the doctor. Who is this putz? What kind of car does he drive? Mercedes, you bet it's a goddamn Mercedes.

In addition to making stupid, irritating observations like "the doctor really likes your father," your mother looks like hell. She's too skinny, she looks as breakable as a dime-store comb, but she's trying to be brave, brave and jaunty, like one of those teeny plastic swords stabbed through an orange wedge in Polynesian cocktails. Try to imagine other kinds of inanimate snappable objects your mother resembles. Your little sister, who has driven up in a pouring rain, is wearing the oversize tortoiseshell glasses that she had in high school, in lieu of her contacts. The only one who looks okay is your father. He looks great. He's in the driver's seat. You are just the terrified passengers.

"What's so weird," he says, "is I feel fine. I feel really good."

Later, he confesses that his back hurts; what he thought was the aches and pains of playing squash at fifty-five is cancer wrapped like lace around his spine. "All that helps," he says, "is alcohol, especially red wine. *Expensive* red wine." Make a note to buy red wine when you're out at the store today. Remember a goofy T-shirt you once saw, LIFE IS TOO SHORT TO DRINK BAD WINE.

I. Should you buy it?

2. Should you buy one of those baseball caps with a ponytail sewn inside it?
3. Pray that your father doesn't lose his hair.
4. Try to keep yourself from imagining his bald skull.

C. Imagine Cancer

The doctor says that visualization is very important in combating your illness. Try to imagine the cancer, the doctor says.

Space: Your father's lungs are a constellation of cancer cells. Exploding stars. Once in a blue moon, a cell will shoot like a comet across his lungs and land somewhere else in his body, someplace soft and spongy, like his kidneys, maybe. There it will burn like an asteroid.

Nature: His body is a hive of cancer with worker bees pollinating cancer cells throughout his body as if it's a garden, rubbing their cancer-covered legs up and down his spine, poisoning his vertebrae with fast-blooming tumors.

War: Cancer cells are an army of soldiers intent on taking your father's life. Colonizing his body, they plant land mines and flags, claiming body parts as their own. Blowing up vital organs that are the territory of the well body. Seizing the heart, conquering the brain.

Slapstick: Cancer cells are stainless steel ball bearings careening around his body. Somebody could slip on those and really get hurt.

Home: Cancer cells are ill-mannered houseguests who keep showing up each day with more and more children, and won't leave no matter how many Slim Whitman records you play. Cancer is a houseguest you can't get rid of without burning your home to the ground.

3.   Take Charge

A.   Write the doctor, who has your father's trust, a very angry letter, threatening that if he doesn't save your father you will make his life a nightmare. You will stalk him. Kill one of his children.

Scare yourself. Are you a good daughter or what?

B.   Fear that if you send it, the doctor will intentionally let your father die. Don't send it, but *keep* it.

C.   Go to the store and buy all your father's favorite foods. Chocolate Häagen-Dazs, hard pretzels, lard-fried potato chips, and a cheese-steak sub with fried onions and pickles. "Fat," you say to the cashier, "is no object."

Buy yourself a pack of extra-strength mentholyptus cough drops. You can't get breath anymore, your lungs feel like someone is squeezing them, flattening them like an accordion. *Lungs, the oompah organs.*

D.   Buy books about living with cancer. Do not read them, or open them.

E.   Buy all the Joseph Campbell books your credit card can suffer. If there's an answer to the question *Is there a God?* this guy likely has the answer. Never open them.

F.   Think about Dr. Linus Pauling. King of the Cs. Lived to be an old, old man. Buy a life's supply—it would seem—a thermos-sized brown jar of vitamin C with rose hips. What is a rose hip? Are there iris hips? Tulip thighs? 1000 milligrams, that's a lot of oranges. Present the vitamins as though they were frankincense and myrrh. Don't be hurt, when your father says, "Thanks," but doesn't even take one. You're not giving up. Wonder why it is that people in health food stores always look like they are sick or dying? Is it all that kelp?

    G.   *Metastasize!* It sounds like a laser shot out of the palm of a superhero.

Metastasize, it stings.

3.1   *Just Me and My Anger, Strolling down the Avenue*

    A. Hate everyone. Everyone is evil. Even babies, babies are evil because they've got their whole lives ahead of them. Stupid babies don't even know what they've got.

    Except for your baby. Your baby makes your father laugh. Your baby can stay.

    On the M14, make an argument for extinguishing nearly every life on the bus: Mean to Kids, Stares at Women's Breasts, Old and Smells Bad, Doesn't Give up Seat to Pregnant Lady, Addict, Homeless, Wouldn't Be Missed by a Soul, Tax Cheat, Likes Little Boys, Gets off on Making People Cry, Ugly Sweater, Dumb Mustache . . . until there's just you and the guy you need to drive the bus.

    B. Be short with your friends when they kindly inquire about how you are feeling. Say, "Fine." Think, Nobody wants to hear a sad story. Alone, gorge on self-pity like it's ice cream. You make yourself nauseous.

    When your best friend asks why you seem so hostile these days, say, "Oh, I don't know, I guess because my father is dying of cancer." Relish the look of horror wilting her features.

    C. Be cruel to your husband because he can't do anything right—i.e., save your father. Feel justified and comforted when your sister says her boyfriend is an asshole too.

D.   Hate everyone some more. Wonder if you can get addicted to hate. How would you come off that high, what would the cold turkey be like? Would you be forced to watch slides of Mother Teresa feeding the poor, your eyelids held open with toothpicks? Would you be considered healed, clean, if all you felt was apathy?

At night, crying in your bathtub, decide that the only people who should be allowed to live are you and your sister and your mother and father, and maybe your husband, and your sister's boyfriend, but even they have to build their own life raft.

E.   Wonder how anyone in the world can stand you, forget about like you.

F.   Wonder why it is that you have two healthy grand-fathers, both in their eighties, and your fifty-five-year-old fa-ther is toast. Are you a bad person for not even thinking twice about offering their lives to God in exchange for ten more years with your father? You're not greedy, you're not asking for twenty, just ten. Do I hear five?

Wonder how you will explain to the grandfathers that your father is dead, since neither has been told he has cancer again. How many business trips can a guy take?

Think, There's some kind of dark comedy to be formed out of all of this, but that's another story.

4.   Embrace Treatment
A.   "Basically they kill you and bring you back to life," your father says.

"Oh, is that all," you say.

B. Feel grateful when the doctor, who likes your father, respects him, gets him into a program that he really isn't eligible for because he isn't sick enough. Wonder at that. Not sick enough? That sounds good. Still, we start. Chemotherapy. Therapy—therapy—that sounds good. You are in therapy. It's a science, they say, but they're really just high-end bartenders expertly mixing chemicals, layering poisons like a pousse-café. Chemotherapy, the word sends shivers. It's what the outside world knows of cancer, the hero of cancer stories: Caped Crusader Chemotherapy and his sidekick Radiation Boy. Think of all the chemotherapy clichés. Hair loss. Vomiting. Yellow skin. Numbness. Imagine Deadly Disease Roulette: *Okay, Alex, I'll take Bloody Stools for a side effect, and spin again. Come on, Remission! Daddy loves Christmas!*

C. Offer to shave your father's head before he loses even one hair. Contemplate who you are really doing this for. Your father says, "I always did like the way I looked in a drug helmet," folding and unfolding a dark blue bandanna.

Pledge that if you do shave his head you will not cry. Pledge that you will save his hair, but not let him know. He wouldn't understand.

D. Go to the hospital and sit with your mother and father while he has a series of bags filled with various chemo concoctions, liquid hell, dripped into his veins. Say, "That's not chemo, that's antifreeze!" Don't stare at his arms, or the tubes, or all the tape they use to keep the tubes in place for eighteen hours. He looks like a bungled arts-and-crafts project from the children's wing. Don't get hurt when your father ignores you. When the nurse comes in, clipboard in hand, looking tired and bored by all this dying, say, "Oh goody, another Intoxicating Drink of Love." Your father says, "That's my daughter." Think you will never get tired of hearing your father say that. *That's my daughter.* Roll up your sleeve, slap the inside of your arm, and say, "I'll have the Zombie, no chaser, and hold the umbrella." Try to make the nurses laugh. Be nice to them, apologize for ringing the bell when they don't materialize as soon as one bag has been drained and it's time for the next. Be nice to the nurses in the hope that they will be nice to your father. Give him confidence in his treatment. Make him unafraid. Like they can save him, these white-frocked witches in their silent white rubber-soled shoes. When your father has to urinate, excuse yourself to go get a snack. Say, "Man, have I got a hankering for a microwavable cheese product hotter than the core of the earth." See the silhouette of your father behind the curtain peeing into a plastic bottle. Later, see the bottle sitting on the windowsill in the sunshine. It's chartreuse.

Try to distract your father from the cramps that keep shooting up his legs, the lava flows of nausea bubbling up his throat; try to make him laugh, but keep staring at the plastic trash receptacle for needles and other sharp objects. When he falls asleep, leave the room, it looks too much like he is dead. Make your mother come with you to the lounge to watch a soap opera. Recognize the evil temptress by her expressive eyebrows.

Wonder why the television is always on so loud in the lounge of the cancer ward.

Smile at families who look just like people you see in the supermarket, people buying cheap ground chuck and boxes of ice-cream cones in the wintertime. Everybody seems to be either in fancy sweat suits or rugby shirts. You are wearing all black, like a crow.

E. Scour New York City for a roll of an obscure English brand of large, extra-chalky, extra-strong peppermints— the only thing your father can stomach after chemotherapy. It's what keeps him from vomiting in the car. It allows him time to get upstairs and vomit in his own toilet. Consider this a triumph.

Remember:

Just last summer your father was mistaken for a movie star in a third-world country. The proprietor of a Thai restaurant took a Polaroid and insisted on an autograph. Your father protested, then went along with the ruse. He purposefully misspelled the star's name, *Warren Batty*. He rolls his eyes when he tells you this. Your father pretends to be no one but who he is. Wonder, if he was that movie star, would the doctors be breaking their humps to save him?

Remember:

The doctor has said that right now your father's cancer is sluggish. You never know with cancer, the doctor says. Think of lazy, recalcitrant Boy Scouts ambling in the wilderness of your father's body, up the path of his spine, poking his organs with sticks as though they were torturing frogs, carelessly spilling cancer seeds everywhere.

Remember:

Your father has beaten cancer before. He's been in remission on and off for fourteen years. He is unstoppable. Superman. Everyone should just remember that.

F. Your father can't sit down to eat his birthday dinner,

his back is in too much pain. He stands, palms pressed to his lower back, and stares down at the table frowning, not touching his plate of duck à l'orange and steamed asparagus. Nothing tastes good. He picks up his wine, sucks at the glass. His skin is as yellow as old newspaper; he is going deaf from the drugs. Still, he is hopeful. At your father's insistence, your mother has bought napkins and balloons that have the number 77 on them. Your father insists that you are all celebrating his seventy-seventh birthday, not his fifty-fifth. This is supposed to make life make sense.

Your father has beaten cancer before. Everyone should just remember that.

Your sister looks at you across the table, spits a mouthful of food into her napkin, and asks to be excused. Her skin is gray. Even her eyes look gray. Wonder if she even swallows her food anymore, how big the masticated food ball in her hand has to get for her to start a new napkin.

"It's strange," your father says, "but I'm not angry. I guess I should be, but I'm not."

Pat his arm and say, "Don't worry, I've got enough anger for the two of us."

In truth, your father has rages too painful to recall, spitting out hurtful things in a voice that isn't his own. He makes jokes about the men he imagines your mother having sex with after he's dead. The doctors tell my mother it could be the cancer attacking his brain, or all the steroids he's on. Sometimes your father looks like he could rip a phone book in half. When he is angry, try to make yourself small, try to speak slowly and softly like you're trying to charm a grizzly bear or an angry weight lifter.

Your father has beaten cancer before. Everyone should just remember that.

5. The Holidays
    A. Get Through Them
      1. Buy ridiculously lavish gifts for family members
      2. Drink: Aperitifs, after-dinner drinks, beer, Bloody Marys, champagne, egg nog out of a carton, glog, red wine, shots of Aquavit, shots of tequila, a shot every so often.
      3. Hang on to your father like he's a fancy purse you're afraid of leaving somewhere, something that could be stolen.

6. When Treatment Number One Fails
    A. Wonder who in the hell it saves. Have you seen these wonder patients or their families in the hospital? Do they have kids? Do their kids even like them?
    B. Try not to grimace when your father says (a little too loudly, for he's quite deaf now), *I WANT TO KEEP TRY-ING.* Your father clings to science like religion.
    C. Try to stay *positive.* Be encouraged when you hear from a woman in the waiting room that her husband, who is ten years older than your father, has been taking a drug made from the sap of some rain-forest tree and it's cleared up his brain cancer, as though it were just a bad strain of acne.

Try to remember at what rate the rain forest is being depleted. Should you send Sting a check?
    D. Contemplate Eastern remedies, even though you feel

like you are settling for the first runner-up, the hunchbacked bridesmaid.

    I.   Acupuncture, attacking cancer with long, blade-sharp pins, like cancer cells are fat caterpillars you could stab to a card, and bleed.

    2.   Think that all of those Buddhas your parents have collected over the years can't hurt.

    3.   Wonder if sacrifices really work. What does God like? Do I know any virgins?

E.   When people say, "You should be thankful that you've had this much time together," wish a pox on their house. Tell them your father has beaten cancer before. Everyone should just remember that.

F.   Wonder why your own back hurts, why your arm is numb, why your entire body aches as though you've been beaten up and down with baseball bats. Monkey see monkey do. *What did you say?* If your father jumped off a cliff, would you? *Come again?*

What are you missing?

G.   Fantasize about your father dying. Never at home or in a hospital. It is always quick, painless, and exotic, quite possibly on vacation. Your father deserves a remarkable death. No bedsores. No bedpans. No bed at all. A wild passing. Every time your parents take a trip you pray:

    I.   Your father is eaten by a lion while on safari in Africa.

    2.   Your father is eaten by a shark while diving in Indonesia.

    3.   Your father is eaten by an unnamed beast that

will prowl/swim/thunder around with him in it's belly, so he will live eternally.

H. What can you do about this eternity thing?

I. Remember being sixteen and wanting to kill your father for not letting you borrow the car one Saturday night. You imagined incredible violence. A gun, an ax, a rope, a club, a hacksaw, a table saw, a vat of acid. You didn't have enough hands for all the ways you wanted to kill him.

J. Fantasize about your father dying again. This time he is bedridden, blind, drooling, and wasted on morphine. He can hardly speak, but he touches your hand and his lips mouth, *I, love, you.* You are selfish enough to choose this.

K. Fantasize about your father growing old. That is the most impossible thing you could pray for.

7. The Second Go-Round

A. Suspect that the doctor who likes your father is only continuing to treat him because he's known him for fourteen years; your father *was* his success story. Maybe he just wants him to have hope. Perhaps it's a favor. When your father complains, "This new treatment is shit. It isn't making me sick enough to possibly be doing any good," be afraid.

B. Your father calls to you from the back porch, where he is sitting in a kitchen chair clipping the branches of a bonsai tree and wrapping the amputated limbs with copper wire, bending them into the position of branches being blown in a gale-force wind. This is his new hobby.

"Come talk to me," he says, gesturing at the porch steps. He is wearing moccasins without socks; his ankles are knobs; his skin looks shiny and white, like bark on a birch sapling.

"People expect that I'm gaining some kind of wisdom or insight through dying, but jeez I'm not," he says, pruning the new growth of a blue spruce. He has told me all this before. "I don't have the answers." He laughs and uses his sleeve to mop the sweat that drips from his brow. "Right now, at this point in your life you know as much as I do, sweetheart." Is he trying to tell you that you can live without him? He has no idea what he is talking about. Wonder why you have to psychoanalyze everything your father says. It's exhausting.

Your father has beaten cancer before. Everyone should just remember that.

8.   Father in the City

A.   For the first time your father comes to a gallery show. A rinky-dink group show in the Village. You are nervous. You've done very delicate, very small pencil drawings of animals and women, intentionally childlike and sexually fraught. You feel self-conscious. He peers at a dark scribble of pubic hair. You want him to be proud of you. He looks at you, and he smiles, sweat rolling down his face, dampening his collar. You told him he didn't need to come to this one, that there would be other shows, shows when he didn't feel so bad, but he insisted.

Afterward, he is weak with hunger. He can't eat the five-dollar chocolate bar you bought him at Dean & DeLuca; it makes his gums bleed. You climb into a cab; he closes his eyes and lays his head back against the seat. You wonder if you could chew the chocolate up like a mother bird and feed it to him. He's your father. He would do that for you.

You go out to dinner, he just drinks wine, he takes your hand. "I'm proud of you," he says. You cry, big hiccuping baby tears.

Finally, the two of you are getting somewhere.

B.   At home he can't get out of his jeans fast enough and he shits on the floor of your bathroom. You don't see this happen, you smell it. A smell worse than shit, like death. Behind your bedroom door you laugh and laugh, then feel as though you will vomit. Your father doesn't seem embarrassed, but he doesn't want you to know, your mother tells you this as she carries his clothes downstairs to the washing machine. You can't forget that smell.

C.   Your father is in sky-blue pajamas, in bed on your pullout couch. On his chest is a paperback book; he's recently become interested in maritime novels. Your mother is reading a fashion magazine beside him. When you bend down to kiss him good night, he holds your face between his hands and kisses you on the mouth. He tells you, "Sleep well."

You say, "I will. I love you."

"Good girl," he says, and goes back to reading his book.

You say, "Wake me in the morning before you leave."

Your mother says, "You need your sleep, sweetie."

Your father says nothing. In the morning, you hear the rustling of your parents in the other room. You think, Get up. Your body says, You said your good-byes. Then you hear the door gently close. They don't want to wake you.

9.   Come to Me Now

A.   The Phone Call

Your mother says, "Your father is in the hospital, he dropped a glass this morning, and—"

You interrupt her. "Boy, you sure know how to punish a guy."

Your mother laughs a little. "He didn't feel well—it's probably coming off all those steroids—so I drove him up here. Why not."

You say, "I'm coming down."

Your mother says, "No, I don't think that's necessary. Wait. You know, sometime in the future I'm going to need you to come down and help, but I think we're okay. I want to save my favors, okay?"

You are not convinced everything is all right. Why didn't your father call?

Your mother calls back half an hour later, frantic. "Your father is deteriorating," she says. "The doctors say come now." You don't believe there is reason to be panicked. It's just the first of many frightening and sick-making steps we will take down the steep slope of sickness, until we're forced to walk into the sea of it.

B. The Car Ride

You put your suitcase in the car. You didn't know what to pack. You packed shorts and T-shirts, a silk nightgown, lots of underwear, and no socks. You packed a pair of high heels, and some sneakers. You've packed for the beach, or a honeymoon. Your husband drives. The baby sleeps in her car seat. Sitting in traffic, the cords in his neck pop out and vibrate with his swearing. "Shit. God damn it, people. Come on. Come on. Let's get a move on here."

You don't know why he is so testy. He drives up on the shoulder. People stare. Children strain against seat belts to catch a glimpse of you.

"Settle down," you say. "Everything is going to be all right. Daddy's just dehydrated from treatment. For Christ's sake, who wouldn't be?"

Look at all the cars driving over the George Washington Bridge, look at how the sunlight bounces off the silver girders, look at all the people, if your father was dead none of this could be happening. The sun would be blotted out, the world tipping on its axis.

Tell your husband, "My father wouldn't die without me."

Remember the sound of the lock tumbling in the door when they left. Your father wouldn't just slip out of your life like some thief.

"He would wait," you say. "He loves me," you say, feeling yourself getting angry, light-headed with rage. Your husband says nothing. Your goddamn husband can't even make small talk with you. He is driving eighty miles an hour, like it's some kind of race.

Insist that your husband pull into a rest stop so you can go to the bathroom and put on fresh lipstick so you'll look pretty for your father. Look at yourself in the restroom's warped mirror. Think, That is the face of a daughter. The fact that you can stop and urinate and put on lipstick is proof your father is alive. Press your lips together. You couldn't do this if he were dead. As you cross the Pennsylvania state line, wonder, Did he just die? Think you are crazy. Wish you were the kind of person who is so sensitive she would know such a thing.

You remember the sound of the lock tumbling in the door when they left.

C. The Hospital

Your mother meets you in the hall. She is wearing blue

jeans, brown moccasins, and a short-sleeved orange sweater. You've always hated that orange sweater. Around her neck is the gold necklace your father bought her on their last trip to Thailand. It looks so yellow to you. Your mother takes your hands—she's just had her nails done—she smiles at you, she looks sorry. Her eyes are red and swimming behind her glasses. Her mouth opens and she says, "Honey, your daddy is dead."

You fall to the floor. You are not a fainter, you are not a faller—what would your father, lying there in the next room, say?—but you lie there C-shaped on the cool floor, eyes closed, a snail. Your mother kneels beside you, you feel her hand on your hip. "Oh, honey," she says. A nurse comes with smelling salts, the floor is moving under you, you don't want to get up. Stand up. Hold on to your head as though it's loose, a button barely hanging by a thread.

"I'm sorry," your mother says, wiping your eyes, "about the way he looks. I asked the doctors, I told them my daughter is coming, I don't want her to see her father looking like this, but they said there wasn't much they could do."

You see him in the bed. He's twisted on his side, contorted in pain, his left arm reaches up over his head. His mouth hangs open. His head is tilted up. He looks frightened, like he's trying to crawl away. His eyes are rolled up in his head, either in surprise or pain. You want to believe the look is the recognition of God, not agony and disbelief. You're supposed to see his body and think this is some sign that he couldn't wait for you—*Look*, he's saying, *my life was taken*—but you can't believe it.

How could he leave without saying good-bye?

Stand there and look at him. Touch his skin. Be surprised

at how very cold he is. Just like they say in the movies. Pull the sheets up over his chest, under his chin. This is the first and last time you will ever tuck your father into bed. Kiss his forehead. Touch his cheek, it doesn't feel like his cheek. Hate this. Stand for a second in the room. It's big, just one bed, with a window looking out on a brick wall, swathed with orange and red curtains, a private dying room. Stand very still, see if you can feel his soul hovering in the room, some sense of spirit; Come to me now, you think, but there's nothing there. Not one fucking thing. All you hear is the low roar of the air conditioner. The nurses are talking as you leave. As you pass, they say in unison, "We're so sorry."

Don't want them to feel bad for you.

Your mother is wearing your father's wedding ring under her wedding band. She's also got his watch on, she's wearing two watches, like she's living in two separate time zones, the living and the dead.

D.   In the parking garage, the car won't start. The battery is dead. Laugh. Realize the car just isn't in *park*. Feel robbed of a good metaphor. There's no fitting end to the anecdote.

10.   Home

A.   Your sister is waiting outside in the driveway. By the time your mother tracked her down your father was already gone. She has already been in the house and made up your parents' bed, cleaned up the broken glass. She couldn't stand to be in that house alone.

Inside, you go through the house with your mother, a white tornado with a trash bag.

"I want all this shit gone," she says, throwing out can

after can of Ensure vitamin shakes, all of his drugs and pain-killers, morphine, hydrocodone, Valium, Gaviscon, Titralac, cortisone cream, Aveeno oatmeal bath, extra-extra-strong peppermints, it all goes into the trash, every goddamn thing that says cancer.

Your mother throws out death. She bags it all up and carries it to the curb. It should weigh a ton. Your mother throws out death, but hours later there it is, still sitting out there by the road. You go outside, pick up the poisonous bag, and move it down the street to the edge of your neighbor's driveway, where you leave it. You walk away. But you can't do it. You drag the bag back up the street and leave it in front of your house, where it sits, looking cursed and lonely, until morning.

A poll is taken and it is determined that no one has eaten in twelve hours, so you order a pizza, you order pepperoni with green peppers, which is your father's favorite, and no one else's. You pick all the pepperoni off, your sister pulls off the green peppers. Your mother isn't hungry. Your father is dead and there is still pizza delivery. Wonder if you should have told the delivery boy your father just died; would he have given you a discount?

B. People are drawn to the house like flies. They light down and sob. You cry with them for a while, listen while your mother recounts the day, the broken glass, the drive there—your father not speaking—how fast it all went wrong. You pour wine, you mix drinks, you pass out tissues. Be hugged, hug back. Find it interesting to see how different people look when they are crying. There are little bits of tissue clinging to your neighbor's stubble. Your mother's best friend has large purple splotches on her face, so her face resembles a globe with the African continent right between her eyes. Notice that some people look really terrible, while others are enhanced. As the people leave, they say: "Next time I'll bring a meal." "It's so unreal." "Take care of your mother." "Anything you need, you call." "There was no one in the world like your father."

No shit.

C.   Notice that out back, a white water lily has bloomed in the lower pond. Wonder if this is your father's soul. How did it beat you home? Wish you believed all that psychic bullshit. Wish you believed anything. Stand out on the back deck your father built and wait, wait for him to show himself to you. To put his ghost hands on your shoulders. One last kiss. Did he not love you best?

No. No he did not.

D.   Go down into the basement to be alone. Rest your head on the washing machine. See your father's boots (boots you see on his feet when you imagine him, when you *can* imagine him) under the workbench, which is still scattered with tools left out mid-project, a bookcase for his almost-one-year-old granddaughter, your daughter. Your father made dollhouses, bird boxes, and chairs, but this bookcase, which would once have taken a weekend for him to bang together, was too much to accomplish in six months. Hammers, screwdrivers, wrenches, a jeweler's saw—his prints are on everything, but nothing holds any warmth. You wonder what he touched last. Is his smell anywhere in this house?

E.   When the people finally go, insist your mother take a Xanax so she can sleep. Put it in her mouth, lay it on her tongue, and make her swallow it with wine. She lets you lead her upstairs like a little kid. Sleep in your parents' bed with your sister and mother, your legs all tangled together. Every time you wake up, your sister is awake and looking back at you. Do you look as empty as she does? You think about how you are sleeping on the same sheets your father slept on last night. You think that it is almost certain that your mother is going to die in the middle of the night. Perhaps from that pill you gave her. It could happen, couldn't it? Keep checking her breathing. Kiss her forehead. Remember all those stories you've heard about people in love dying within hours of each other. Think, There is no other couple as in love as my parents are. Were.

F. When you wake, think, Every day for the rest of my life the first thing I will think when I wake is, My father is dead. My father is dead. My father is dead. It still doesn't seem real. You say it out loud. "My father is dead."

You are a fatherless daughter.

II. Here's the Funeral

A. Buy a dress at the mall suitable for a funeral, something dark and mournful but with flowers. Your father loved flowers. Buy a dress that feels disposable. You will never wear it again. When the salesman says, "That looks nice on you," you say, "Does it matter?"

B. Before the memorial service you go to the funeral home to see your father one last time. He looks like a stranger. He looks like his driver's-license photo, only worse. His hair is brushed straight back and there is dirt under his nails from his bonsai class the night before. This would piss him off. He would hate being immortalized with dirt under his nails.

Wonder: Would you rather remember him twisted in pain and horror in the hospital bed, or peaceful and plastic? Choose pain.

Open a bottle of sake you've snuck in and make toasts to your father. Ask him, Dad, why aren't you drinking? Laugh uproariously. One by one, step up to the casket to be alone one last time with your father, step up and say your good-byes. You stand there and think, *Okay, this isn't funny. Get up. How could you do this to me? How could you leave me alone in this world? I will never forgive you, you know that.*

On his chest place a box of sake, in his lapel an oncidium from his greenhouse, in his breast pocket his passport. In his coat pocket your mother hides a pair of her bikini under-pants—she always used to pack a pair in his suitcase when he went on business trips.

"You know, your father believed he was going on an incredible adventure," she says, facing her children. "Death was just another trip."

Sure, except it's one way and postcard delivery is a bitch.

No one says anything.

C.   At the church, gather in the vestry and peek out the window at all the people filing up the walk and into the church, it's like the pre-awards show for the Oscars. You don't even know half of them, but they look important. Your mother is doing color commentary: Oh my gosh, I never thought they'd come. Well, how nice. That would make your father happy. She is touched. The minister says, "I can't remember there ever being this many people here for a memorial service." Think that he's thinking, Especially somebody who rarely went to church. Think, Man, imagine if Dad was a churchgoer, we'd have packed this place.

Stand and speak at the service. Talk about dancing with your father. You feel your father's hands on your shoulders. Or want to feel them. Want to hear, *You done good, kid.* Think you hear it.

D.   At the reception at your house think how it was all the same people at your wedding. Your best friend, your father's old lab partner. At some point in the evening, it's hard to tell it's a memorial service. Everyone is getting smashed. You hear stories. Your father was the best friend to so many people. Toasts are made, glasses are raised over and over to your father, a wine bottle is hurled off the back deck in his memory. Everybody stays too long, then goes home. There's so much food.

Sit on the kitchen floor and break plastic forks, spoons, and knives. Break every single one. Every time there's a satisfying snap, and a satisfying sting; your palms are getting red. Your mother and sister laugh and leave you alone. Wish you'd broken all this plastic cutlery before the guests arrived.

12.   Ashes

A.   Have your father cremated without having any clue if this is what he wanted. Your parents never discussed this. Think this is odd. Think it makes sense. When you pick up his ashes at the crematorium, be shocked at how heavy the brass urn is. Say *Urn, urn, urn* . . . You sound like a constipated goat. Strap your father's ashes into the backseat with the seat belt. Before you go into the liquor store, lock all the car doors and ask your mother, "Should we leave the radio on for Dad?" Be afraid to look at his ashes. Curious, but afraid.

13. Home Is Where You Are

A.   You don't need to think anything at all to cry, it just happens, caused by nothing, it's a sickness, it's organic to who you are, you cry. Some people have rashes, or tics, you cry, always, steadily. Asked to give one word to describe yourself, you say, *Constant.*

If you stop remembering, you are afraid you will forget. You must be the constant daughter. You thought when your father died, you would die too. You have no plan for living with this.

When people ask you, "How do you deal?," joke, "Grief is like arsenic—you only swallow as much as you can without it killing you."

Your back aches, your arm is numb, you can't breathe, you can't hear, you have sores in your mouth, on your tongue, it hurts to swallow, you can barely lift your head, your pulse has slowed, you are sure you are dying. Your body is thrumming with disease.

B.   Take baths. Take baths at midnight. Notice in the tub that there is a delicate, almost infinitesimal spray of shit on your white shower curtain. Your father's shit. You don't ever want to wash that shower curtain. Wonder if this means you are some kind of freak. Smell the spot. Smell nothing.

C.   Don't sleep. Watch nature shows. Just the late-night stuff. Animal-kingdom porn. Sex and death. Watch gazelles running as if in high heels across the Serengeti plains, watch the cheetah bob and weave, know the cheetah is going to win, watch anyway. Watch the gazelle stumble, get taken down hard and ripped apart like a sandwich. The blood on the cheetah's mouth looks like lipstick. You like to see this.

D.   Feel so angry all the time, you think you could kill a man with your bare hands and a ballpoint pen.

E.   Wonder if that it-gets-better-after-a-year marker is really true.

F.   Try to read *When Bad Things Happen to Good People*, think it's a bunch of shit. Get angrier.

G.   Ask God Questions

"What the hell is your problem?" You could give him/ her a list of people who *deserved* to die. "Come on, you watch the news, you're omnipotent, why him?"

H.   Ask Your Father Questions

"What the hell is your problem? You don't call. You don't write. Didn't you ever love me?"

13.   Ashes II

A.   You find yourself alone in your parents' bedroom with the urn, which sits on your father's nightstand. You sit on the side of the bed that your mother never sleeps on, indeed the side that never even gets untucked, so it must still feel as though there is a presence there, a lack of open space for a body to move into. No void. You pull the brass stopper out and peer inside. The brass casts a peachy light on the gray talcum-fine ash; the bits of burned white bone look like miniature marshmallows in pale cocoa. What would happen if you added water, would you get a paste? Some kind of cement?

B.   You can look at the ashes, you can shake them, you

can touch your fingertip to a hill of ash and feel it cling there. You can wonder if your father would think this is sacrilegious, disgusting. If he would care at all. You think he would be displeased. Your heart is pounding as though you're stealing, which perhaps you are. You can stick your hand down inside the urn, stick your index finger deep in the mound of ashes, right up to your knuckle. You wait to feel something. You want to feel something other than emptiness and pain. Before anyone can come upstairs and discover you with your hand in your father's urn, you can pull out, rub your thumb and fore-finger together, rub the ashes off the pads of your fingers and back into the urn where they, or he, belongs.

No, no, you don't do that.

C. Instead you do this: you lick your finger and stick it deep in the urn, then you stick that finger, coated with your father's ashes, into your mouth. You press that finger to your tongue and wait for it to kill you, but you don't even gag. You swoon. The ashes are gritty as sand, they fill your mouth, then, as you swallow, they cling to the back of your throat. Little bits of bone grind between your teeth like boulders, then dissolve into a gray stripe on your tongue. Evidence. You wonder how you could ever explain this to anyone. Or explain that you want to keep doing it, you want to keep doing it to see if it keeps horrifying you. Maybe you will learn something this time. Maybe your pain will be replaced with something else. Maybe you will be saved. You plunge your hand back in, and hold him in your fist, you can't get enough of his ashes in you. You shouldn't be left alone with this urn. You cannot trust yourself not to eat the entire thing.

IN HEAVEN,

DEAD FATHERS

NEVER STOP

DANCING

On the first anniversary of my father's death, when the phone rang for the fourth time in an hour and the caller didn't leave a message, it occurred to me that the caller was the boy I was flirting with earlier at the Cinnabon stand in the Christiana Mall. What could I say, I was starving.

Luckily, my mother rarely answered the phone these days. When she did, and she got a salesman, she seemed to take delight in saying, "Mr. Wakefield can't come to the phone— he's dead." "Mr. Wakefield isn't interested in an Acapulco vacation, he's dead." "Mr. Wakefield can't take part in the March of Dimes walkathon, he's dead."

Was it possible? No. Maybe. Maybe that incredibly cute guy was calling me! My hands were all trembly, despite the Xanax I'd popped after getting home from the mall. I helped Billy buckle Annabelle in her car seat for a trip to the playground. Billy ought to be a hit with the local moms in his teal Hawaiian shirt, holey black jeans, and motorcycle boots, his dark hair standing up on top, still damp from the shower. He'd actually gone for a jog this morning. Anything to get away from us.

"Are you all right?" he asked, as much out of habit as anything. He asked this so often he sounded tired out by it.

"Go, have fun. Yes, I'll be just fine here. I'm with my mother and sister, for heaven's sake." I kissed the top of Annabelle's head ten times. "Your mother loves you. Give me a head bonk." She leaned toward me and we bonked the top of our foreheads together.

"Okay, vamoose, you two."

I felt like some giddy fifteen-year-old again, trying to get rid of my mom and dad before some bad boy in his parents' car showed up to drink Bud and make out to Led Zepplin records.

"Is this okay, me taking Annabelle like this? I thought you and your mom and sister might like to be alone, have some space, talk," Billy said, sliding into the driver's seat.

"But if you think her presence might help Mom, you know, distract her..."

"Go," I said, shutting the car door for him.

Next time the phone rang I would just answer it, and in my best French accent, I'd tell the Cinnabon boy he had zee wrong number.

On the first anniversary of my father's death, we didn't look at pictures, or plant a tree, or release butterflies, we didn't bury Dad's ashes on the Blue Mountain where he grew up (so far to drive, let's not waste them), or even sit around and watch Dad on television, even though my mother had a stack of videos, most taken from Japanese board meetings. There are hours of my father scratching his ear with a pen, doodling boxes and arrows (none of his trademark orchids or naked women), the sound was bad, as it always is when he tries to talk in my dreams—like he's scrambling his voice so nobody but me can understand, but I never understand it. Here, you could hear him cracking wise about dinner the night before at a sushi bar where a live fish was pinned down on a tatami board and filleted to death.

"Fresh enough for you?" he says.

Hot enough for you?

Mom turned these videos on like background noise. She knew every chair scrape and every cough. It was the most boring surveillance footage you could imagine. Spying on Daddy living. Sometimes my mother would just stick one in, then go off and clean, or do yoga, or talk on the phone, and the tape would run but nobody would be watching it. Then you'd hear that laugh, my father's laugh, and it would freeze you, and there he was, my three-inch-high daddy sitting in that fluorescent-lit conference room, again and again, in hell it appeared, and none of us was paying any attention.

There was no clean way to do mourning.

On the morning of the first anniversary of my father's death, my mother, my sister, Annabelle, and I went to the mall. There would be no crying or tearing of hair for us. No banquet, no light show, no speeches—no indeedy. Just shopping. And what do you buy when you're mourning? Diamond stud earrings. Yep, expensive studs—such a bold, *we're really living now* statement, right? We were living high on the h-o-g, like a bunch of nighttime-soap-opera heroines. *Falcon Crest* bitches, get out of our way.

It took about fifteen minutes. We picked, we pointed, we paid. It was exhilarating, in a strangely joyless way.

"Wouldn't your father love this?" my mother said, handing over her credit card. "Wouldn't he be proud?"

"Now we've got something to remember this day by," Dee says. She kisses our mother's cheek. I do too.

Like, who could forget.

I went into my mother's handbag and found the ubiquitous pack of sugarless gum. I felt nauseous.

While my mother and Dee were in the bathroom changing Annabelle's diaper—"It's a novelty for us," they insisted—I slipped in my new studs, then ambled over to the Cinnabon stand. As I was paying for a sticky bag of twelve cinnamon rolls—what can I say, I was out of control—I saw a boy from out of my past. Not really, I mean he was the sort of boy who'd have sent my panties into a twist years ago.

The girl behind the counter smiled at him, flashing him a blinding wealth of orthodontia. He smiled back. I wanted him.

He was just my type. One of those precious, slightly arrogant boys who look as though they could have been raised by wolves, sensitive and a little mean, with dark brown eyes, a straight, prominent nose, and shaggy blondish-brown hair that hung in his face, so he had to keep brushing it out of his eyes. He was wearing a Hang Ten T-shirt, dark blue Levi's, and Vans. I think he was really, really stoned.

I wanted him. I made a deal with myself: if he talked to me, it was meant to be. Kismet. You could never guess what the gears of destiny were churning out for you. At seventeen I believed in kismet. Here, today, in the food court of the Christiana Mall with Grotto's Pizza, Arby's, and Mr. Steak, I believed in kismet.

I asked him for a cigarette, and somehow—I haven't smoked in years—executed a French inhale without choking to death. For some reason, men think this means you give good head—that, and being able to tie a cherry stem with your tongue.

He smiled. He was checking me out. This boy who had not suffered one day in his life.

I prayed my mother and sister and daughter wouldn't come back from the bathroom just yet, for it occurred to me how no one thinks I'm beautiful anymore. How even if Billy tells me I'm beautiful I think he's full of shit. He just wants to get laid. But here, this boy thought I was hot.

How incredibly pissed off would my father be if he could see me now?

Wasn't that too fucking bad.

I inhaled, felt the smoke swirling under my nostrils. Why had I stopped smoking?

I wasn't me anymore. I was someone else. I wasn't some old married woman with a kid, going into a power slide toward thirty. Suddenly, all I wanted to do was for this boy to go down on me in the backseat of his car. His friend's car. I didn't care.

It was morning. Ten o'clock in the morning, and already my life had changed. Anything could happen.

"So, you at the U of D?" he asked, licking a piece of tobacco off his lip.

"Nope."

I smoked. This is a boy girls throw themselves at, I thought. I checked his sneakers for lip gloss.

"You work in the mall?"

"Nope."

If you can't be scintillating, be mysterious. Always say no. Men want what they think they can't have.

"So, how would a person find you?" he asked, as though he couldn't care less.

"A person, or you?"

"Me."

His name was Dean. I wanted to chew on that Dean boy's mouth. I wondered if he would want to make out for a long time, or if we could just get to the good part. If I were seventeen I'd make him wait, and wait, I'd grind my pelvis into his groin, and then I wouldn't sleep with him, and then we'd break up. I'd leave him wanting me. Then, months later, we'd get back together, I'd sleep with him, and then we'd break up again. But no more, this boy was going to get lucky. I bet the girls he'd been with didn't even swallow.

Because I wasn't me, and because my whole body was just jazzed and ready to ride, I scribbled down my mother's phone number on the back of a Cinnabon napkin. What was the harm? Dean was stoned, and that kind of boy never called. As he walked away—he had almost no butt!—my hands started to shake. How did he miss that wedding band?

He wasn't yet old enough to even think of checking out the left hand.

I was asking to be struck down. Watching him give some girl at the piercing pagoda the high sign, I wished I'd at least kissed him. It didn't matter what I did.

On the first anniversary of my father's death, in the bra department of Macy's, I looked at underwear and wondered what Dean would like—a tiger-striped G-string, a black garter belt—compared to what Billy liked—anything white, girlish, and defilable.

Dee bought lingerie, a dark blue teddy, a long pink negligee, some white lace tap pants, and a pair of mules with a pom of pink feathers. We egged her on. As she paid, my mother told us a woman from her yoga class wanted to fix her up with some widower who, like my father, also "liked plants."

"Some old fart," my mother said, turning her back on her image reflected from four angles in a set of mirrors. "Can you imagine?" She laughed her widow's laugh. "He likes plants! I bet he's got one of those, what did your father call them? You know, Ev."

I did know.

"The amazing potted closet fern. Grows in the dark, needs very little sun or water. You can't kill it. Indestructible. Great for nursing homes, dorm rooms, and bomb shelters."

"Exactly." She smiled broadly. "See, that isn't lost."

It is my job to remember. Word for word, in my father's voice whenever possible.

My mother is obsessed with what has been lost since my father died. Information. Like the name of a restaurant they'd visited in Turkey, a kind of blue stone a Sherpa in Nepal had showed them, the title of a jazz song they'd heard in a club in Chicago and then listened to all the time in graduate school.

What is definitely lost is my mother's hair. It was one of the first things to go. For the past year my mother had been getting her hair cut at a beauty school that practiced on convicts, the criminally insane, and old people. Her wild honey-colored curls had been chopped off in favor of an undyed, dour brown dome that resembled a hacked-up hedgehog. This hair fairly bellowed, Don't even think about it!

"Mom, how are *you* set for underwear?" I asked, then felt like a jerk.

Dee pretended I hadn't said anything. She smiled at the cashier. My sister wanted the cashier to like her. My sister put that cashier's smile in her little wallet like a penny for a rainy day. My sister had her eyes on the future.

At Christmastime, Mom had really thrown down the suffering gauntlet while we were disposing of the figgie pudding—drunkenly flinging it off the back deck and into the woods, where we'd decided Dad's spirit resided. Mid-fling, her blouse came untucked and I could see the white waistband of her underwear sticking out. My father's underwear, a pair of old white BVDs.

She had seen me staring, and sort of laughed.

"Mine are dirty."

"Yikes," I said. "Is the creek frozen, or did the washing machine crap out?"

"Mother," Dee said. She shook her head, her mouth pulled down into an exaggerated frown. "This is not good."

"Who would know?" she said, and shrugged, tucking the elastic waistband back down inside her skirt.

"Oh, okay, Mom," I said. I looked at her for bunchiness. Could you make out the crotch? Had anyone else noticed, were people whispering?

"I wear it to garden in," Mom explained. "Puttering."

Dee grimaced. She looked like she wanted to shake my mother.

"Sure," I say. "Is that all? Puttering? And by the way, it's December . . ."

She shrugged. That's all. I couldn't possibly compete.

On the first anniversary of my father's death, my sister, Dee, announced she was a Jew. Secretly, in her heart, where it mattered most.

None of us mentioned the man that she'd started dating after my father died, or the fact that he was Jewish. He was a partner in the firm she worked for in Philadelphia, an unreasonably pretty man, who wore one of those big heavy gold signet rings that screams good school, good breeding, and does double duty for wax-sealing important documents. He liked to go hang-gliding on weekends. He didn't laugh at my jokes. He held Dee's hand like she needed protecting, and kissed her fingers when he didn't think we were watching.

My mother took the news well. She just blinked, as if the news that her Presbyterian daughter was now a Jew was a stone being throne at a rhino; it bounced harmlessly off her armored skin.

As my mother drove us home from the mall, my sister read us the Kaddish, the prayer for the dead. Every day for a year you say the prayer and mourn. Dee had a Daily Prayer Book in her handbag. I wondered why she'd taken it to the mall. She half read, half recited it. Her voice rising on the part "He who creates peace in his celestial heights, may he in his mercy create peace for us and for all Israel; and say Amen."

"How nice," my mother said.

"You see," Dee said, "we have nothing like that, no official prayer or mourning period. Our religion is inadequate," she explained in her proud and zingy defensive-attorney voice. "You yourself have said it's unreasonable, Evie."

"I have," I said, trying not to laugh. I couldn't imagine Dee as a Jew. Since my foray into a convent before Annabelle was born, I was off religion. *Take this lamb of God and shove it!*

"Casseroles and cocktails," Dee said. "That's what we WASPs do, you said it yourself, Ev. That's no way to grieve, right?"

"Hello, don't forget TV and Valium."

"Not everyone likes pills, Evelyn. Not everyone is comfortable going through life half stoned," she said, rather meanly, I thought, but then again, I was a little out of it—all that sugar and nicotine, I guess.

I did know I didn't want to fight with Dee. We never fought. Ever. I loved Dee, and I didn't want to fight with her, especially today.

"You'd never blow a little weed, would you, counselor?" I said. "Thank God they don't subject you upholders-of-the-rule-of-the-land to drug tests, huh? Deirdre?"

Dee went pale. To be fair, it was only the second time in her life she'd gotten stoned, and she'd only gone along with it because Mom and I were doing it—chemo weed. Talk about peer pressure.

Mom had since killed off the stash.

"Evelyn Anne," my mother said. That's all she could say.

We drove in silence for a few miles.

"I'm going to stop at the liquor store," my mother said. "I hope that's *all right.* We don't have one thing to drink at home."

Because we were in mourning, officially, and because Dee and I both suspected it would cheer our mother up, we bought some chardonnay, in a box. A big old juice box of vino with la spigot you could drink from. When you got down to the end, you could rip the top off the box, remove the bag, and squish it in your hands. It was fun to hold the silver bladder over your head like an astral wineskin and squirt the last bit of wine into your mouth. It was a happy sight.

With Billy and Annabelle gone, and Mom and Dee inside, I prowled around the yard surveying the damage my father's absence had wreaked. Out back was a full-scale gardening debacle. The tiger lilies had ravaged the austere irises, the black-eyed susans cowered like schoolgirls trying to escape a strangling vine, while the peonies were rangy and heavy-headed, like they figured, Oh what the hell! Out front it was slightly better, the danger more contained. By the front door the holly bushes bulged menacingly, like fat men with switch-blades, and the forsythia bushes that lined the drive poked out their branches like vandals ready to gouge any car that dared cross our property line. My mother had tied up the weeping Chinese maple to keep it from collapsing like a drama queen into the grass, but she can only do so much.

I could only stand so much.

Inside I lie down for a second on the sofa. Every time I come home there are new pictures of my father, on the re-frigerator, on the walls, in the bathroom, in the hall. There are outtakes, and boyhood pictures, some hand-tinted as though by a funeral home cosmetologist so they impart a rude health. And, because there will be no more pictures, and be-cause we need to be reminded that my dad was really sick and in pain and should have died, there are pictures of Daddy ill. I can't look at these.

Instead, I stare at a gold-framed photo from the fifties, my mom and dad, in each other's arms, leaning up against an old blue Mustang. My dad seems to be whispering a private joke into my mother's ear. She's laughing, her eyes half-closed. Young and in love, they are all promise. They can't lose. I hate how clueless they are. I can't even stand looking at them. I want to scream, *It will only end in sadness. Don't be fools. Save yourselves.*

I go into the kitchen for the wine. My mother is sitting out on the back deck alone. Dee is in the hall talking to her boyfriend on the phone. He was listening to her feelings. Listening to how rotten we all were, and how we scoffed at her announcement. She told him how I'd crashed the car into the garage wall yesterday and cried. She was such a traitor.

He was the one. Really, the one, she'd assured us in the lingerie department. Not the one *right now*, like the other boys she'd been in love with. He was different. He made her feel safe.

I carried the box-o'-wine outside to Mom. I knew she'd appreciate somebody waiting on her for a change. She was sitting at the table, which sported a pale array of food—Brie, Triscuits, a bag of microwave popcorn, cashews, and a little bit of spinach dip in a Chinese bowl.

"Did you check messages?" she asked.

"Zero," I said. "All hang-ups." I tried not to smile.

When Dee came outside she looked refreshed. She'd put on lipstick and changed into white pants. My sister had become one of those women who can wear white pants.

"Dee, would you like some wine, or perhaps a gin and tonic? I've got rum—it's almost summer. I'd be happy to make you whatever you like," my mother said.

"I'm fine, Mommy, thank you," Dee said, but my mother pushed a glass of wine in front of her anyway.

"So," my mother said, "I think we're doing pretty well. I think your father would be proud of us."

"Me too, Mom," Dee said. She reached out and squeezed my mother's hand.

"We're moving on," I said. "Now, wouldn't that make a great PBS show? *Move On!* There's my new job. Forget this art crap, I could be the host of a show dedicated to mourning. We could make armbands, share, I'd give them helpful tips for surviving in the real world, like how to drink on the job—the old coffee-mug trick, the wash-your-hair-with-baby-powder trick, when you can't bear to bathe—there'd of course be a little scripture reading, done by some kind of animal—a lamb, maybe, or a lion, or both! *Move On!* I like it."

"Oh, Ev," Dee sighed. I listened to the sound of her golden charm bracelet tinkling as she lifted her glass. The charms sounded like little trophy cups knocking together. Then they both drank their wine, and sat there. They looked like they were waiting for something to happen, for somebody to do something that seemed grief stricken or profound.

"You know, Dee, Jews don't believe in heaven," my mother announced, as though she'd just remembered it, as though heaven were an exclusive gated beach community Dee wasn't qualified for membership in if she switched sides. Like Dee would miss out on all our family volleyball games in the hereafter if she started going to temple.

"Heaven." Dee laughed derisively. "Ha! Heaven is supposed to make all this horrible stuff people endure on earth worthwhile." She was tan, and had recently acquired wrinkles around her eyes. "What a ridiculous argument," she said. My sister had become absolutely beautiful.

I poured myself some wine and congratulated myself on not mentioning Mom's own conversion.

Since Daddy had been diagnosed the last time, my mother had been steeping herself in the Buddhist religion of golden happy reincarnation. Mom wasn't going to heaven, she was going out to pasture in her next life as a Zen Holstein.

Every time we visited the house, it seemed another stone Buddha had taken up residence in the backyard, plopped down in some wavy ornamental grass or lurking at the edges of the woods. When the morning mist hung low over the trees and you unfocused your eyes, the Buddhas looked like tombstones.

Yesterday, I'd made some lame joke about how she could spray for that Buddha infestation—"They're like raccoons, or crabgrass"—but she'd just let it go, playing with her bracelet of carved jade prayer beads.

"For your information," Dee said, flashing me a snarky look, "the Jews *know* suffering, they understand grief. Judaism makes sense. It's much more humanistic. I'd think it would appeal to you, Ev."

"No, thanks, I'm hip deep in green bean casserole and sidecars, sis. Oops, got to go pop a Percocet." I was teasing; in truth I was devoted to Xanax. *Was.* No longer, nope, I was moving on!

Dee sighed.

I yanked open the top of the box, yanked out the bag, and shot a stream into Mom's empty glass; it looked as though I were dumping a catheter bag. My father would have appreciated the humor in that, but nobody here would, so I kept quiet. There was a whole realm of things I'd never say, jokes I'd never make because he wasn't here to hear them. To egg me on.

My sister frowned as wine splashed on the table. She checked her watch. It pained me that it seemed she was just counting the hours until she could return home and say, "I survived it."

I wish I'd thought to have a T-shirt made, I MADE IT THROUGH THE FIRST ANNIVERSARY OF MY FATHER'S DEATH, AND

ALL I GOT WAS THIS LOUSY T-SHIRT. He'd have smiled at that one too, even though it was a cliché.

"Well, religion is the opium of the people, that's what Dad would say." I thought I heard the phone ringing inside the house.

"Your father would never say that," my mother said in horror. "Your father was a Presbyterian."

"Dad didn't say that, Karl Marx said that," Dee said.

"Yeah, right," I said, settling back in my chair. "Whatever."

I did that a lot, attributing things to my father that he hadn't said, but that felt like things he might have said. Could have said. Things I wanted him to have said, if only because I remembered them. Half the time I made him sound like Noël Coward, the other half, John Wayne. Superman or Superdick. Sometimes I feared I'd never listened to him at all. Sometimes I couldn't hear his voice, or remember one thing he'd said. As if I'd been parented by Casper the Friendly Dad, all his words had infinitesimal half-lives, they'd just burned off.

On the first anniversary of my father's death, I realized that it was possible that because I'd been building him up in my mind for so long, preparing for the day when I'd lose him, I'd missed the man altogether, and now he was irretrievable.

If I could forget him, he who was everything to me, what hope was there that anyone would remember me when I was gone?

"You don't know what you're talking about," Dee said.

I couldn't let anybody have one piece of him. It was like it came out of my pie.

"I know what I know," I said. "You don't even know what religion you are."

"Dad wouldn't want us fighting," Dee said, narrowing her eyes.

"You don't know what Dad would want," I said. "Unless, along with becoming a Jew, you've also acquired ESP."

The phone rang. It really rang. I hoped it would ring just once, this would mean it wasn't the boy, but one of the shepherds from the outreach program from church calling just to let us know they were thinking about us. That would show Dee. Years ago, when Mom and Dad went on a marriage encounter weekend, the same thing happened. Your shepherd would call and hang up just to let you know they were praying for you. It gave my father the creeps. Me too. The thought of another couple praying for my parents seemed just one step away from wife-swapping.

"Anyway, we're not fighting," I said. My mother just stared blankly. No doubt, in her mind, she was twisted up in one of her yoga positions, hands over ears, legs over head, knees clamped on hands, to ensure nothing seeped into her ears, the Denier pose.

"Girls," my mother said, and made like she was keeping us apart. "Think of your father." And of course we had to shut right up.

"So," Dee said, "Mom says you've been getting some good work as a stylist for photo shoots, that's nice. The fall *Vogue*, right? That's an American institution, is it not?" When did it happen that she became the big sister, and I became the little one?

"Yeah, whatever, no big deal," I said. I didn't tell her

that this sweet gig was basically thanks to Mary Beth, who was an editor in the fashion department and who probably held the photo editor at stiletto-heel-point, forcing her to give me work. I hadn't wanted to go, Billy made me go.

"And some gallery downtown is interested in showing some work?"

"Yes, and they don't even serve food or have bar service." Up till now my few pieces had hung in cafés, or dark bars who took pity on artists. They weren't exactly discerning. She frowned, she was really trying to be nice. I wanted to be nice. I didn't know if she would understand that none of these good things meant anything to me. That when the curator called I'd burst into tears. That without my father here, success and happiness meant nothing.

"We'll see," I said. Really, who gives a damn.

I'm inside using the bathroom when the phone rings. Maybe Annabelle is in the emergency room, maybe Billy got a flat. Maybe, maybe.

"Hello?" I said, trying to sound breathy and slightly annoyed like this call was interrupting a grand party. I was just about to grab ahold of the crystal chandelier and swing out over the heads of my guests, when *ring ring ring* ...

"Hello? Evie, how are you, dear?" It was one of my mother's friends. "How are all of you?" she asked, holding her breath for a moment, as if she expected the room to fill up with my tears.

"We're good, really, hanging in there, you know," I said, then the other line beeped, so I said, "Sorry, hold on." I hadn't imagined that all those earlier calls could have been thoughtful friends.

"Hello?"

"Hey," a voice said, "it's Dean." It's Dean. My heart started pounding like mad, my palms got wet. It was amazing.

"Hey," I said, trying to muster up a husky, devil-may-care voice. I dragged the phone into the closet and shut the door. "Hey you," I said, surrounded by coats. I stuck my hand in a coat pocket, it felt like my dad's old jean jacket. I felt a wadded-up Kleenex, some change, a piece of paper, perhaps an old shopping list. How many pieces of paper with his writing on them were left?

It was wrong, I knew that. I was out of control. I couldn't stop, I just couldn't help myself. I didn't want to help myself. Why couldn't I have this one thing? This one good thing?

"What's up?" he asked.

"Not much," I said. There was a long, uncomfortable pause. I could hear him smoking, maybe doing bong hits. Bong hits would be nice.

"So," he said. "What are you up to?"

"Not much," I said. God, why couldn't I think of anything to say!

"So, do you want to get together or something?"

"Yeah," I heard myself say.

After that we both loosened up. He told me he lived with his mom, that he just read *On the Road* and had been taking a lot of acid.

He asked if I lived in North Star, because a guy on his water polo team had the same exchange. That kid lived up the block. I described our house, and he swore he knew which one it was. I told him I couldn't meet him until after eleven. He didn't mind. "That's cool," he said. "Good."

He suggested a bar in Newark, the Deer Park, near the university. I was heartened to find he could meet me in a bar, that must have meant he was twenty-one. Maybe Dean and I could be friends, I thought.

When Billy came home, tired, Annabelle in one arm, his hands holding bags of CDs and penny candy, a daisy chain on his head like a crown and, under his arm, a bouquet of goldenrod, I couldn't even look at him. When he handed my mother a bag full of corn and tomatoes he bought at a road-side stand, and the bouquet, I went to him and kissed him on the mouth. It surprised him. Of course I wasn't going to meet Dean, and by tomorrow we would be gone and this would all be over. Still.

I picked up Annabelle and savored her weight in my arms. I loved the smell of her. She wrapped her arms around my neck and yawned hugely, like a cat. I wondered if she would remember my father. Remember how he held her and kissed her behind the knee. How he adored her.

Since my father died, Billy had become the de facto man of the house. A role he'd seemed to slip into with surprisingly little resistance, the same way he'd become a father. Therefore the responsibility and privilege of charring the clan's meat fell to him. Billy set up the barbecue outside and started grilling the steak my mother had been marinating all day, although she was now a vegetarian. He cut up red and green peppers, tomatoes, and mushrooms and made brochettes while Dee and I shucked the corn.

"Vitamins," Billy sang, raising a cold Corona with lime, "You girls need vitamins."

"You should have brought your guitar," I said, then wished I hadn't. Ever since my father's death, Billy seemed to think I wanted him to get a real job instead of taking the random studio-musician gig and fact-checking for *Rolling Stone*. It was true. His need to succeed and the uncertainty of the music world made me too anxious. I needed him stable. At least for a little while.

I knew he heard me, but he just kept painting olive oil on the brochettes, and finished his beer.

It was so lovely out, we all agreed, it would be a shame not to eat outside on the deck. In truth, since my father died we only ever spent time in two parts of the house, the kitchen and the bedrooms. Any room where my father had held court—the living room, family room, or dining room—we avoided. The deck was like an anteroom, a place to hide from the body of the house.

When no one was looking, I slipped into the dining room and kissed my father's chair.

Billy put Annabelle down for the night. Then he joined us out on the deck, with five nice wineglasses and a bottle of the good stuff. A bottle of my father's Chateau Margaux we had been saving for A Special Occasion. I guessed one was happening. Billy turned on the outside lights so we were no longer pleasantly resting in gloom. Now it felt like we were on a stage, surrounded by darkness, waiting for something to happen.

"Annabelle walked today, again." Billy yanked the cork out in one swift pull. "In the grass, at the playground. She's got incredible balance."

"Really?"

"Good."

"How nice..."

This was how it went. The day before, Annabelle had taken her first steps in the front yard. She walked from Billy to the weeping maple. Mom and I were sitting on the front porch watching. When it happened, I caught my breath for a moment. I looked at my mother; she looked back at me, her mouth tightening. I checked the skies. Did you see that? I thought. Then and only then did I go to my daughter, hug her. What a shit I was for not jumping up straightaway.

On the first anniversary of my father's death, I didn't think it unreasonable to expect a miracle.

Billy poured for all of us, and we raised our glasses. My father had always made the toasts. Then Billy poured some in a glass and set it in front of the empty chair and framed photograph of Daddy in Kathmandu we'd set up on the table in front of us, just as we had done at Thanksgiving and Christmas, and as I had then, I kept waiting, glass after glass, fool that I am, for the wine to disappear, like that statue of Ganesh in India that drinks milk.

I pretended I wasn't watching, but I was. I lit a match, and another. I surprised myself by realizing that I'd forgotten about meeting Dean. I checked Dee's Rolex, it was nine-thirty.

Just one drop. Hell, I was willing to can any skepticism about evaporation.

The brown bats did acrobatics over our heads, feasting

on the insects drawn to the porch lights, a regular smorgasbord of moths and mosquitoes.

"Girls, do either of you remember that night in London when we first had Indian food?" my mother asked. "It was London, right, not Edinburgh?"

"It was London," I said.

"Edinburgh," Dee said.

My mother frowned.

"You know what I remember?" Dee said. "Dancing with Daddy. He was an incredible dancer."

My mother nodded. For the first time all day, I thought she might cry.

"I know," I said. "Remember how people would sort of make way for him at weddings? It was amazing. My God, I'd be ready to keel over and he'd be like, Come on, it's the Stones!"

"I will never forget dancing with Daddy," Dee sighed. For the first time all day I thought *she* might cry.

Then it occurred to me, hearing that sigh, seeing those tears well up, that all girls with dead fathers must remember dancing with them. That intimacy of being in his arms, the public spectacle of it, the feeling of your father's hand on your back, owning you. Being allowed to love him a little in that way. It bothered me. I couldn't remember my father making me a sandwich. I'm sure he did, hundreds of times, but I couldn't remember it, and I wanted that memory. I wanted to remember that, some keen or poignant personal thing, not this stock footage of a girl, any girl, and her father dancing—even if it was to "Brown Sugar" and he was doing a Chuck Berry duckwalk—I was scared it could be somebody else's memory.

Heaven was filled with dead fathers dancing away like wind-up toys.

I excused myself. I could feel myself about to say something mean, or stupid, so I got up. I went into the dining room and sat in my chair, the one to the left of my father's chair. Then, out the front window, I saw Dean standing at the edge of our yard staring at the house, his foot resting on a skateboard, like he was waiting for me, like some idiotic kid. He flipped the skateboard into his hands, then held it behind his head, stretching. His T-shirt rode up so I could see his flat stomach, the hair leading down to his groin. I wondered what he smelled like. I remembered the boy Billy was when I met him in Amsterdam; he was just twenty-one, his stomach concave; I remember the smell of kissing him there, feeling his breath quicken. How I'd look at him naked when he slept, just amazed by how pretty he was. How lucky I was. I thought I'd never get tired of touching him, or hearing his voice. We were so young then.

I just stared at Dean. I didn't know whether to run, or hide. Instead, I panicked. I went straight out the front door, I tried to look casual. I wondered if the neighbors were watching. As soon as I got close enough to see him, really see him, looking at me sideways and sort of shy, I was undone.

"Hi, what are you doing here?" I asked. I didn't look over my shoulder to see if anybody was watching me, because I hadn't done anything wrong.

"I was in the neighborhood." He shrugged, then picked up a piece of grass, stuck it in his mouth, and gave me this lopsided grin. I wondered if he was checking out my wrinkles.

"Yeah?" I said. One-word answers. I was regressing

quickly. Soon I'd be sneaking out my bedroom window in my nightgown to drink Löwenbräu and kiss up against the trees down in the woods, as I'd done with Scott Richmond.

"So talk to me, what's your story?" he asked, and made like he was going to sit down on the grass.

"Don't," I said. I grabbed his arm and pulled him back up. I felt the tight biceps, that smooth skin.

"Hey," he said, reclaiming his arm.

"Listen, I have to go back in." I bit my lip. "We've got this big family dinner thing going on out back, and my dad will kill me if he sees me out here talking to you—I'm supposed to be getting ice. Lots of thirsty people down there," I said, staring at his mouth. I was as hormonal as a horny teenager.

"Your dad, huh?" He smiled like he might want to kiss me.

"He can be a real bastard," I said. I was standing really close to him. I slipped my fingers through his belt loops and then stopped. "He'd kill us both," I said. "That man *loves* his ice."

Dean laughed. I liked Dean.

"Eleven," he said, like he didn't believe I'd come.

"Elevenish," I said, then headed off in a run, a bounding Audrey Hepburn–esque romp across the grass toward the house. Inside, I slammed the front door and locked it. I was shaking and sweating. I peered out the front window the way I used to do when dates dropped me off. I'd watch them walk away and wonder what they were thinking. Wonder if I'd see them again. If I wanted to.

When I went back to the deck, nothing had changed. It was as if nothing I did changed anything. My father smiled back at me from the photograph. He hadn't had one drop.

. . .

It was almost eleven when I checked Dee's watch again. When my father was alive, this was the time when my mother and sister and Billy would start making noises about bed, and my father would look at me and say, "Nightcap?" And I'd say, "Sure."

Now when we visited I went to bed early, and my mother and sister and Billy all stayed up. Maybe for my father's sake. Me, I saw no reason to stay up.

If I was going to go and meet Dean, I should leave now.

I lit another match. Not one sip was missing from the wineglass, or evaporated, or whatever. So I drank it. I reached over, and without the nicety of a toast, or even a here's-looking-at-you-kid, I slugged my father's wine back in one gulp. I now know I should have passed it around, so we all could share.

Blood of Daddy. But fuck it, I was greedy.

Dee didn't say anything, in that annoying way she had of saying nothing, just looking at you, so self-contained and well groomed, so well groomed you suddenly felt hairy and troll-like, and if you hadn't thought of picking your nose, you suddenly did.

"What?" I said.

"Nothing," she said, meaning *everything*. In the dark the lightning bugs were blinking their green and yellow lights, calling out to each other, here I am, over here, no, over here in the tall grass, come to me, come to me. My father loved lightning bugs. *"I think lightning bugs are just about the greatest thing in the world,"* he'd said the spring he died.

"No, tell me."

"I can't believe you just drank that wine like that. That wasn't right, Evie. Granted, it's just a symbol, but—"

"Fuck you, Dee, it's not a symbol."

Dee moved a strand of hair away from her face very deliberately, like I'd spit on her.

"Oh, that's nice," she said, and sat up straighter in her chair, crossing her legs. "I wish I could say I was surprised, but you always have to take it too far, don't you?"

"Fuck you, fuck you, fuck you," I said. "You don't even know too far. You think you know too far?"

"All I am saying is that it was wrong for you to just take that. Please, just get a grip, why don't you?"

My mother sighed, hunched up her shoulders, and started doing yoga breathing through her nose: sniff, sniff, the breath of fire. It was supposed to make your spine feel like a fiery serpent. This was supposed to be a good thing.

Dee started to laugh. I could sense Billy bracing himself in his chair. He knew the mistake she was making, he'd made it—you should never laugh at a crazy person. To prove that point, I leaned over and took a wild swing at her, punching her in the back.

"Owwwww!" she screamed. Then, for a long moment, there was no sound except the animal-like grunts of me trying to hurt her and her pushing me away, then the scuffling sound of the table moving and her chair falling backward as she jumped to her feet.

"God!" she shouted, and lunged at my chair, pushing it over. I landed with a thump, a shocking wonderful bone-rattling thump that shook me. I'd been waiting for somebody to knock me on my ass. Now I really wanted to kill her. I started slapping wildly, trying to smack her in the face, or pull her hair. We hadn't fought like this since we were little kids.

"Evie!" Billy yelled. "Don't!"

"Girls!" my mother yelled. I saw her hand down in front of my face for an instant. I recognized my father's wedding band on her finger. "Stop it, stop it! Someone will get hurt. Stop it!"

But did Dee stop?

No, Dee fell on me and punched me in the nose, so hard the blood started to gush. Thank God, or I don't doubt she'd have kept on swinging.

"Oh my God," Dee said, sitting back on the deck and shaking herself like she was in a dream. "I've never done that before." She stared at her hand; her knuckles were pink.

"Is it broken?" Billy asked. He looked confused, as if he wasn't sure he saw what he thought he saw. Hell, he probably wanted to sock me too.

I held on to my nose. I was glad. On the first anniversary of my father's death, my sister gave me a bloody nose, and I was grateful.

"Oh, girls," my mother said. She scooped some ice out of her drink and bundled it into a napkin, then handed the little ice pack down to me. She sat back in her chair, closed her eyes, and started doing her yoga breathing exercise again.

As I lay there getting my breath, napkin dripping water all down my face, I said, "You know, I'm pregnant."

Now that I'd said it, it was true. "Ha-ha," Dee said, lying on the ground beside me. I wasn't kidding. I wished I was. I wished to hell I was joking. I wished to hell my sister and I still lay together like this, the way we had as children, sharing the same bed, by choice and need.

"That's really nice," I said, trying to lift my head, then, deciding it wasn't important, I just lay there. I didn't want to get up. I was scared, and scared to tell them. "Do some Starsky and Hutch flip-over Dukes of Hazzard shit on a pregnant lady. Just you wait, Daisy Mae," I said. "Your time will come. You and your fancy-pantsy boyfriend."

Now, she knew.

Billy dropped his wineglass on the table, a nice dramatic touch. But it didn't break. It should have broken.

"You're joking?" he said. "Us?" He was grinning like crazy.

"I'm sorry," I said, apologizing, I guess, for springing it on him this way. For springing it on Mom and Dee with no warning.

"Oh God," Dee said. "I'm sorry, oh God. I'm so sorry. A baby," she said, turning toward me to rest her hands on my stomach.

My mother had stopped doing the dragon sniff. I thought she might have stopped breathing altogether.

"So," I said, lying still. I knew it hurt her. Nobody did anything for a minute. We were not happy, not unhappy, just thinking how impossible it was that this kid was going to be born without my father knowing it. How impossible it seemed.

I wondered if Dean was waiting for me at the bar. I wondered what he drank, something boyish like a black diamond, or a madras.

"Are you sure?" Billy said, plopping himself down on the other side of me. He kissed my hands.

"Yep." I propped myself up on one shoulder. It felt like I was talking about a leaky pipe that was going to cause trouble, not a baby. "Two months at least," I said. I'd just assumed the tiredness, moodiness, nausea, and headaches were all part of an anniversary reaction to my father's dying. That was what I wanted. Even the missed periods—that was grief. I wanted to feel that kind of connection, not this, not now.

"But the pills. Oh God." He grinned, hands over his mouth for an instant, like he wanted so bad to smirk. He was so proud. I messed up my pills—who could remember?—and so Billy had performed the penile equivalent of shooting an arrow into an apple on the head of a whirling dervish.

I said, "You realize, of course, I hate you."

My mother smiled, looking out at the yard. "Well, that's wonderful, kids," she said. "No, really," she said, her eyes dry.

"A toast," my mother said. I couldn't recall her ever making a toast before.

She raised her glass, and said nothing. Then she said, "To you both," her voice not at all wobbly. "I am so happy," she said, where once she'd have said *We.*

"It's almost midnight," Dee said, a little anticipatory smile on her lips. "It's almost over."

On the first anniversary of my father's death, we were supposed to move on.

I didn't want to go forward.

"You know what? I'm going for a walk," I said, standing up shakily. Feeling, for the first time in three months, really pregnant. I didn't want to walk. I just wanted out of there.

"I'll come with you," Billy said, taking my arm. I loved Billy.

"No." I squeezed his hand. "I want to be alone for a little while. I think, if it's okay with all of you, I'm going to take a little drive."

"Baby," Billy said, "it's late."

"Your nose," my mother said. "You're pregnant. You need sleep."

"You're joking," Dee said. I waited for her to say something about how I'd crashed into the garage yesterday, but she just looked sad and worried.

I couldn't stand it.

"I'm just going to take a little drive around the neighborhood, that's all," I said. "Once or twice around the galaxy, to remember Daddy."

No one would argue with this. I got into the car and rolled down the windows. Drive, my father said. Just drive. I flipped on the radio. On the first anniversary of my father's death, we were supposed to move on. I was moving on.

I didn't want to. It was as though I was a refugee being chased from my true home, prodded into the future with the stick of forgetfulness. Turning my head, trying to catch a glimpse of something I could never see again, the lights of a place I'd never wanted to leave, a place I'd never return to, a place that in memory would become more beautiful, more irreplaceable the longer it was out of my sight.

HERE IS

COMFORT,

TAKE IT

How many other women are you going to wake up with?

This is what I wonder when I roll over and see Charlie dozing at my side, a wet halo ebbing out on the sheet behind him, his arms flung out, claiming the center of our bed as his own. When I start to wonder this, I can't just let him lie there and sleep, no, I have to kiss his cheeks, the sweaty back of his neck, his pale stomach where the skin is so silky it feels almost unseemly to touch it. Almost. I nibble and suck his earlobe until he rolls toward me, burrowing into my side, his fingers working the buttons of my nightgown, his head nuzzling my breasts, and then he sucks. While he nurses, I close my eyes and stroke his head, fingering his blond curls, enjoying the pleasurable throb I've become a stranger to even with my husband, especially with my husband. "I won't ever let you go," I whisper in my son's ear. "Never, ever."

This morning Billy isn't hanging on the edge of our bed, clinging like some kind of flightless cliff-dwelling bird that can adapt to even the harshest conditions, such as the ubiquitous wet spot, though at one time, long ago, he'd gallantly offer to sleep on it. That was when it was his, of course. This morning Billy is crashed out on our four-year-old daughter Annabelle's floor swaddled in a Little Mermaid sleeping bag, his head stuffed in a beanbag chair. For a second I feel like shit.

The first few times Billy had fled I'd felt guilty, as though Charlie and I had chased him away. Later, I didn't mind, actually I preferred it. I'd stretch out and luxuriate in the room his being gone gave me and Charlie. But since Billy and I are trying to salvage our marriage I feel sort of rotten. Still I cling to Charlie.

How many women will you kiss? How many hearts will you break? Will they pick up your socks for you? Will they feed you?

I never think about Charlie loving them. Why would I?

When Charlie tears himself away from my breast—it's always tearing himself away—a rivulet of milk runs out of his mouth and down his neck like he's a milk-drunk Bacchus. I smell my milk on his breath. I taste it on his lips when I kiss him. It's sweet like almonds and vanilla. It's wrong, I know that, kissing him like that on his lips, but he likes it. I like it. I kiss him again, and hope Billy doesn't walk in. There's this frisson between Charlie and me, we both know it. It's like we're having an affair, we have to steal our moments, but when they come they are delicious. They make you want to keep on living.

Weaning is hell.

Sometimes, at La Leche meetings, I just sit there and sob.

"I can't do it," I say, tearing a Kleenex into snow. "I'm not ready."

They all support me, of course. They say, "You've got to do what's right for you, sweetheart, for you. The rest of the world shouldn't matter."

But Billy and I have agreed it's time.

"It's hard on Annabelle," Billy says. "She needs more of your attention, and she's not getting it."

"I'm here," I say.

"Charlie will be three this fall," Billy reminds me. "He can't go to nursery school and have you loitering around the schoolyard waiting to stick your tit through the fence. He can't. It's not fair to him."

"Fair?" I say. I resent the implication that my son and I are some kind of freak show. Not that I don't know what people say, the way they look at us, then look away. The whispers: "This is not a third-world country." And "You have to wonder what's up with the mother."

Even my friends, even my oldest friend, Mary Beth, rolls her eyes. Mary Beth, who listened to me wail after my father died, who has been the one constant in my life. I'm beginning to wonder if maybe she hasn't been avoiding seeing me because of the nursing, if maybe it makes her too uncomfortable. After all, she'd nursed her own daughter, Ondine, for only two weeks and then quit.

"Darling," she explained, "my body is a shrine, not a breakfast bar."

Mary Beth has never suggested I should stop. I know it's an act of great friendship for her to keep her mouth shut. I'm sure it's just killing her, but she wouldn't dare say a thing. Still, I know how she feels. How everybody else outside of the La Leche bubble feels, including my mother and sister. No one can make me stop nursing my boy. I won't be bullied.

It's like when my father died, every helpful Hannah who had ever read Elisabeth Kübler-Ross or any of those *Grieving for Dummies* handbooks said, It takes a year for the hurt to get better. Meanwhile, members of the Daughters with Dead Dads Club said, It takes two years, and the second year is worse because nobody remembers or gives a shit about your pain.

We don't all go crazy the same way.

I imagine this year, year three (we're off the grieving time line altogether), I'll probably forget it's the day and I'll be out ballroom dancing, or shopping for suede hot pants, or eating malossol caviar on toast points when suddenly it will hit me: he's never coming back.

I pull Charlie closer, belly to belly, it's delicious. His round little-boy stomach, it's like a cupcake you can't resist eating.

In the spirit of honesty and reconciliation that Billy and I are tacitly pursuing with each other, I should have told him last night that I was going to a nurse-in today. A rally to boycott Mama Robino's Italian restaurant. Seems Mama asked a nursing mother to nurse either in the ladies' room or outside. So today we're all going with our children to sit outside and nurse with our placards reading MAMA ROBINO IS A BAD MOMMY. And NO NURSING NO PEACE.

People don't understand. I can't just make my son stop wanting me. You don't own your children, they own you.

So Billy and I have decided: no more snacking on the breast, no incidental sucks, just night-night nursing and boo-boos—comfort sucking. That's it. We both agree, the gradual approach is only humane.

But what about me? I feel like asking Billy. What the hell about me? But I don't. Things between Billy and me are better than they've been in a long time. I've been selfish. Incredibly mind-numbingly selfish. What makes it worse is that after my father died Billy was incredible, a real pillar of strength and goodness, truly, his halo was goddamn blinding. He took care of the children, and the apartment and the bills, and life while I fell apart. Drinking Dewar's in the tub—reminding myself that it was possible to drown in a bowl of chicken soup—and slouching around the apartment in the same black clothes day after day, justifying it as a European artist thing (even though I hadn't been making work), thinking, God knows the French aren't obsessed with washing their clothes after one wearing, those Frenchwomen bought a few nice pieces and wore them into the ground—difference was, my clothes were black stretch pants and a turtleneck.

Sometimes when Billy left the house with Annabelle in the stroller and Charlie strapped to his back I felt like he was wearing a neon sign advertising: SENSITIVE CARING IMPREGNA-TOR. GREAT SECOND HUSBAND MATERIAL.

Billy got tired. Any man would get tired. Especially a man whose wife looked like a fat melancholy beatnik.

One night sitting at the kitchen table paying bills, smelling of baby shampoo and roasted chicken, he said, "I'm burned out," knuckling his bloodshot eyes for effect.

"Burn, baby, burn, disco inferno," I said. I know he wouldn't appreciate this, seeing as how I hadn't so much as folded a tea towel in days.

"I'm serious," he said, in his new and unsettling grown-up voice. "What about me? What about us?" *Us* meaning *sex.*

I didn't say anything. He'd been patient, it wasn't until Charlie was six months old that he snapped.

"I'm tired of it. Sometimes I feel like I am comforting you on the death of *your husband.* It isn't right, Ev. It isn't right."

I couldn't say anything, but for a moment I was proud. Wasn't I some daughter? Then I was ashamed. How my father would hate the way I have carried on. He wouldn't understand how I could just stop working, how I could estrange myself from anyone who wasn't family, or one of my La Leche sisters, or one of the few friends or acquaintances who had actually known my father. I didn't understand completely. I did know that the idea of sex, of surrendering my body, was out of the question.

Right after Charlie was born, Billy started playing piano in a bar downtown. A self-consciously chichi little French Moroccan club with low velvet sofas, brocade pillows on the floor, and red lanterns.

Because it wasn't the old blue Stratocaster that he wanted to drag out, and hang out with a bunch of guys in a smoky club, the wood floors swollen with spilled beer, I was neither threatened nor turned on. I'd fallen in love with Guitar Billy, no-underwear, torn-jeans, three-earrings-in-his-left-ear Billy. Not Piano Billy in boxers and black cords, the piercings now invisible, you could only just feel the scar tissue. That idiotic line *If this don't turn you on, you ain't got no switch* surfaced in my mind over and over again. Forget a switch, I'd blown my fuse box.

I kept thinking about how turned on I used to get as a girl thinking about Pete Townshend smashing his guitar, because, as he said, he could never get the guitar to make the sound he wanted. I'd always wanted Billy to do that, but he wasn't the type, it was too obvious, too emotional.

"Maybe if I had one of those Mexican-made cheapy Fenders guys buy just so they can smash them," he said. "That'd be fun."

"You're joking," I said. It was like finding out the woman of your dreams has a silicone core.

"I need this," Billy had said, like he thought I'd deny him this one thing. "Shit, sometimes I look at myself and I don't even know who I am anymore, what with the new job, the suit, the kids, and the—"

"It's fine," I said. "I get it." I did. I didn't recognize myself anymore, either. But I envied him. Billy had transformed his life. Three years ago he had started a small software company that was among the first to create RealAudio Web sites for bands. And though Billy would say the job nearly killed him, it saved us.

"So, are there piano groupies?" I asked. He'd just laughed.

Playing piano worked like a tonic on my husband. "I haven't been this jazzed in a long time," he'd said to me after playing his second set. "Okay, okay, so it's not exactly Max's Kansas City, still..."

In the beginning I'd go and watch Billy play. I'd sip Maker's Mark at the bar, pretending I wasn't his wife, seeing if that might deliver some sexual kick, the way it used to. But nothing happened, I'd just get sad. Even when women in short skirts sidled up to him after a set and stuck tips in his jar as if they were reaching into his pants, I didn't flinch.

I didn't care when he started hanging out afterward at the bar, coming home late, and later. I was tired, I didn't want to go out. I went to bed and took Charlie with me. I curled my body around his. He made me feel loved, irreplaceable. He was who I wanted.

I knew. Even without all the clichés. There was only one hang-up, there was no lipstick on his collar, no phone number on a cocktail napkin. I knew there was another woman because Billy was happy, and in some small way, deep in my grief, I think I was glad she existed. No one would believe that, but I had no time for Billy and all his wants. I wondered sometimes if he still loved me. If he had ever really loved me. If anyone could ever love me enough.

With Billy, I felt like the Blob. Sure, I was shapeless, slow moving, and boring as sin, but I still managed to devour everything good, then spit out the bones. There was the quick thrill of feeling like I could annihilate him with my rage, but it was followed by great waves of guilt. I'd hurl my blobby self at his feet, beg for forgiveness, and then later I'd be angry at him for making me feel like such a monster. It was an ugly cycle. Occasionally when Billy guilted me into it, I worked. Mary Beth continued to set me up with photographers who needed assistance, throwing stylist work my way. It took all my strength just to make it to those silly photo shoots, where I was basically a robot obeying orders shouted by dictatorial photographers. *I want less ankle sock and more shine on the Mary Jane—think, sadistic schoolgirl—not school marm.* All I could think was, Please don't let me start crying here. Please just let me get home to my children. Home was where my heart was.

It wasn't until the affair ended, until I saw how distraught Billy was, how he looked gray, like he'd been washed in gravel, his eyes half opened like there wasn't enough oxygen in the air to sustain him, how even Annabelle's dadaist jokes about chickens and rubber boots couldn't coax a laugh, how he'd explode in anger and throw things at the slightest provocation, denting walls with drinking glasses, angry at us for not making it easy for him to go to her, that I saw him passionate, really feeling something, something big and deep, that I felt like I was dying. I remembered that boy, and I wanted him back. That was when I sank my claws into him. That was when I agreed to give up the nursing.

I cheat. But I am trying.

Billy tries to be nice about my La Leche meetings.

"I understand this is in some way about sisterhood or whatever, but can't you be friends with these women even though you're not nursing—it's not like the Moonies, right? They're not going to excommunicate you."

"You don't understand," I say. I don't understand either really, why I can't give it up.

Billy looks suspicious when I jokingly tell him that we've come up with a La Leche cocktail. Every organization needs their own emblematic cocktail—ours is the Naughty Mommy Slammer. A shot of breast milk, a shot of vodka, and a dribble of grenadine. If you want to use tequila, it's a Naughty Mamacita.

"What's next?" he says. "Don't tell me you're going to start baking with breast milk, are you, like those women did in the seventies—some sort of Bundt boob cake?"

"Oh, honey, don't be silly. Remember, people ate alfalfa back then too."

He doesn't get it. It's not the milk.

While Charlie lolls in bed, I take off my nightgown, pinching the flesh around my middle; even though I'm back to my normal weight, I'm not skinny like I once was. It's depressing to admit, but my mother has a better body than me. Though you never see it under the gauzy saffron and sage colored robes she's taken to wearing, her hair hanging down to the middle of her back in a heavy gold braid, like some sort of suburban Tibetan priestess. How did I turn into a woman who prays that one day someone will design a chic black bathing suit that doubles as an evening gown?

Mary Beth doesn't even look thirty, and she has a child only a year younger than Annabelle. No, Mary Beth is a dead ringer for her college self, only better dressed and with the benefit of all-body salt rubs and shiatsu. It isn't fair.

"Mommy, am I going to die?" Charlie asks.

"Oh, heavens, no," I say, lying down beside him. I realize how absurd it sounds. He is lying back in bed, arms behind his head, in his Elvis T-shirt and Superman Underoos, staring at the ceiling like a man deep in thought.

"Can you hear music when you're dead?"

"No," I say, getting up off the bed. "You can't hear anything. Nothing."

"Oh," he says, disappointed, like for the first time maybe death doesn't sound like such a good idea.

The death of Annabelle's hamster, Archie, has shaken our household. I've had to insist that she stop digging him up out of the garden. (He was too big to flush. Last winter we'd had an unfortunate incident with a pair of gerbils—Ernie and Bert—that required plunging.) I just couldn't deal with this whole burial thing. Annabelle says she misses him, but I suspect she just wants to see his skeleton, obsessed as she is with bones. My sister, Dee, had done this as a girl too; our backyard and the woods behind it made a spacious pet cemetery. She exhumed the rodents pretty regularly, unwrapped their toilet paper shrouds, only to find them desiccated and coated in ants, skeletons still not exposed. Blossom, my Siamese cat whom we'd had to thaw out before burying her—we'd been in France and my parents insisted that the house-sitter freeze her—was eternally secure, once she had defrosted enough to fit in a nailed-up wooden wine box, otherwise I'm certain Dee would have had her way with her too.

We'd made such a big deal out of pet funerals, scattering flower petals on the fresh graves, my mother lighting a little of the sandalwood incense she burned for dinner parties. I would read passages from our *Good News for Modern Man Bible*, and the four of us would sing a hymn or song, or both, my mother elbowing my father as he checked his watch, always so much to do.... We crooned "Yellow Submarine" and "They Will Know We Are Christians by Our Love" when we buried Blossom. We were singers.

It's funny how we've still not scattered my father's ashes. It's been over three years and still we can't part with his body.

Gazing at my supine golden-haired boy sucking his thumb, weighing the pros and cons of death, I can't believe that I'd once wished that pregnancy test was wrong. I can't believe that I'd willfully denied my pregnancy, drinking and smoking and flirting like mad with anybody who would have me. I couldn't stand the idea that my father would never know my son. You see, I knew it was a son, it had to be, and this made me giddy, for I had this creeping suspicion—no, hopeful expectation—that I was going to give birth to the reincarnation of my father.

I believed it.

Charlie likes the idea that he's named for my dead father; he likes the idea that, as I once, regrettably, put it, my father is "his angel." I've overheard Annabelle telling him, "Grandpa keeps an eye on us, he protects us, you know."

Sometimes I wonder why I've filled their heads with such shit. It's one thing to not tell your daughter she can't be an actual mermaid when she grows up—after all, she could be one of those synchronized swimmers at some pleasingly cheesy Florida resort—but it's another to tell her my father is keeping her safe from traffic accidents and bee stings. Because she suspects it's important, Annabelle tells me she remembers my father. "He loved me," she says, clasping her hands behind her back like she's doing a recitation. "I remember that."

Downstairs, Billy is at the kitchen sink finishing his second cup of coffee. He's already painstakingly brushed out Annabelle's long coppery hair, pinning it back out of her serious brown eyes with glittery butterfly barrettes. Dressed her and fed her.

I am surprised at how handsome Billy looks this morning in his dark gray suit, his black hair cropped close, his cheeks pink and freshly shaven. Frankly, it's scary. I remember how I used to stand at the foot of the stage at CBGB's and watch Billy, his hair streaked with safety orange paint, play the bass, screaming incomprehensible lyrics about doom, plastics, and Kierkegaard. Here was a classically trained pianist playing three chords. I thought he was a genius.

This morning Annabelle has chosen her cream-puff party dress, and he's chosen the dark blue leggings she wears underneath. It's a constant compromise. She puts on a halter top, he gives her a cardigan. A war of attrition. Out back on the deck, Annabelle is practicing her mermaid walk, legs pressed together in imitation of a tail. She despises her feet.

"Ah, it's the drunken rodeo clown," Billy says, mussing up Charlie's hair.

"Billy," I say, but I don't push it.

I put Charlie down, and immediately he protests, arms up.

"No," he shrieks, climbing back up into my arms and clamping his legs around my middle. Charlie would rather his feet never touch the ground, preferring instead to be buffeted through life in our arms, or upon the golden litter of his stroller, preferably in the fully reclined position.

"For Christ's sake, Ev." Billy scowls, looking very grown-up in his suit. I still can't get used to the fact that from time to time he'll ask me, "Does this shirt go with these pants? Is this tie too loud?" This from the man who used to consider a vintage bowling shirt dressing up.

"My radio!" Charlie shouts, spying his tape player in the now-emptied cabinet beneath the kitchen sink where he left it last night. He wriggles free. Charlie's world was forever rocked when he discovered an old box of tapes in Billy's office. Sex Pistols, Ramones, Buzzcocks. *Hasta la vista,* Raffi—our boy was a sucker for that 1-2-3-4 beat. His tape player is his sacred object, he even sleeps with it.

"See, that's why he got into bed with us last night," I say. "He didn't have his radio."

"Right." Billy nods, not at all convinced. We both know it's a lie.

The tape player provides music for Charlie's "spaceship," and within seconds he's happily stowed under the sink, doors shut.

"Ground control to Major Tom," Billy calls out, waiting for Charlie to pop his head out. He doesn't. "Look at my ribs," Billy says, untucking his shirt and sucking in his stomach. "I've got bruises," he says in that husbandy I'm-still-a-baby-too voice. There's not a mark on him. From under the sink we hear Iggy Pop scream, *Now I wanna to be your dog!* and then there's the sound of Charlie doing a modified pogo, his head banging on the cabinet doors.

I kiss Billy's tummy. "Poor baby."

"Remind me again who you are," Billy says. He takes my head in his hands and pulls me up, then slips his tongue in my mouth, his hands sliding up under my shirt. He can't keep his hands off them. Who can blame him? Finally I have tits, real stop-traffic-oops-sorry-about-your-fender tits. The guys at the deli talk to my chest like it's an intercom. It's a marvelous novelty. Billy will miss these breasts, I know it.

"Mmm..." he says.

I close my eyes and try to give in. Then, just as I knew he would, Charlie comes crashing out of the cabinet. "Owwwww, Mom!" he shrieks, holding on to his head. He's smacked it on the pipe below the sink.

"Remind me to kill myself later, okay?" Billy says. "Really." He makes his hand a gun and points it at his temple. "Pow."

I sit down and pull Charlie into my lap. I unsnap the left cup of my bra; the left is Charlie's favorite. I lap his tears. When Charlie was a baby, his eyes were so beautifully bright and blue, we kept expecting them to change. It seemed impossible that they could stay.

"I swear that kid's got radar, he knows the minute we kiss. The second I touch you, touch *them*..." he says, waving in the vicinity of my breasts. He turns his head in disgust as a spray of milk fans droplets across Charlie's cheek and forehead. Charlie laughs, delighted.

"Oh, that's real nice," Billy says.

"It's comfort, asshole."

My nipple juts out of Charlie's mouth like a wet pink cigar. He taps his toes to Black Flag's "TV Party."

We've got nothing better to do than watch TV and have a couple brews! Don't talk about anything else, we don't want to know!

"Hey, they're playing our song," I say. I feel light-headed for a moment, as I always do when Charlie first latches on. I didn't feel this way with Annabelle. Maybe because I was an anxious new mother. But when Charlie latches on it's like the first kiss —for a minute you catch your breath in surprise at its loveliness, you forget how much you liked it, how that intimate skin-on-skin contact connects you to yourself, to a wellspring of feeling, and your body. After a few sucks I start to feel good, calm, and a little dopey. I get that erotic tingle in my crotch. The tingle no one talks about. His hand strums my breast like it's a fret. I feel great. Maybe my boy will be a guitar god. When my father got sick the last time he told me that that's what he'd have liked to have been in another life. Not a guitar god exactly, but a rock 'n' roll star. It was hard for me to imagine. I thought he was kidding, but he wasn't. My father said, Isn't it every boy's dream?

I imagine the cherry red Fender Jaguar I'll give my boy on his thirteenth birthday—was that what Thurston Moore played? Or maybe one of those Buddy Holly specials, a Gibson, I think.

"Ev," Billy sighs. "I thought—"

"He's hurt. Okay? We discussed this—right?"

"What the hell happened to Band-Aids? It seems an Elmo Band-Aid and an ice cube worked just fine with Anna."

"Anna was different," I say.

"You're different," he says. I wonder if Billy weren't such a success, if my nursing wouldn't bother him so much. If maybe he would care so much what people thought.

I haven't told Billy that the milk has already tapered off, that Charlie isn't nursing as much. He hasn't wanted to. Without the protection of that pleasing, narcotizing fog, I'm irritable and anxious, always anticipating my next fix. If Billy has noticed my shrinking breasts, he hasn't said anything. One day the milk won't be there at all. I'll be empty. Never again will I nurse. Never again will my son need me like this, want me. Never again will I feel that warmth and intimacy, that closeness, that tingle. Soon he'll move on.

These thoughts are what pushed me to try it. Sitting on the toilet, weeping, I'd finally sucked at my own breast. Just for a second, then I'd stopped. It was so ridiculous. Then, I thought, just once more, just to see. I was surprised at how warm and soft the nipple felt between my teeth, how large and alive to my tongue's touch it was, as it flattened it on the roof of my mouth, sending a gusher of sweet, fatty milk down my throat. I was surprised at how fast milk filled my mouth, how I gulped it, that pearl-colored elixir coating my tongue, its aftertaste waxy like coconut milk. I sat and sucked, eyes closed, mouth latched onto breast, a perfect unending circle.

It wasn't until I started imagining what I would look like if someone walked in on me that I had to stop, it was like catching a glance of yourself masturbating. Actually, masturbation would be much easier to explain.

· · ·

"What's your plan for today?" Billy asks, putting on his running shoes. He walks the three miles to his brownstone office on the far side of the park.

"Mary Beth and Ondine are coming for a play date."

"Ondine, what kind of name is that? Doesn't she have any clue about the Factory gang? Ondine was the big speed freak, right?"

"It's pretty. Mary Beth was determined that her daughter have a fabulous name. In college she used to say, If there's a more dreary name than Mary Beth I'd like to hear it—we struggled to come up with a good nickname for her, but she's just not the nickname type."

He shrugs.

I neglect to mention the nurse-in. I am surprised that I haven't canceled lunch with Mary Beth. I really prefer socializing with other nursing mothers. I cancel on everybody else, but Mary Beth, she would act like it didn't matter, that she wasn't hurt. "Don't worry, darling," she'd say, but she has *abandonment issues*. There would be other rallies.

I also didn't cancel on Mary Beth because it was almost spring. The time of year my father died, and in this season I am always hungry to be with people who knew him, if only tangentially. Actually, that is best. I prefer that. I like feeling as though I knew him better than anyone. When people recall my father I can see him in a new pose, imagine him in a fresh setting, but it's still just a snapshot, his image flat. Unmoving. Sometimes I might hear his laugh, but that was it.

Mary Beth, unlike Billy, unlike my other old friends, doesn't think my grief is inappropriate, or strange, or if she does, she's never said so. I appreciate that. Sometimes I wonder how much of our friendship was founded on keeping our mouths shut.

"We're going to talk about work," I tell Billy. "She says she can set me up with a regular gig at the magazine, in the art department doing layout. Some stylist work, back-breaking stuff—you know, swiveled-up lipsticks, prepubescent super-models slathered in seaweed. Good stuff."

He sighs. I know this appeals to Billy. We aren't desperate for cash but he believes I need to get out of the house more. He's also been at me to rent some studio space with some other artists. Last Christmas he bought me new brushes.

"I don't trust her," he says. I'm surprised. Billy so rarely gets personal about anyone, but he's uncomfortable, noticeably so.

"Why not?" I wonder if it's because she's cheating on Lars. I should never have told Billy that, now he'll hold it against her. I should never have told him that she said, "Divorced people are the only people with grown-up lives." Maybe, despite the fact that we had sex last week, and I'm weaning Charlie, he's still considering it.

"Forget I said anything. She's your oldest friend. You have feelings for her. Just forget it."

"You always flirt with her," I say. I'm teasing him, of course, but he does. I like it. Mary Beth is a flirt, and Billy, like any man, flirts with her. It makes me jealous, of course. The attention of another woman always brings out the best and worst in a wife. We always used to have sex after seeing Mary Beth.

"I do not," he said. "And what do you two even have to talk about anymore? I mean, she's become even more of a caricature of herself, with the darling this, darling that. She's turning into Truman Capote."

"We have the past," I said. "That's something."

Mary Beth had met my father when we were in college, and though she didn't know him well, how could she, she had known him. I know she'll let me rattle on about him if I want to.

This time we aren't going to go out for lunch, we are going to have tea at my house. The last time we'd gone to a local Brooklyn bistro and at one point I thought Mary Beth might fall off her chair when a surly four-year-old wrestled her sobbing toddler brother out from under Mom's tap and took his place. The mother barely looked up from her *Holistic Root Vegetables* cookbook.

Then Charlie, who was wearing the incredibly expensive French-made sailor suit Mary Beth had given him last year for his birthday, clambered out of his stroller and climbed into my lap. "Noonie na nas!" he demanded.

"Cookie?" she said, and began to summon the waiter to bring Charlie a sweet.

"No, no," I said.

"Oh, heavens, I let Ondine eat those chocolate Snackwells like mad."

"Na na na nas!" Charlie chanted, pawing at my blouse.

"Excuse us, just a minute," I said, and swatted Charlie's fingers from my buttons. That invariably caused eyebrows to raise, the unbuttoning of the shirt, as though he were a randy teenager and not a hungry toddler.

Mary Beth blanched.

"I'm sorry," I said, and halfheartedly made to pull Charlie from my breast.

"No, it's fine, really."

Charlie sucked, peeping out from under my shirt at Mary Beth, who gamely wiggled her fingers in his face like a giant squid preparing to suck his face off.

"You were saying."

"God, they're like Mormons the way they lurk around, watching your every move. Waiting for any opening: Does your child have earaches? Look at that poor woman, she has no chance! She's absolutely destroyed. Sleep-deprived, insane ... Oh, honey, I'm sorry. You know I'm just being bad. I'm sorry. You're different," she said, looking suddenly stricken with embarrassment. "You're you."

Today Mary Beth and Ondine are going to take a taxi from the Upper East Side out to Park Slope, and while the kids play, the two of us are going to sit on my little deck and drink tea like civilized people. If she leaves early enough, I'll race over to the rally with Charlie and nurse. Surely, that was okay. I mean, this was a political statement. Surely, that wasn't breaking the pact I'd made with Billy.

I wake up Charlie from his nap with a kiss.
I wonder, Who will steal you away from me?
No. Who will try?

. . .

Mary Beth and Ondine are right on time. Ondine is in a feather boa, Dorothy's ruby slippers, a long gold lamé gown, and a tiara. She looks like a tiny drag queen.

"My name has an umlaut," she says, stalking into the living room. "And who is that creature?" Instead of her usual Caribbean accent, which she'd picked up from her nanny, she sounds like a jaded thirty-something Manhattanite.

Charlie grins at her and beats his chest like a gorilla. Then he grabs his radio and shuts himself under the sink. I don't think I've ever seen him move so fast.

Roadrunner, roadrunner, running faster miles an hour, gonna drive past the Stop and Shop . . .

"I'm bored," Ondine moans, and collapses on the floor. She lifts her head dramatically. "Do you have any windowpane?"

"She means Windex, not blotter acid, and incidentally, ignore her," Mary Beth says, taking me by the arm. "You look thin," she says, kissing my cheek.

"You too," I say. This is the way women tell each other "I'm happy to see you." It's code.

"No cleaning, Ondine. Annabelle will be home soon, and then you two can disappear and do whatever it is you little people do behind closed doors. No," she says, holding up a hand, festooned with her acorn-size diamond wedding ring. "Don't tell me, I don't want to know."

Mary Beth and I retire to the deck with iced tea, improved by a shot of rum and some lime. Inside, Charlie creeps out and spies on Ondine who is polishing our small and motley collection of silver. She's very meticulous, dipping the flatware into the pink goo, rubbing it, rinsing.

"Come on out here, baby," I call to him, but he ignores me; he has a good view from his cabinet.

"So," I say.

"So," she says, sipping her drink. "I quit smoking, it's been three months. Aren't you proud?"

"Bravo," I say.

"This is the longest I've ever gone. And I think it's going to stick."

"Good for you."

"I do miss those pretty little tubes, oh, and those divine and stinky Gitanes," she says. "I smoked those like a demon. Remember?"

Mary Beth and I talk about family the way old friends do. A little awkwardly, spilling all the intimate details in a newsy, slightly canned voice. I tell her my sister is going to be made a partner in her law firm, that she's going to marry her boyfriend this fall, and that we talk on the phone a lot. I miss her. I tell her how my mother is in Tibet this summer with a women's group and writes me weekly. Mary Beth tells me how her mother has stopped drinking and married a Belgian man who imports ceramics. Her father is on his fourth wife, and just got a neck job.

"He looks about forty," she says, and rolls her eyes. "I think he's finally happy."

Maybe it's the cocktail, or the rush of well-being that comes with seeing an old friend who you believe knows the real you, a friend who knew you before you became who you are. Maybe it's that Mary Beth talks so easily about her marital troubles with Lars, and how she fears Ondine picks up on the stress between them. In any case, I am just about to tell Mary Beth all about how it is with me and Billy—how he had been having an affair with that other woman for almost a year, and how I knew, but I didn't let myself really know it. How it was over, but I was just realizing how scared I was of him leaving me.

Instead I say, "Well, don't even ask about my father. We are completely out of touch. He never writes, he doesn't call."

Mary Beth frowns, then her expression shifts to one of pity.

"You know, I remember the first time I met your father, I liked him straightaway," she says. "Of course, your mother is wonderful too."

"Of course," I say. "When was this?"

"Some parents' cocktail thing. Neither of mine were there, so I glommed onto yours, remember? We went to that Tahitian place with the parrot noises and the waterfall; they float your pupu platter out on a little raft."

"Didn't we go there once before for some awful pre-fraternity gala thing?"

Mary Beth shrugs. "Probably. Lovely bathrooms, too. Big clamshell sinks."

Mary Beth always remembers the bathrooms.

"Your father was so funny," she says, and though it is a familiar refrain, I never get tired of hearing it.

"I know. I don't laugh like that, or rather in that way, anymore."

"Do you know, I remember him telling about his first trip to New York City, and how he was terrified to leave his hotel because he'd never seen so many people and cars in his whole life."

"Really? I didn't know that." I laugh, though I don't think it's funny. And I don't like Mary Beth laughing like that, as though my father had been some kind of rube. I didn't believe her.

"Can you imagine?" She laughs. "Your father?"

"My father?" I say. "No."

She looks surprised.

"I'm sure he didn't say that," I say. "That's bullshit. I mean, my father wasn't afraid of anything—I mean, nothing like that. That's just stupid," I say, surprised at the edge in my voice.

"He did. It was at our graduation brunch, at the house, remember? We were out by the keg. I clearly recall drinking champagne out of one of those glass boots we got from the cowboy bar. If memory serves, I rode that bull longer than any of you girls," she says proudly.

"He wasn't afraid of anything," I say. I can't remember my father ever admitting he was afraid—no, that's not true, there was the first time he saw a shark while scuba diving.

"I nearly shit my wet suit," he'd said, laughing. Still. I could allow that.

"I'm sure you misunderstood," I say.

Then I remember him after the last set of test results, a profusion of cancer cells tripping across a glass slide.

Of course I'm scared, damn it.

"Oh," Mary Beth says, as though I'd insulted her.

"Can I get you another?" I ask her, getting up to refill my drink.

"Dreamy," she says. "How's Billy doing?" she calls into the kitchen. "Has he made his first million yet?"

Digging into the freezer, my hands are shaking. Why do I care what she says? Why did I even ask? No one knew my father like I did, no one. Why did I even ask?

I watch Charlie sitting cross-legged next to Ondine. He's watching with solemn intensity as she polishes my fish forks and sings what sounds like some kind of calypso music. After she cleans each one, she hands it to Charlie, who lays them in a row.

I take a deep breath, then head back out to the porch. Mary Beth has kicked off her shoes and is resting her feet on the railing.

"Are they playing nice?" she asks.

"I think so," I say. I don't know if I really want to sit back down.

Mary Beth takes a long sip of her drink. "Then there was Amsterdam," she says. "Oh my God." She pauses. "I don't think I ever told you this."

I sit. Charlie appears and tugs on my pant leg. "Up," he says.

"What?" I say, annoyed at his pulling on me. Suddenly, the sky seems too close to the ground. I ignore my son.

"Tell me," I say. "What is it?" I can feel my entire body get hard, like glass. Don't break me. Don't hurt me, I think. Don't.

"Oh, it's nothing, really, it's almost next to nothing, I don't even know why I'm telling you. Oh, Ondine, darling, no, I don't think Evie wants you to straighten up her spice cabinet."

"I don't care," I said. "It's fine. Go on."

"No," Mary Beth says, shaking her head. "Ondine, be a dear and take baby Charlie outside, run around, be a child, for heaven's sake."

Ondine skulks over and grabs Charlie round the waist. He holds on tight to my leg.

"Come here, child," she whispers in her Caribbean accent. I make like I'm going to peel his fingers loose, but I don't. I wouldn't.

Who do you love best? No one but me.

Charlie lets go and wraps his arms around Ondine's waist, and allows her to drag him back inside. "Can you believe this cleaning obsession?" Mary Beth laughs. "I actually have to tell her the vacuum cleaner is asleep. At least the accent, that dreadful accent she picked up from Philomene, is gone. Firing her nanny was the smartest thing I could have done. Can you imagine her going off to Sacred Virgin Academy saying, 'Hey don't you know that I love the sour sop!' We spent thousands of dollars getting her to say *th*, instead of *t*. Remember, she'd trill, 'Don't you know I'm trrrreee...'"

"Finish what you were saying," I say.

I watch through the window as Charlie follows Ondine out the front door, stopping only to pick up his bucket of chalk.

"Stay on the stoop!" I yell. "Keep the gate closed." Though I don't have to worry about Charlie going anywhere.

"Go on," I say, though I wonder why. Obviously there's nothing she can tell me I don't know. I just want to hear anything and everything. I want for a moment to feel like he's here.

She looks at me. "Are you all right, darling?"

"I'm fine."

"Well," she says with a big sigh, as though this is going to be a long story. "You remember how we all went out for dinner—we drank bottle after bottle of wine, you had just fallen ass over teacups in love with Billy, he was always coming in through the fire escape day and night—"

"We went out," I say. I don't remember too much of the rest. "The restaurant had views of the canals."

"I can't recall," Mary Beth says. "It was a wild night, you were drunk too."

I nod. I remember. My father had just had lung surgery. He looked pale, but fine. Every time we spoke on the phone that summer it seemed he'd make some joke about how he was getting old, or needed glasses, there was always something. It bugged the crap out of me. I remember he'd traveled all the way from London just to have dinner with me.

"God, how do I put this?" she says, pausing for a long moment. "We kissed. There, I've said it." She cringes, and covers her face as though she's afraid I might hit her. She's grinning. For a moment it occurs to me that she's talking about the two of us, that we kissed, we fooled around in some drunken stupor and I didn't remember it. It's so funny, I nearly laugh.

"What?"

"I kissed him, your father."

Silence.

I think, This is just like when he died. That moment when all the air got sucked out of the world, and it was just a vacuum, a howling hole. I wish I could fall down, but I can't move.

"It was a huge mistake," she says. Two bright spots of

color rise up on her cheeks, and her hands fly up to her throat. "Oh God, you're mad, aren't you?"

Vacuum, I think, there are two *u*'s in vacuum, you and you. Them.

I stare at her. I think I must have misunderstood, but I look at her face. Her mouth is loose like a rubber band. I have never seen her cry.

The truth settles down around me like fog. I don't want to talk. I don't want to listen. I want to close my eyes, but I can't do that. I think, This is just like what happened with Billy. How can this be? No one can be trusted. My men don't love me. They can never love me enough. Everyone leaves.

"Oh God," Mary Beth says. She wipes the back of her hand across her eyes. "I am so embarrassed. Why did I do this? It's this liquor. You know I didn't mean it. It was a bad time for me. You know. I was drunk. He was drunk. It was a mistake. You know what, much like now." She laughed, a little hysterically. "Perhaps, it's best if I go, I think."

She starts to stand up.

"How?" I say. I feel retarded trying to make sense of it. I don't want to know, but I have to know.

"What do you mean?" Her hands are in her hair, pulling it into her face, she sits down on the edge of her chair.

"Did he kiss you back?"

"Oh, Ev," she says, then, "Listen, I'm far too blasted to sit here and . . . Don't hate me, darling. Don't hate me, please. I couldn't stand that."

"Answer me," I say.

"Don't," she says.

"How many times?"

She laughs. "Oh, honey, it's not like that..."

That is enough.

"You should go," I say, nodding. It is wise. I wonder what my mother is doing right now. Did she know about this? Had he told her? Had he told her after they saw Mary Beth at the silly little art show in the Village? Had he mentioned it to her when I told him Mary Beth had assisted me in the buying of chemo weed for his nausea? Did my mother know when Mary Beth took the train down for the funeral? Or was it my father's secret? Death made us know things we never needed or wanted to know.

Everything is wrong. Even the air feels wrong. It's as though my molecules have been scrambled. I don't know what I know anymore. I do know that tonight when Billy comes home tonight I will crawl into his arms. I will give myself to him. I will make promises to make him happy, to keep him, to keep us all together.

"You should go," I say again. "Now."

"You know, Ev, your father thought you were just great, he loved you," she says, her voice breaking. "You're lucky."

"Why would you say that?" I ask, hating her, hating her so much.

She hunches her shoulders, and twists the bit of paper napkin in her hands. She looks down in her lap. Her nose is starting to run. She licks her upper lip, then brushes her bangs back from her eyes.

"It was a mistake," she says. "Everybody makes mistakes," she says. "He was a human being, Ev."

"Don't talk to me," I snap. "You don't know one god-damn thing about me or him."

I close my eyes. I'm afraid I'm going to cry too and I don't want to give her the satisfaction. Then, for the first time since my father died, I can feel him. I can see him in my mind, unfrozen, breathing. Alive. I've watched him on videotape, but this is different. He is alive in my mind, just for a moment, but I can see him standing there, he's healthy, his hair is dark, his eyes full of spark, his hands are in his jeans pockets, and he's got on his red work shirt, his watch is glinting on his wrist, and he's moving to some music in his head, waiting, waiting for me to do something. But I don't know what I am supposed to do.

I get up from the table. I can't look at Mary Beth, even though I know it is the last time I will ever see her. I want to hold my son. I want my baby.

Outside, Ondine is on her knees pulling weeds from around the stoop. She has straightened up the hallway, lining up the buckets of chalk, jars of bubbles and umbrellas, centering the doormat. She has wisely removed her tiara and left it by the door.

"Where's Charlie?" I scan the bushes where he sometimes likes to hide. I see her boa and some beach towels, which we put on the steps when we want to sit outside in the evenings, spread over the bushes.

"He was right t'ere," Ondine says, gesturing with her sunglasses to the steps. "But he left, you know. He was so bored."

Mary Beth stands behind me in the foyer. She lights a cigarette, and she exhales loudly.

"What do you mean, he left?"

"Oh, he went adios, bon voyage, adieu." Ondine throws kisses, waving her arms as if she were bidding farewell to an ocean liner.

"Some stranger came by, don't you know," Ondine says, her voice trailing off. I swear, she thinks it's a joke. There's no one on the block, the street is completely empty, except for the trash barrels and cardboard boxes that the neighbors have put out for the morning pickup.

I take the stairs two at a time. I rip the towels off the bushes, half expecting Charlie to jump out and scare me, but he doesn't.

"He left?" I ask Ondine again. "Are you sure?"

"Sure I'm sure."

Immediately I start to compose a police description: Elvis T-shirt, green shorts, red high-tops, side part, blond hair. Three years old. Blue eyes, blue blue eyes. He's beautiful. First my father and now Charlie.

No, I think, my father, the angel, came and got Charlie. That's it. He'll protect him.

Bullshit.

Charlie is not a wanderer, he doesn't slip off. He's here. *He wouldn't leave me.* Something horrible has happened. I was out there on the goddamned porch with that woman and now my boy is missing. It isn't possible. My breasts ache.

"What are you saying?" Mary Beth asks Ondine, sounding for the first time, to me, like a real mother.

"Oh, can't you see I'm a-working here," Ondine sings.

"Stop it," Mary Beth shouts.

Ondine's lower lip begins to tremble. I head back up the stairs to call the police, to call Billy. He'll know what to do, when I notice a large cardboard box out on the curb beginning to move. I am sure I am hallucinating, willing it to move, and then, in a flash, my boy leaps out, screaming and waving his arms. His fluffy blond hair stands up as if he and Ondine have been wrestling. He dashes through the gate and leaps onto Ondine, who bursts out laughing, and the two of them giggle uproariously, hugging each other and jumping up and down.

I feel tricked and stupid. In three bounds I have my son by the back of the neck.

"Not funny, Charlie." He squinches up his shoulders and starts to whimper. I've never done that before, grabbed him like that. Like I wanted to hurt him. I shake him hard. His feet fly out in front of him. Then I pull him into my lap. My whole body is shaking.

He yelps.

All at once I feel terrible. I am terrible.

"Oh, baby, I'm so sorry, baby, but you scared Mommy. I was afraid I'd lost you, I was afraid something terrible had happened to you," I say, stroking his hair, kissing his temples, his eyes. I can barely breathe.

I glare at Mary Beth, her and her disreputable strumpet of a daughter. "You can call a car inside," I say.

"Ev," Mary Beth says, then sighs. "Shit," she says. "Ondine, I believe it goes without saying that you shall have no Cinderella or Sleeping Beauty videos for the rest of the week," she says, grabbing her daughter by the arm and pulling her inside, but I don't believe her, she's got no backbone. I want her gone, I don't want any more memories of her. I just want her out, vanished, gone.

She reappears a few minutes later, she's still got Ondine by the wrist. "We're going to go now."

I stand up, it feels so formal.

Ondine's crown is crooked, her bottom lip thrust out in a pout. "I didn't get to the linen closet," she says apologetically.

"All right then," Mary Beth says. She gathers Ondine to her side and checks up the street for their taxi. Neither of us knows what to do.

"You know what, we'll take the train," she says, and the two of them start to walk away.

It's too much leaving, too much.

"Don't go," I say, surprising both of us. I reach down and pick Charlie up off the step. "Just one more thing." Mary Beth knew my father, she knew something I didn't know, something I wanted.

"I really don't think—" she starts to say.

"Please," I say.

Mary Beth sighs, then she says, "Until the car comes, and you have to make me a drink, and not a weak one this time. A real drink."

I hold open the door, and she enters tentatively. She sits on the sofa, at the far end where there's some shade, and stares down at the floor. Ondine climbs up and curls up beside her, resting her head on her mother's knee.

I sit across from them in my old velvet armchair, the chair I've nursed both my children in. Charlie is in my lap, slumped against me.

"There's something I need to ask you, something I want

you to tell me," I say, my voice nearly a whisper. I'm glad she's not looking at me. It almost hurts to talk. "Do you think I loved him too much?"

Mary Beth stiffens, and for a moment I'm sure she's not going to answer me, then she looks up at me, fixing me with a terrible stare. "I wouldn't know."

Charlie and Ondine have started making faces at each other. Ondine crawls into Mary Beth's lap and starts sucking her thumb. Mary Beth strokes her hair. I pull up my blouse and unsnap my bra; I nudge Charlie's head toward my weeping breast. He pushes away, shaking his head.

"No," he says. "I want to dig up the hamster," he says, kicking his legs, struggling to get loose. "I want to show her Archie."

"No." I hold him fast in my arms. I won't let go. He gives up and goes limp.

"Mom," he says. "Am I going to die?"

"You mean right now, right this instant?"

"I am, right?" Charlie says. He is serious.

I don't say anything for a moment.

"Yes," I say, "but not for a very, very long time."

"So when I'm old you're going to die?"

I don't say anything. Then, "Yes. When you're old. I hope so."

Charlie starts to cry. I don't want to cry in front of him. I push his head toward my breast.

"Here," I say. Here is comfort, take it.

He refuses, turning his head away.

"Oh, honey, it will make it better," I say, but it's not true. The truth is, I'll feel better.

He struggles to climb out of my lap, but I don't let him. I won't let him. He turns around in my lap and faces me, frowning. "Charlie." I say his name like I'm begging him to stay.

"Listen," he says. He sounds like my father. Then he drops his head on my shoulder and sighs.

I close my eyes for a moment, and there he is. My father. The sight of him in motion takes my breath. He's still in his blue jeans and red workshirt, but now he appears to be holding an imaginary microphone in his left hand, his right hand stretches out toward me, toward an imaginary sea of people. He's singing, *Wild, wild horses, couldn't drag me away. . . .*

"Let me go," Charlie says. "Let me go."

What can I do?

I let go.